Never Date a Roommate

NEVER DATE A ROOMMATE

PAULA OTTONI

Recycling programs for this product may not exist in your area.

ISBN-13: 978-1-335-57479-4

Never Date a Roommate

For questions and comments about the quality of this book, please contact us at CustomerService@Harlequin.com.

Harlequin Enterprises ULC
22 Adelaide St. West, 41st Floor
Toronto, Ontario M5H 4E3, Canada
www.Harlequin.com

Printed in U.S.A.

To the Viking roommate I married.

One

Today I'm going to quit.

End it all and go back to Brazil.

Because my dream of happiness in the happiest country in the world ends when my lease does, in ten days.

I climb the stairs to the second level of Scorpio Games, and the familiar scent of freshly brewed coffee and brand-new Apple devices welcomes me. The lack of typing or chatter in the open office is explained by the circle of people standing in the empty space between the desks.

I swiftly leave my purse on my desk and join my teammates, squeezing myself between the quality assurance lead and Chiara, the sweet Italian QA tester who sits next to me and is the closest I have to a friend here. It's the second time this week that I'm late for our daily 9:00 a.m. stand-up meeting, and everyone but Chiara ignores my arrival as they listen to Ellen, the 2D artist, listing the tasks she must tackle in the next few hours. Chiara announces she'll be looking for bugs in the latest version of *Beetle Battle Match 3.* I then tell everyone my goal is to make three more puzzle levels before the weekend and tweak the difficulty on some of the ones I've already made.

My answer is almost the same every day, and I always fulfill my promise, even if that means working a few extra hours. Sometimes I even make more levels than I say I'll do, just because I'm efficient. My passion is long gone.

I wonder when I lost it.

I like the place, but I don't like my place in it. I'm ready for more challenges, to use my skills and creativity without so many boundaries.

But that won't happen here. And even if it did, it wouldn't matter. Because the lease on my small studio apartment in the center of Copenhagen will expire in ten days with no possibility of extension, and I have nothing else in sight.

Once I sit at my desk, I open my phone to the *Beetle Battle Match 3* app and play level 679 to remember what I've already done so I can do something *slightly* different for level 680. A notification then pops up at the top of the screen. I'm ready to ignore the message, but Mom keeps spamming me, so I open the chat.

Mom: Nada de apartamento ainda?
Mom: Seu quarto está te esperando aqui! 🏢♥☀👄🙏👍

I take a long, deep breath. She's asking me if I found an apartment, is saying my room is waiting for me, and is illustrating it all with a row of emojis to remind me of all the love and sunshine I'm missing.

To top it off, she sends me pictures of the room I had in her house. I was sharing it with my cousin Mariana, who was in college and couldn't stand living with her parents in a satellite city an hour away from the centrally located University of Brasília.

Neither of us paid rent to my parents, which would have been an insult. (Mom would rather pay *me* to live with her.) I'd have given anything to have my own place—where I could be independent, make my own choices, and find out who I wanted to be in peace and solitude—but I couldn't afford my living expenses with the jobs I had in Brasília. Besides, Mom wouldn't have left me alone, no matter how many buses she had to take to visit me.

I get an empty feeling at the bottom of my stomach looking at the tiny room with pink walls full of outdated stickers and posters. The emptiness hits my heart with a punch as I stare at the bunk bed I know still creaks, the narrow desk that hardly accommodates my towering pile of office supplies, the plastic computer chair—all the stuff I left behind.

Which doesn't at all seduce me or make me nostalgic. They are only reminders of why I shouldn't go back.

"How's your apartment search?" Chiara asks me. I blink at her, lowering my phone.

She raises an eyebrow and ties her pink hair up in a ponytail. "Have you found anything yet?"

I shake my head. "No…nothing."

"Look, I think you should—" she rambles on, and I stop listening, my eyes staring unfocused at the HYGGE mug I bought in a souvenir shop the day I arrived in Denmark.

Everyone tells me that something will come up. They give

me names and links. I visit apartments, but other people get them. I find something online, but it's too expensive or too far away, or I'm applicant number 379. That's how hard it is to find a place to live in Copenhagen.

I no longer expect I'll get a place in the next few days. Just as I no longer expect to feel excitement about my work. I've accepted that my dream of living a Danish life will never be more than just a dream.

"You need to give it a try, Sol," Chiara says, her voice startling me out of my thoughts.

I have no clue what she's referring to. Probably another website for finding rentals. But her words bring out the stubborn part of me I've been fighting against lately—the optimistic, hopeful side of Sol Carvalho that says I need to give it another try, *just one more.*

I look down at the photo. This is what I'm going back to if I give up now. A life where fear suffocates me. Fear of never having enough money to be truly independent. Fear of never having a family of my own with a man who loves me and respects me. Fear of not getting home in one piece when I walk alone in the dark after long hours in an underpaid job that is far from my game design ambitions.

My heart races, and I make a quick decision.

I go to the eleven o'clock design meeting with my hands sweating and my pulse throbbing in my ears. I avoid everyone's eyes, but when they start discussing new features for the game, I swallow my shyness and pitch a detailed idea I've been entertaining for the past few weeks and never dared to bring up.

When I finish, my manager, Lars Holm, says, "That's an interesting idea."

Other people nod, agreeing with him, and my heart does a *thump-thump-thump* in what feels like hope…

Then Martin Olesen, game designer, raises his hand.

"I see a few problems with this," he says and goes on to destroy my idea.

Ripped. To. Absolute. Pieces.

I want to murder him. But I keep a calm face.

"You might have a point, Martin," Lars concludes. People nod. "Let's just keep doing what we've been doing and monitor player response. Jessica, do you have any data for us?"

I look at Martin. He acts as if I'm not in the room. Everyone pays attention to Jessica's slides, and I want to storm out.

Why is Martin Olesen so fu—*fantastically* annoying? It's not the first time he's obliterated one of my suggestions. He's always showing a feverish need to be the cleverest, most accomplished person in the room, regardless of who he steps on.

For the rest of the meeting, I don't see the numbers or charts displayed on the big TV. All I see are the percentages surrounding the current possibilities of my life.

Chance of getting more interesting tasks at work: 0%.

Chance of finding a place to rent in the next ten days: 1%.

There is no future for me in Denmark, that's the harsh truth. I sigh, looking at my perfect self-manicured nails. I have beauty salon skills because, since I was twelve, I've been helping Mom in her business. It's the job I'll have the moment I land back home under my mother's overprotective wings.

When we're leaving the meeting, a hand squeezes my

shoulder. I look back at Lars, who's smiling at me. "Are you ready for our one-to-one?"

"Sure." My stomach sinks. *No, I'm not at all ready.*

We walk to another empty meeting room and sit across from each other.

"So..." My boss interlaces his fingers on the table, speaking English, the official language used in the company. "Sol."

I wish Lars would say my name right, with the Portuguese pronunciation (sounding similar to *Saul*). *Sol* is also "sun" in Danish though, and my boss calls me that, with the closed "o" (more like *soul*). I could tell him to call me Marisol instead, but I didn't correct him the first time, and doing so now would be awkward.

"It's been more than a month since we had a one-to-one, so I'd like to hear how it's all going."

These monthly meetings have been meaningless because I always say, "It's all great, no problems!" That won't happen this time though.

I woke up ready for this moment, but now that I'm here, a void opens inside me, sucking down all my dreams and hopes.

I take a deep, painful breath. "I think it's time we talk openly."

"What about *closely*? I need that door shut, sorry," he says, laughing at what he seems to consider genius wordplay. He rises to close the door and sits back heavily, hands clasped. "Go on!" He smiles. Lars is a friendly guy. He's always joking around and seeing the glass half full.

If you told me to think of a stereotypical Danish person, I'd think of him. He's tall, slim, blond, and blue-eyed. He has good taste in design and dresses soberly. He has a wife named

Lotte and two teenage sons, and they live in a beautiful white house in Frederiksberg, one of the best neighborhoods in the city. He bikes to work every day and is a fundamentalist when it comes to eating organic food. I know all this because he's not afraid to share details of his life with anyone in the office, no matter their role.

Unlike me, who stays quiet unless I'm positive people won't think I'm the odd one out.

"Lars, I..." The words are stuck in my throat. After a moment of awkward silence, my boss takes over.

"Listen, I think your ideas are great."

Wait, what?

"You're a very promising young woman, Sol. I've been impressed with your performance."

Okay, I was *not* expecting that. I lean back and let him speak.

"In fact, I think you might be able to handle more responsibility."

"What? Yes, absolutely," the words rush out of my mouth. "I'd love that!"

"The question is where we should place you." He scratches his shaved chin, thinking to himself. "You've only been with us for six months, but I haven't forgotten that you've worked with games for five years in Brazil at Vortex."

I nod, a prickle of gratitude tickling my stomach. It was thanks to my hard work at the Brasília-based indie game studio that I got my opportunity at Scorpio.

I joined the Vortex team the year the company was founded. Their mobile games didn't have the scope and reach of Scorpio's high-budget, high-profit games, but we were innovative and passionate—which, to be honest, was our driving force, considering how little we got paid. At one point, I earned a low salary. Then I worked part-time unpaid for half a year in the hopes our game would sell enough to keep me there full-time on a livable wage.

That didn't happen.

And then fate intervened.

One of the three founders got sick and couldn't go to São Paulo for the biggest video game convention in Latin America, so I offered to take his place. There, I met some amazing people from several international game studios, including Scorpio Games.

That day changed everything for me. I had a pleasant talk with Scorpio's recruiter and got an interview with Lars a few days later.

I look at him now, remembering our first video call, how nervous I was. My English kept failing me, but that didn't ruin my chances. He saw how much I wanted the opportunity, how ready I was to move across the world and make it happen.

Maybe the dream doesn't have to end yet.

"After the Fun Season, we'll be doing some rearranging and internal hiring," he says.

"Fun Season?" I ask, not familiar with the term.

Lars smiles. "Every year, from October to the end of December, we have a series of fun events to warm up the team, lift the spirits, and get to know each other better." I nod, listening eagerly. "You might call it a tournament, but we are a game company, so we're not so competitive," he says sarcastically.

I laugh, curious to hear more.

"New people are joining the company all the time, and I appreciate the opportunity to get to know my coworkers on a more personal level." Lars rests his elbows on the armrests of his chair, staring at me. "I look forward to learning more about you, Sol, and finding the best place for you in this company." He then adds, "Oh, that sounded weird. Please don't misinterpret me."

I smile back at him and wonder if what he means is "If I like you enough, you get a promotion."

"We'll start to work on a new project next year," he continues. I sit straighter, my heart pounding. "There's nothing defined yet, but we want it to be different from what we've been doing so far. It could be any kind of game. We're open to innovation."

If I could use one word to describe what I love most in this field, it'd be *innovation*, so my heartbeat rises another level.

"That's great news!"

"We'll be hiring a game director internally to lead this project. We want someone creative, proactive, and full of ideas. A leader with vision. Someone who's *really* in for the ride."

Instead of beating even faster, my heart stops for a fraction of a second. Did he say *game director*? I thought I was at the descent of the roller coaster when I'm actually on the climb. Or the loop, perhaps.

This should be the moment when I pitch myself as a great fit for the position. I sense that it's not necessary though, from the way Lars is looking at me. Just from telling me all this, it's obvious he's already considering me. But he can't promise anything yet. He wants the right person.

Someone who won't just suddenly go back to Brazil.

Someone he likes.

I'll have to work for this promotion, but I'm *so* in.

My smile fades, however, when he says, "Martin was talking about a truly innovative idea the other day. A dating game of sorts."

My insides boil. *Not Martin the Beetle.* Yes, he is just like Marlin the Beetle, the annoying insect in our game that blocks your tiles and prevents you from making matches.

"Are you considering Martin for the role?" I dare ask.

"He's been showing his potential, just like you." Lars drums his fingers on the table. "There are many talented people here. I'm keeping my eyes open. Let's see what happens, shall we?" Lars winks at me meaningfully, and I take my cue to leave.

Okay. Change of plans. I won't be quitting today after all.

Now I must beat Martin the Beetle to get my dream job.

Which means I need to find a place to live. Like, *now.*

Once I sit back at my desk, I ask Chiara, "What were you telling me before about apartments? What is it I should do again?"

Her eyebrows rise as if she suspects I didn't pay attention but won't blame me for it. "You should talk to Mark," she answers patiently. "He knows someone."

A flush of excitement washes over me. "Oh. Right. Thanks!"

My phone buzzes. It's my mom, desperate to know where I am because I haven't answered her messages.

I take a deep breath and stand up to look for Mark, a programmer I've never talked with before.

"Erik Storm is renting out a spare room," Mark tells me once I find his desk. "You should call him," Mark says, and gives me Erik's number. "He was a programmer here but quit last winter to work on a personal project."

I thank him and walk back to my desk, watching my mom's messages piling up. She saw I saw them, and is annoyed that I'm ignoring her, because she's been *very* worried. I'm about to answer that I'm at work and can't talk now. Instead, though, I tap on the new contact I've just added.

With a hopeful smile, I say a silent prayer.

Erik Storm, please give me a room.

Two

Erik Storm doesn't give me a room.

I dive into my pillow and scream in frustration. My phone chimes, a quick succession of *dings* that make me detangle from my sheets at lightning speed, hoping to read Erik saying, Sorry. The other person bailed. The room is yours.

But it's just Larissa, my best friend from Brazil.

Larissa: What do you mean, he said NO?

Larissa: Why?

Larissa: What exactly did he say?

I tell Larissa that I called and said, "Hi, I got your number from one of your former coworkers at Scorpio Games. I work there too. I'm looking for a room to rent in Copenhagen, and they told me you have one."

He said, "Yes, I do, but I've been talking to some people already, and I'm about to close the deal with one of them."

I then said, "Oh. But they might back out. You should interview me. I'm an excellent person to live with. And I really need a room."

I was about to pour my heart and soul into an emotional application bordering on a plea, when he cut me off. "Sorry, but I don't need to interview you. Good luck with your search." And he ended the call.

I shouldn't have mentioned that I work at Scorpio Games, I write to Larissa. That was probably the wrong thing to say.

Why would working there be a problem? Larissa asks.

I don't know, I write. He quit his job. He might not want anything to do with the people there.

You're overthinking this, Sol, she replies. He already found someone. It happens.

I groan, throwing the phone on the bed. My urge to curse compels me to babble unintelligible sounds like a cartoon character. I don't say bad words. It's a life mantra my religious mom taught me with resolute fervor.

I'm not done with you, Erik Storm.

This guy's apartment is my last chance, and I'm going to fight to make him change his mind.

I open my computer and search for him on Facebook. There are five people with variations of the name, but filtering through location and educational background, I find him—or at least the one most likely to be him. A thirty-one-year-old, long-haired, sunburned dude on a tropical beach wearing a white T-shirt, sunglasses, and surfer shorts.

I check his public posts, and the latest, the only one from

this year, is about the apartment. He posted it a week ago, and it's written in Danish, but I translate it, confirming that he has been asking his friends if anyone is interested in living with him. There are no pictures of the place, just the rent (not too bad), the neighborhood (Østerbro, very central), and when it's possible to move in (ASAP). It sounds great. I need it.

I call him again the next morning. Maybe if I invite him for lunch, he'll say yes, and we'll be able to talk properly. But he doesn't pick up. I consider texting him, but Larissa says I should stop before he thinks I'm a creep.

I stare at my phone screen, sighing. On impulse, my thumb opens Cinder, the dating app topping the charts in Denmark since its release seven years ago. It's just like Tinder, but its Cinderella theme was both so praised and so mocked that many people decided to try it—and then it became so popular it's the top choice of those looking for a date in Copenhagen. I find it fun and, at the same time, uninspiring. I wish there was a dating app with less focus on looks and more on matching like-minded people.

That's because you're not supposed to look for a life partner in those apps, Larissa said one day when we were discussing the subject. *Most people there* are *just looking for a hot person to spend the night with.*

I'm aware of that, of course, but I'm an incurable romantic who keeps telling herself she'll eventually match with a cute Dane who also didn't delete the app because he's a hopeless optimist.

I study my Cinder profile. My picture is great, and I'll forever claim it's because Larissa is a talented photographer, while she'll always say it's because I'm the best model she could have.

In the photo, I'm smiling brightly, laughing at something Larissa had said. My skin is darker, tanned by an excellent Brazilian summer, and my hair is falling nicely over my shoulders in loose waves, all dark brown—before the honey-colored *ombré* I let Flor do on me one afternoon when there were no customers in the salon and we got bored. It hasn't even been a year since I posed for that picture, yet I already feel like it's not a faithful image of who I am now.

Knowing these might be my last days in Copenhagen gives me the unanticipated wish to be naughty. To enjoy this wonderful city while I can. To kiss a hot Danish guy. And maybe do a little more…

My heartbeat rises as I watch the typographic Cinder logo glint over the slogan: Find the one who fits your glass slipper.

For once, I won't be Cinderella looking for her Prince Charming.

I go to my profile settings, and under the "I'm looking for" section, I uncheck Relationship and tap on Casual Encounter.

If I'm not staying, there's no point in finding my soulmate in Denmark. But that doesn't mean I shouldn't bring back memories of one dreamy date. I'm on my third "like" when the next man on the list makes my heart stop.

Erik Storm.

It's the same surfer dude photo from his Facebook profile. I'm not usually attracted to men with long hair, and his face is barely visible in the picture. But his level of attractiveness doesn't matter. That's not what's keeping me in his profile.

It's the chance to talk to him in person.

I chew on my lower lip, staring at his picture.

Should I do it?

It would be wrong…

I do it. I give him a glass slipper.

Giggling into my hands like a teenager, I spin in the desk chair, round and round, until I'm dizzy. He won't like me back anyway…

He likes me back.

I jump to my feet. *Holy Fairy Godmother.*

You are a match!—the notification pops up on my screen. Two glass slippers meet, twinkling as they form a pair, and a message prompts me to interact with Erik Storm.

I spend a minute laughing and pacing the room, then I send him a date request. Tonight at 9:00 p.m., at a pub in the city center. It's in three hours. He would never say yes…

He accepts it.

I laugh out loud again. Unbelievable.

He doesn't know I'm the woman bugging him about the apartment. I never gave him my name. When he finds out, he'll probably flee. But I'm desperate. I can't let this opportunity slip by.

It's fate…

Three

Erik Storm is no surfer dude.

He is a Viking.

And he is hot.

"Hi," he says, and it's impossible to tell if it's in English or Danish, as the *hej* greeting sounds exactly like *hi*. "Sol?"

I nod, smiling. He pronounces it right. My stomach leaps.

"*Dansk?* English?" He gets up from the bar stool to offer me his right hand. I'd usually go for a one-arm hug or, as is common in Brazil, a cheek kiss, but I shake his hand like he wants, looking at his prominent muscles. He was way skinnier in his profile picture. It was probably taken years ago.

"English," I say with no shame. Nearly everyone in Denmark speaks English. It's why I haven't bothered taking Danish lessons in my limited free time. "And yes, Sol. Well, Marisol. But people call me Sol."

I look up at his face—he must be at least six foot two while I'm five-four—caught off guard by his rough beauty. I'm used to seeing blue eyes everywhere by now, but his are especially bright. It looks as though he was sculpted by Odin himself. His nose is beautiful, his teeth are white and aligned, his eyebrows are expressive, and there is a toughness in his jaw that matches his thick beard.

A lot more beard than I would normally find interesting.

And a lot more hair too. Only now his golden-blond locks are tied up in a bun.

Well, it's good that I'm not here to date him.

"How are you doing?" I ask, trying to keep my nerves under control.

"I'm good. Take a seat," he invites, and I accommodate myself on the stool next to him. He is wearing a plain black T-shirt and jeans, and the combo looks fabulous on his body.

It's an English pub, crowded at this hour, so we can't take one of the tables, but that's fine. It's cozy to sit at the bar, with the warm light of old-fashioned lamps reflecting off the wooden surfaces and duplicating in the mirror behind glinting bottles of liquor.

"Do you want a drink?" His voice is rough and deep… Rather sexy.

Don't think about that.

I'm here for the apartment. I can't throw away my future for a night with Erik Storm, no matter how Asgardian he may be.

"Sure," I say, swallowing hard.

"So, tell me a bit about yourself, Sol."

The bartender comes, and Erik orders two pints of lager for us. As I conclude that I should wait until the alcohol lightens up his mood before revealing why I'm here, I lift my glass, and we toast.

"Skål," he says. "It means cheers."

"I know. I've been here for almost six months."

"Where are you from?"

"Brazil. And you're Danish, I guess?"

He nods, swallowing a big mouthful. "Brazil? Wow. I've always wanted to go there."

"Rio?" It's always about Rio.

"Of course. Which city are you from?"

"Not Rio." I drink too. If I'm doing this, I better be tipsy. "Brasília," I tell him.

"The capital."

I give him an acknowledging nod. "You know that. Ten points for you."

He laughs at my random scoring—a little game I used to play with my best friend. Erik clinks his glass on mine, and we both drink.

"Is it nice in Brasília?"

"It's fine, but the nearest beach is over six hundred miles away," I say, wincing like I always do whenever I'm reminded of the biggest con of my always warm—and half the year too rainy, half too dry—hometown.

"Oh, I couldn't imagine living so far from the sea," Erik says, reflecting what I'd probably say myself if I'd lived on the coast all my life.

"Where were you in your profile photo?" I drink faster now to see if he will follow. The quicker we get inebriated, the better.

"Colombia," he says, and I lift my eyebrows.

"Oh, so you've been to South America!" I don't know why that surprises me to the point of making my heart race. He's probably lived a financially comfortable life that allowed him to travel the world. So what?

"I love your continent," he says with a light shrug and a carefree smile that makes my breathing fussy.

"Then why haven't you visited Brazil? I'm offended." I tilt my head, assessing him with a critical eye, even though I'm not truly offended. He laughs, and I attribute the unwelcome fluttering in my stomach to the beer I'm consuming too fast. It's definitely *not* because of the golden strands of hair slipping out of his bun and falling over his face, where he lets them be.

"It wasn't in the itinerary, sadly," he answers in a casual tone, and I'm somehow glad for the vague explanation. The lighter and more impersonal we keep this exchange, the better. "Your country deserves a dedicated trip, north to south," he adds.

I put my hair behind my ear in an instinctive reaction to looking at his loose strands, which I can't move away from his face.

"Good save," I reply, his smile convincing me of nothing but his seductive intentions, which I'm intent on keeping at bay.

We keep talking about traveling while drinking our pints. I learn that he had two "gap years" between high school and college in which he worked at a restaurant to earn money for a four-month backpacking trip across the world. Universities are free in Denmark, and his grades were good, so when he returned, he had no trouble getting into his desired program—a bachelor's degree in software engineering at the IT University of Copenhagen. Right after graduating, he started a master's in games.

I tell him I have no master's, only a bachelor's in design.

Before I reveal that I work at Scorpio Games, I stop and gulp down the last of my beer.

"What did you do after your master's?" I ask, pretending not to know that he worked at Scorpio.

"I'll need a stronger drink before talking about that part of my story," he says jokingly, but a shadow crosses his eyes.

I smile with sympathy, but to myself, I'm thinking, *Was Scorpio so bad?* "Let's get you some liquor then."

"No, no," Erik says with a grin. "It's too early for that." He winks, and I feel another little quiver in my stomach, both because he can be so charming and because the implication that there might be a later for us will be crushed when I reveal that he has fallen into the trap I've set up for him.

I can't let this continue any longer. It was a mistake.

"I'm sorry… I shouldn't have invited you here."

"What are you talking about?" Erik frowns a little, amusement still playing on his lips. He's affected by the cheerful vibe of the alcohol, the laughing crowd, and the upbeat music in the background.

He thinks I'm joking, and it's tempting to let him believe that. I can't though. As I remain serious, his smile starts to fade, until his brow furrows in confusion.

"You'll hate me when I say it…" I look down to avoid his eyes.

"Say what?" His voice is louder now that the noise in the bar has increased. He comes closer to my face, making it hard for me not to look at him. We're surrounded by people. It's feeling a little claustrophobic.

"I should leave." A flush of boiling heat rises to my face,

threatening to burn my cheeks. I'm getting up, but Erik holds my wrist.

"Come on, Sol. Say it. What's wrong?" He blinks, confused.

"I'm the woman who called you about the spare room in your apartment," I say, the words spilling out.

Erik bangs a hand on the counter like a true Viking. I examine his face, my heart hammering. He doesn't look angry. Wait. Is he…*laughing*?

"Good job, Sol. Very clever move. Ten points for you." He lifts his empty glass. "Cheers!"

He's annoyed, yes, but also amused, as if he's mocking himself for having believed he could have a pleasant night with a girl he met on Cinder. I can't let this hurt his confidence. That's not fair. This is all on me.

"Listen." It's my turn to hold his wrist as he gets up. "I'm very sorry I did this. I regret it. It wasn't nice."

"You think so?" His sarcasm is so natural it might pass unnoticed. I keep holding him in place. It's too hot in this bar. I need to breathe the cool air outside, but I'm not leaving until he forgives me.

"I never expected to find you on Cinder. I was honestly looking to have a last night of fun, then your profile popped up, and it felt like…fate." I look down, overly aware of how much I'm flushing and perspiring. I wipe my hands on my dress.

"It's fine," he mutters. His hand is closed in a fist though.

"I'm desperate, Erik," I say, a bit more firmly, gazing at him.

"It's noticeable," he replies with an aloofness that gets on my nerves.

I stand up too, now so hot that a drop of sweat trickles

down my spine. "You turned me down without even telling me why."

"That's how these things go, Sol." He opens his arms as wide as the crowded space permits. "The one who contacts you first wins."

"That's not true," I say, hiding my shame in the bottomless pit my stomach has become. "You didn't close the deal yet or you would have said so. You want the best match, not the first—"

He chuckles. "And you think you're the best match?"

"I need this room—"

"This is not charity," he interrupts me again, and I'm getting so irritated my voice is rising.

"I know that!" People are looking at us now. Erik notices and makes a gesture for me to sit down. I don't want to make a scene, so I take a deep breath, relax in my seat, and lower my voice. "Listen, I pay on time and I keep things tidy. Besides, I'm up for a promotion. We can help each other out."

Erik blinks at me with his long golden lashes, his jaw tight, and I hurry to give him the rest of my convincing speech.

"I only made this desperate move because I finally have the chance to get my dream job," I say, and as he doesn't interrupt, I continue, eyes on his. "If I have a place to live and I impress my boss in the next few months, I might get a promotion, and then I can stay here, living the life I always wanted, away from my family's influence and the lack of opportunities in my hometown." I keep speaking, afraid that if I take a break, he'll walk away. "You don't know where I came from and how hard I had to fight to arrive where I am." The words are coming out so fast I'm barely breathing.

"Things never came easy for me. I'm used to moving mountains to get what I need."

Saying all this to a stranger feels awkward yet…liberating. My chest is suddenly lighter, even though my lungs are working almost as hard as they do when I go for a run on a cold Danish morning.

Erik stares at me, and I can't tell if he's moved by my monologue or if he doesn't care at all.

"Where are you living now?" he speaks at last, maintaining his poker face.

"In a studio apartment I need to move out of next Monday." Every time I'm reminded of this, I feel like I'm being punched in the gut. That apartment became my home—my precious sanctuary of silence and solitude—but it was never mine. "I have nowhere else to go. Not even a friend's couch." I flush when I admit this, but it's the truth. Except for Chiara, whom I chat with at the office, I haven't gotten close to anyone here. And letting him believe I have friends—or anyone else in the city who cares—wouldn't help my case.

"And you're getting a promotion?"

"Yes," I say a bit too avidly. Then I pause. "Maybe. I was going to quit, but my boss told me I might become game director if I stay."

"At Scorpio Games?" He remembers I said I work there when I called him, of course. There is bitterness in his tone, but that shouldn't surprise me. He left the company. Mark told me it was because he wanted to work on a personal project, but I'll probably never know the real reason.

"Yes. And I need that promotion."

I watch his face for any reaction. His left eyebrow trembles almost imperceptibly, but that's all.

"Why did you come to Denmark?" he asks, intertwining his fingers on the bar top. "You mentioned your family and a lack of opportunities, but why not Rio or England?"

Is he interviewing me for the room? I hope so. At the same time, I don't feel very inclined to tell him my very personal reasons for being in his country. All I've laid bare in front of him tonight was enough.

So I just give him the answer I give everyone who asks that question. "I needed a fresh start, and what better place than the happiest country in the world?"

"Is that it?" One of his eyebrows climbs in an unconvinced expression that is sexy and irritating at the same time.

I blink slowly, not letting myself be affected—that is, if my heart pounding madly doesn't count. "Well, there's Denmark's quality of life index, the free health care, the low crime rate, the work-life balance, the hygge…and games jobs that pay a good salary."

"I didn't ask you to quote a 'Ten Reasons to Live in Denmark' blog post," he says, cold, rigid, and large as a stone. No, a statue. A pretty one. Michelangelo level. But even prettier.

Stop thinking about his inhuman beauty, Sol, for the gods' sake.

"I'm sorry to disappoint you, but I did read plenty of those articles before deciding to come," I say, treating him with his own indifference. I sip from my glass to illustrate how much his tone doesn't bother me—even though it does.

"Then you found a job here?" I catch a glint in his eyes that wasn't there before, but I'm not entirely sure what it means.

"It was the other way around," I tell him, still in my shrug-off mode. "I got the job, then I read up on Denmark."

"How did that happen? Did Scorpio headhunt you?" He seems a tiny bit more interested now, so I sit straighter and seize the opportunity. I might not want to share, but I want him to *care*, and I'll do what it takes. I didn't come this far to give up.

"I used to work at this indie game studio in Brasília called Vortex Games," I tell him, running a finger around the rim of my glass. "One day, I went to a video game conference in São Paulo and met game developers from all over the world, including people who worked at Scorpio."

Erik nods, showing me he's listening. For the first time since I revealed why I asked him out, he looks interested in what I'm saying. There are still remnants of the poker face in his features, but now his eyes tell me he's concentrating on my words, not on a plan to get rid of me.

"I talked to the recruiter and some designers," I go on. "They liked me and I liked them. But there was one person who made the biggest impression."

I lower my eyes to the bar top, the nodes in the wood turning into shapes that build a full picture of that day in my mind.

Cristina—so beautiful, confident and successful. Mikkel, Cristina's handsome and kind Danish husband, who followed her around not only with love and devotion but with all the attention and help she needed. I watched them, fascinated—and more than a bit jealous.

"Who was it that made the biggest impression on you?" Erik asks me after my long pause.

"A game director I met," I say, looking down, thinking back to that day again.

I wasn't prepared for what I'd feel when I talked to them. To *her.* This successful young woman who had everything I suddenly needed in a dreamy land that felt like the one and only place to live the life I always knew I wanted.

She was proof it was possible.

"I realized I wanted to get where she'd gotten," I tell Erik.

Cristina wasn't Scandinavian. She was Spanish. She told me how she had adapted. How Denmark had changed her habits and turned her into the best version of herself. She was excited about the prospect of being a mother in the near future because Denmark was such a great country to raise children.

She convinced me. She lured me. And after that I couldn't think about anything other than getting the kind of life she had.

"What was her name?" Erik asks. "Maybe I've met her."

"Cristina." I'm about to say her last name, but Erik doesn't need it.

"I've worked with her. She left a month or two after me."

"Yeah, I never talked to her again. She wasn't there when I started. I heard she got an even better opportunity at another studio."

"Yeah, she was great." He looks down, his fingers distractedly folding a napkin. It's like his aura changes whenever Scorpio Games is mentioned. His shoulders tense up, his voice gets weaker, and his eyes roam around as if seeking a way out. I want to ask him why *he* left, but I'm not entitled to that question. This interview is about me.

"What is your role?" Erik's gaze finds mine again.

"Level designer," I answer in a tone I judge as neutral, but the minimal way his lips stretch up reveals he saw right through me, all the way into the corner where I bury my hostile feelings toward my current position.

"And now you have the opportunity to get the job you actually want?" His gaze stays firm on mine as he studies me. I fight against the urge to look away. *This is how you win*, a voice in my head encourages me. *Laying yourself bare.*

"Yes," I answer his question, swallowing hard because I feel like I'm naked under this man's stare, and such a thought makes me blush from head to toe. *Gosh, Sol. Pull. Yourself. Together.*

"And then you'll find your fairy-tale ending in the happiest country in the world?"

I empty my lungs with a sound that resembles laughter. I'm not letting his teasing, his skepticism, get to me. "Yeah, exactly. Dream life, dream career, and maybe even a prince. Sadly, the princes and counts of Denmark are either already married or too young for me. But you never know."

Erik pretends not to laugh, but I see the corners of his mouth turning up. His approval of my humor makes me want to smile too, but I stop myself.

"I'm sure you have dreams too," I say, looking at him. "Come on, Erik, help me save mine."

He puts on another poker face, this one gentler but impenetrable nonetheless.

I add a new entry to my "desperate moves" list. "I'll pay you two thousand crowns more for the rent."

He snorts. "I won't extort you."

"*Please*, Erik." I hate begging, but I'm doing it.

He takes a deep breath and leans very close to my face. He smells of beer and some fresh citrusy cologne that gets my hormones dancing. I repress them.

"Since we are being honest with each other, I'll tell you why I turned you down." As he is basically whispering, I get my ear closer to his mouth, eager to hear the truth. "Because you're a woman," he says, and I almost fall off my stool. The anger that was gone returns in a boiling wave.

"What? I can't believe that's—" but he doesn't let me rage out.

"It was unfair, I know. I'm sorry I jumped to conclusions when having so little knowledge, but I was right in the end." I shake my head in disbelief, and he raises his hand to make a point. "I don't want to live with an attractive, straight, cis woman, okay? I assumed you were that by your voice, which was wrong, but I was right in the end." He sounds much less confident now, embarrassed even.

I laugh to digest all I heard. "That is simply—"

"Don't judge me when you don't know my history," he says, clear and sharp as a razor.

And then I understand everything.

"Your former roommate broke your heart, didn't she?"

Erik's short, mirthless laugh and the way he averts his eyes tell me I'm right.

"Why do you even want to be a game director?" he asks me out of the blue. The interview—or should I say *interrogation*—is not over yet, it seems.

I fix my posture and look straight into his eyes. He needs to see how much I care. "Because I want to have creative freedom and decision-making power over a project." Martin's smug face pops into my mind, and I smirk. "And it wouldn't be bad to wipe the smile off Martin's face."

Erik goes rigid. "Who?"

"My nemesis." I shiver as if Martin disgusts me. "The guy I'm competing with for the promotion."

Erik's mouth opens in an O. "So, you have competition, and Martin..."

"Olesen, big jerk, will try to take me down, but I won't let him. No, sir."

A crease deepens on Erik's forehead. He nods slowly, thoughtful. "Do you smoke?" he asks suddenly. "Own a pet? Any habits I should know about?"

I blink at him, surprised.

"No to all three." My heart is thumping. Is he considering me? "I'm a sweet, respectful, considerate person free of addictions. I'm the best roommate you could ask for."

He drums his fingers on the table, lips pursed, forehead furrowed in thought. I keep looking at him with a straight posture, waiting patiently.

"I respect your hustle, your dream," he says, getting my already fast-beating heart to the speed of a hummingbird's. "I have dreams of my own, of course. And I like you," he adds reluctantly, and my stomach does a cartwheel in response. "The other deal did fall through, so..."

"So...?" I encourage him. *Just stop killing me and say it already.*

"I'll choose you."

I can't help my smile. Erik isn't done though.

"But listen well." He leans closer again, his eyes locked on mine. "You in your room, me in mine. Shared kitchen, shared bathroom, but boundaries are *always* in place. Do you understand?"

I nod, so overwhelmed I keep the silly smile on my face.

"I have rules," he continues, "and I'll share them with you.

But there's one *absolutely* nonnegotiable condition." Erik takes his jacket off the counter, and at this point, I'm not smiling anymore. Or feeling any part of my body. He points his index finger at my nose after putting on the jacket. "We will never, *ever* be romantically involved."

I stare into his glassy blue eyes. I can easily stay away from him. He is an attractive Viking, but I'm a Prince Charming girl.

"Do we have a deal?" Erik Storm holds his hand out to me.

I shake it. "Deal."

Four

I move into Erik's apartment on September 29, a rainy Sunday, and because I have no one else to help me with my boxes and suitcases, Erik kindly offers a hand. He borrows his cousin's car, and since his cousin can't join us, Erik does all the muscle work, carrying my things up the stairs and into my new bedroom. He's being polite and formal, speaks no more than is necessary and keeps a respectful distance, making it clear this is a professional relationship.

The apartment is on the second floor in a cute historical building without an elevator, facing the northern end of the Copenhagen Lakes in the Østerbro area. It's all so wonderful, I can hardly believe it. Given that most of the furniture and appliances I had been using belong in the studio apartment I just vacated, we are done after a few rounds of climb and descend.

My room has a built-in wardrobe, large windowsills that can be used to put things on, and the former tenant left a chair, a standing lamp, and a cheap night table. I don't have a bed yet, but I'll fix that.

"Do you need help with anything else, or should I leave you alone to unpack?" Erik stands in the doorway, slightly out of breath, wet with a mix of sweat and rain. My eyes keep returning to his muscles, but every time I realize I'm staring, I breathe and make myself busy with something.

I should talk about the bed situation, but I don't want to bother him more. Online shopping is here for people like me. "What about a little tour of the home and a quick presentation of your rules?"

"Sure. Maybe some water first?"

Erik leads me to the fridge, where he takes out two bottles of mineral water, and we drink while he shows me where everything is.

The kitchen is a narrow room with a long counter containing all the appliances you expect to find in a typical Danish kitchen, which are marvelous for someone who grew up in a humble Brazilian home. There's an induction cooktop, an electric kettle, and a dishwasher well disguised behind a cabinet door. The fridge is packed with healthy food, and Erik has a bunch of spices and cooking oils near the stove.

The kitchen opens to a shared area lit up by a big window with a view of the lakes and a geometric lamp hanging over a round dining table matched with four sleek chairs. There is also a bookcase filled with hardcover titles old and new, and a basket with folded wool blankets. Erik stands near the kitchen with his water bottle, letting me explore.

"Can I use everything here?"

"Yes, as long as you are careful." I look at him, and he

smiles. For some reason, seeing him drop the serious face he's had all day makes something inside of me heat up and dance. I'm a happy-atmosphere chaser, no matter who I'm with.

"Is your bedroom there?" I point at the closed French doors facing the dining table. The glass panes are covered by a curtain inside the other room.

"Yep. It was supposed to be a living room, but I chose it as my room because it's the largest space." He moves his eyebrows up and down to illustrate his smartness.

I smile. "Can I see it?"

"This is the only time you'll get a glimpse of my cave. Enjoy the few seconds of this privilege."

He opens the doors to the most organized and beautifully designed male room I've ever seen.

It's bigger than the studio I was living in. Erik has a double bed in one corner with four fat pillows and a thick duvet neatly stretched over the mattress. The other side of the room is a mini living room with a couch facing a big TV and many shelves with books and other personal objects tastefully arranged. There are a few plants and lamps strategically placed, a desk with a closed laptop, and a small wardrobe that seems to contain all his clothes, as there are no pieces dropped on the floor.

It's like an IKEA showroom.

"I'll give you twenty points for this," I say. He looks at me and laughs, closing the doors again.

We go to the bathroom, and Erik shows me how to operate the shower, the washing machine, and the dryer.

"I'm still waiting for the rules," I say when he's done.

Erik leans casually in the doorway with his arms folded, and

I can't help but notice how big his biceps look when they are flexed. "It's basic stuff relying on common sense. Respect my privacy. Clean up after yourself. Wait your turn. Not much more." He shrugs. "We just have to figure out a schedule for cleaning and cooking. And if you want to use the bathroom for long periods, I'd like to know in advance. But in general, don't bother me. The home is yours too."

I nod, relieved. I was expecting a long list of tyrannical rules.

"You said cooking. How will that work? Can I shop for my things and keep them on a shelf in the fridge? Or are we doing some sort of common shopping?"

"No common shopping. No sharing of expenses. You have your things, I have mine." He then relaxes his posture, as if regretting his sudden brusqueness. "Just so it doesn't get confusing," he adds in a humbler tone.

"I understand. No problem."

We nod to each other, an uncomfortable silence filling the bathroom, which suddenly feels too small for the two of us. So tiny it's suffocating. Way too hot. I hold my breath when he squeezes through the door I'm half blocking, his chest lightly brushing my shoulder.

"We still haven't discussed the cooking," I say once he's out and I can breathe again. Sort of. "Do you make your dinner and I make mine, or would it make sense that I cook one day and you cook the next?" I'm not even done with the suggestion, and I already know it was a bad idea.

"I cook at seven every day. You are free to make your food before that or after eight."

I mumble an "okay" and decide it's time to unpack my things.

"And Sol," he calls when I've already started walking to my room. I turn around and look at him expectantly. It takes a moment for him to continue, a moment in which we stare at each other, both now occupying the small corridor. "Welcome home," he says at last.

I give him a genuine smile, drawing all the excitement and gratefulness from the bottom of my heart. "It's all perfect, Erik. Thank you so much."

The smile that stretches across his bearded face makes my stomach react in an undesirable way. I realize it's going to be hard to live with Erik Storm. But I can handle hard.

Oh goodness.

"You're welcome," he says. I want to hug him. And normally if I'm grateful, that's what I'd do. But for some reason, I just stand still, looking at the Norse god I'm living with.

What have you done, Sol?

My conflicting emotions wrestle inside me, and for a second, I think *he* will be the one to hug me. But then he steps back, and his smile fades as he says, "Have a good day."

And he locks himself in his glorious cave.

It's late afternoon when Erik appears at my door. He comes to tell me something about the dishwasher, but when he notices I'm lying on a yoga mat with a pillow under my head as I scroll on my phone, he frowns and says, "You don't have a bed."

I mean, he carried my things up the stairs. Did he think I could conjure a bed out of thin air?

"I'm trying to buy one, but the delivery times are awful."

"I thought you already bought one."

"And that it would arrive tonight?" I lift my gaze to him in a skeptical stare.

"Yes. I just thought you had this better planned out."

"Well, I thought I was going back to Brazil."

He sighs. "Sorry. I don't have a mattress you can borrow. There is only the bed in my room and my couch." He sounds weary. I can easily hear what he left unsaid: *And I'm not letting you sleep in my room.*

That's fine. Because I don't need his help. I return my gaze to my phone.

"You have really looked everywhere?" His tone changes, becoming more sympathetic. But I don't buy his concern. Whatever act of kindness he might do will be strictly for his benefit. In this case, so I don't have to—*God forbid*, he'd think—sleep on his couch.

Don't be so harsh on him. He gave you the room, after all, Larissa's voice echoes in my head. I often have imaginary conversations with my best friend, and the Sol version of Larissa is relentless.

He gave me the room, yes, but I have the impression Erik Storm never does anything he won't benefit from in some way. Charity is not his business, as he made clear to me at the pub.

"Yes, I've looked in every online store, but it will take at least three to five business days to arrive. Suggestions?"

"The biggest furniture store in Scandinavia, maybe?" Erik leans on the door in that casual way that makes his biceps look infused with super soldier serum. "You could go there."

When he sees my incredulous stare, he corrects himself, surrendering, "*We* could go there. In my cousin's car. He won't pick it up before tomorrow." I'm about to say it sounds good when he adds, "Or you can take the car if you want."

"I don't drive," I tell him dryly. "Much less in Denmark."

Erik shrugs, looking more relaxed than he is feeling, I'm sure. "Fine. We leave in ten."

Five

It's a long drive, but the silence in the car is not tense—it's comfortable, expected. We have nothing to say to each other; no need to impress or build a friendship. We are just two people sharing a ride to get something done. No big deal.

I don't feel that Erik is angry at me for forcing him out of the apartment on a Sunday evening for a boring shopping trip. I guess this is so far from what a date usually looks like that it doesn't even bother him. Maybe he is already getting used to my presence. Maybe we will grow so indifferent to each other that we won't have any weird feelings being in the same room.

Once we are inside the store, I quickly discover why he was okay with coming along. He needed something from here. I almost laugh at having a confirmation of my earlier thoughts.

He puts a few hangers and kitchen utensils in the shopping cart as we walk around. It's a huge place with lots of departments, and I marvel at the immense selection and the reasonable prices. Like Erik, I start to grab a bunch of things that will be useful at home. We share the same shopping cart, but he doesn't seem to mind.

When we reach the floor with the showrooms, I point at an elegant living room and ask, "Did you design your room based on something you saw here?"

"My mom helped me decorate the apartment. She's an architect."

I smile. "Oh. That explains it. And what does your dad do?"

We walk slowly, looking around like the many couples surrounding us. Except we are not a couple, and we never will be. And we are not arguing over cabinets and carpets or running after yelling children.

A little white-haired boy grabs my long skirt, hiding from his big sister. I smile at him and politely detangle myself as the dad comes running down the aisle, shouting at his wife, "We are *not* getting those!" I look back and see her dump something in their cart, saying, "Yes, we are!"

"My dad is a physics professor," Erik answers my question with serenity, as if the lives of families and partners are not being built—or crumbling—all around us.

"Do your parents live in Copenhagen?" I ask as we enter the children's department, moving with the flow. Erik is a private person, but if we're living together, I want to know more about him.

"No, they live in Jutland, near Aarhus. Do you know where that is?"

I nod. I studied Denmark's geography before coming, and Aarhus is the second biggest city. "I've seen some pictures. It looks cute there."

He agrees, smiling. "I was born there and moved to Copenhagen when I started my bachelor's."

"Do you have any siblings?"

"A younger sister who lives in Amsterdam." For a moment, I think he won't ask about my family, but when we turn the next corner, entering the area with the bedrooms, he says, "What about you?"

"I have a big, noisy family," I tell him, smiling. "My mom is a hairdresser, my dad is a high school gym teacher. I have a brother three years younger than me who lives in Rio, a grandpa, two aunts, four uncles, and too many cousins."

As if my family had been listening, ready to make a dramatic appearance, my phone rings. I look at the time—7:30 p.m. In Brasília, 2:30 p.m. It's my mom's usual time to call, when she takes a break in the salon.

I reject the video call. I'm writing her a message to say I'm not home when she calls again. I show the phone to Erik: Call from Mãe over a selfie of my mom smiling at the camera with her 7.4 Copper Gold Blond short bob. I suggested it. The color matches perfectly with her warm brown eyes.

"See?" I shake the vibrating phone in front of him, laughing because this is so typical of Rosana Carvalho, calling and calling again. "This is my family. They think I must answer their calls no matter what I'm doing, because I owe them now that I moved across the ocean."

"I can see where you got it from. The persistence." He eyes me, serious in his sarcasm, but it gets a smile out of me.

I answer the call because my mom won't stop disturbing me. I put on headphones so the whole store won't have to hear her say, *"Sol, minha filha! Já estava ficando preocupada!"*

Which directly translated means, "Sol, my daughter, I was getting worried!"

"Oi, Mãe," I say with a half smile and move away from the frame for her to see that I'm in a store. "I'm here to buy a bed, so I can't talk right now," I say in Portuguese. My mom speaks zero English.

"A bed? Did you find an apartment?" Her voice is so loud I suspect Erik can hear it through my headphones. I lower the volume.

"Yes. I moved in today."

"And you didn't think to tell us?" She sounds outraged. If I'd found an apartment in Brasília, or anywhere else in Brazil, she'd be there as fast as public transportation would allow, with as many bags of food and utensils as she could carry. Denying her that, or even the *knowledge* that I moved, is to my mom like excluding her from my life, and she wants to be *involved.*

"Sorry, Mom. It all happened so fast, and I didn't want to jinx it. I was going to tell you tomorrow when I was settled."

Mom nods slowly. "It's fine. I understand."

And from one second to the next, the indignation is gone, replaced by her typical motherly enthusiasm—which goes hand in hand with her instinct to tell the world what her daughter has accomplished.

"Girls, Sol found an apartment!" she shouts to the women behind her—some having their nails done, others with caps on their heads. One of my mom's loyal customers, Edna, a divorced sixty-five-year-old lady who goes to the salon every other week to straighten her hair or dye her roots, lowers the beauty magazine she is reading and waves at the screen.

"Hey, Sol! Congratulations, dear!"

"Let's not celebrate yet!" Mom says. "Sol, you need to give us some details."

I bite my lip. Oh dear. I didn't want to have this conversation in the middle of a home goods store.

"I'll call you when I get home, okay? I have to—"

"Ah, Sol, now you'll tell us all about it!" My cousin that works at the salon, Luana, takes the phone out of my mom's hand and sits with it on the couch. Other women gather around her, including Luana's younger sister and my former roommate, Mariana, my mom, and my teenage cousin, Bruna, who is often there doing her homework while waiting for Tio Antônio to pick her up after work.

"Do you live alone, Sol?" Bruna asks me. She is sixteen and already dreaming of the day she can leave her parents' house. Like me, Bruna can't stand crowded homes, especially when the people living in them have little care for privacy and introversion. I should feel lucky that Erik is so mindful about personal space.

"Do you, Sol?" someone is asking me. Mariana, maybe.

"How much do you pay? Is it near the city center?" a customer I don't recognize asks.

"Copenhagen must be a dream city!" Another unknown voice.

"Sol, you don't live alone, do you?" says Edna.

"The person I live with is nice," I say, taking a quick glimpse at Erik. He is a few steps ahead of me, looking at some boxes on a shelf.

"Is she a student? What is her name?" Mom asks.

I used the word "person" to avoid gender, which is a hard

thing in my language. But I can't escape now. I don't lie to my family.

"Erik. No, he's not a student."

WRONG ANSWER, WRONG ANSWER—their stares scream at me like a wailing siren. My face becomes hot.

"Are you living with a *man*?" My mom is literally shouting now. While her expression is shocked and disapproving, the other women have more amused reactions. Some laugh, some clap, and others tap each other as if they have already made a bet about me. I roll my eyes.

"Calm down, all of you." I'm so glad Erik can't hear or understand this conversation…

But wait, what if he speaks Portuguese? Or some Spanish? He's been to South America. He might have lived in Portugal. I must watch what I say.

"I knew she would find someone quickly! With those big dark eyes and that smooth olive skin of hers…" Edna says to Regina, another customer I know, as if I'm not hearing. "Not to mention the beautiful *ombré* you gave her, Flor," Edna says to my favorite hairdresser.

"Thank you, Edna! It indeed looks lovely on her!"

"Girls, I am NOT dating him, okay? I needed a place urgently, and a guy was renting out his spare room, and that's it!"

"I believe her," Mariana says. "I helped Sol look for apartments in Copenhagen online when she was here, and we couldn't find anything."

"Precisely," I say, glad for the support. "Thank you, Mari."

"What's he like? Show us a picture!"

"Is he there with you?"

"Erik… I like that name."

I lose track of who is speaking. Too many women at the same time. I answer, just so they can let me go find my bed. Erik will get annoyed if I don't focus on it soon.

"Yes, he came to help me buy a bed."

"I want to see him!"

Erik is right ahead of me, about four steps away as we walk along the aisle. I flip the camera so they can quickly see his back.

But that is, of course, a mistake.

They can spot an attractive man miles away.

I should have noticed that his muscles are quite prominent even in a sweater.

"Oh my God, he's so sexy!" Luana squeals.

"Let me see, let me see!" Bruna moves closer to the camera, but they are all fighting to have their noses on the screen.

"You are living with *this* man, Sol?" my mom reacts, and her tone announces her conflicting emotions. She wants her daughter to find a handsome man capable of producing beautiful grandchildren for her, but she fears losing me to a guy who lives on the other side of the planet.

"I love a man bun!" Mariana says when she sees Erik's long hair, now with only the upper half twisted up in a knot.

"Oh, what hair! It's gorgeous! Look at all the tones of blond," Flor comments dreamily.

"I want that color!" Regina says, pulling the phone toward her. My mom takes control of it again and walks from woman to woman so they can all see Erik closely.

"His hair is natural," Luana's voice says. "You can never copy it perfectly."

"Sol, is he your boyfriend?" my mom is asking. Not severe, just serious. She wants the truth.

I'm controlling myself, not wanting to shout or end the call without another word. As annoying and intrusive as they might be sometimes, they all love me and mean well. Besides, I've learned to tackle things with humor. To tease and be teased.

"No, he is not, and I mean it," I say firmly, but with a suggestive smile. They laugh and I laugh back, reassuring them that I am *not* lying.

"Hey, Sol, what about this one?" Erik turns his head, and they get a glimpse of his face—and all the beard. I lower the camera a bit, afraid he will realize I'm filming him.

"Well, that's it, girls. I have to buy a bed now."

"So, you don't sleep in his. Hmmm…"

"Don't buy one! Share one with this Greek god…"

"*Norse* god."

"He looks *just* like Thor!"

"See you, girls!" And I end the call.

Phew.

I focus. Or try to. It's hard when, in my head, I can still hear an entourage of squealing women telling me how hot my roommate is.

He's not my type though. I want a Prince Charming—someone sweet, romantic, stable—not a Viking. They are wild, rough, aggressive, and likely to run off on a whim to fight a battle. They aren't family men. With them, it's all about the fun, and they won't hesitate to use their seduction skills to get what they want. So, yeah, I keep Vikings away from my bed.

But can he *keep me away from his?*

I repress this weird thought and concentrate on the bed. Yes. The bed. A good bed to sleep in. Alone. All by myself.

We find a suitable one. A queen because I'm spacious.

And I don't intend on being all by myself for all my years in Denmark.

The store is closing in ten minutes. We take the elevator down and push our cart through the storage hall, brimming with cardboard boxes of all shapes and sizes. We finally find the correct shelf, but to our dismay, it's empty.

We run to find help. The saleswoman tells me they will have to deliver the bed to me tomorrow. I sigh and give her my address. Erik and I pay for our stuff separately and go back to the car.

We drive home silently, and the dreaded moment comes. Once we enter the apartment, he looks at me, deep in thought. My heart is racing and my palms are sweaty. What do I expect he'll do?

It's in his hands now. Letting me sleep on the floor or...

"You can have my bed if you want," he offers casually, like it's not something he avoided saying at all costs. "I'll sleep on the couch."

"Erik, I don't want to disturb you. I can just—"

"Relax, Sol." When he passes by, he taps my shoulder, and I feel so weird about this whole situation, I stand at the entrance for a few seconds, processing it all.

He is not a jerk after all.

Well, a little bit. But not too much. I guess.

I put on my pajamas—a set of pink silky shorts and a matching top, and it's only then that I realize my sleepwear is a bit on the sexy side. I don't own a set with long sleeves and pants. It's been on my shopping list, but it isn't winter yet, and my duvet is quite warm.

Besides, I thought that when I finally slept in a Danish man's bedroom, I wouldn't be trying to hide from him.

The last time I was in a guy's bed was almost a year ago, in Brazil. I synced up with my cousin Luana to pretend I was sleeping at her place so I could avoid my parents' questions.

It wasn't as if my mom didn't want me to find someone—quite the opposite. While Dad was a hound protecting his little girl, Mom would embarrass me with unsolicited advice. She was always introducing me to the church men, the ones she'd call "the good catches." The two I ended up dating were far from godly—and not in the way you'd want them to be.

I came here promising myself I'd be an adult woman at last, with an active and healthy sexual life. As I prepare to go to my sexy roommate's bed, however, the only "active" thing in my life is my *un*healthy decisions.

I carry my duvet and pillow with me as I move toward Erik's room, and he makes space for me as he holds the door open. I try not to look at him so this doesn't become more awkward than it already is, but I feel his gaze on my body. Is he looking at my butt? My legs are quite exposed...

The bed is ready for me, his blankets and pillows lying on the couch. I lie down carefully, feeling odd and uncomfortable, and cover myself up to my neck. When Erik goes to the bathroom, I look around the dimly lit space. It's cozy in a way I won't be able to make mine, at least for a while.

He has many vintage travel posters on the walls, most of them including beautiful tropical beaches. I find Rio, and that makes me smile. A piece of home in a foreign place... even though Rio is over six hundred miles away from where I grew up.

I'm six *thousand* miles away from home now.

When I think about that, I feel small, happy, and a little lonely at the same time. But when I talk with my family and friends like I did today, the distance feels like an illusion.

Like how I can be in Erik's room, in his bed, and yet be so far away from him.

Six

The night is a mess.

I can't fall asleep, and I sense the same is true for Erik. His couch has a beautiful design, but it's probably not the most comfortable place to lie down, especially for someone as big as him.

The curtains are flimsy, allowing the streetlamp to cast a dim light inside the room, outlining Erik's silhouette. He shuffles several times, and there is occasionally a leg or arm poking out of his duvet, or dangling over the edge of the couch, until he shifts position again. And again.

I feel bad about it, but I'm not supposed to be the gentleman here. Or am I?

I could of course suggest he lie on the other side of the bed—there is plenty of space for both of us—but I know better than to make such an indecent proposal to Erik Storm.

The smell of his citrusy cologne is everywhere, impregnated in the fitted sheet, and when I close my eyes, it's easy to imagine he is lying by my side. Yet, there is no weight on the mattress to balance mine, no source of heat, and there is regular breathing echoing on the silent walls a few feet away.

The breathing of someone who is wide awake.

When I'm coming back from the toilet for the second time, my eyes are drawn to the glow of a phone screen illuminating Erik's face. He's given up.

"You should take your bed back," I say. "I can't sleep anyway."

"Don't worry about me."

I ignore that. "I can be in my room and get some work done."

I sit on the edge of the bed, and he can't look at me unless he turns his head, which he does. "It's three in the morning, Sol."

"It doesn't matter. I've rested enough. And you can't sleep."

He sits up, looking at me through the semidarkness. "It's not because of the bed. It's just…" He hesitates. "It's how all my nights have been lately."

He rubs his face and leans his head back to stare at the ceiling. I stay still for a moment, not knowing what to do.

"Do you have to go to work in the morning?"

He shakes his head. "I'm unemployed."

"Oh. Sorry to hear that."

I'm very curious now, so curious my body drives me to the couch. I move the end of his duvet aside and sit down, leaving one seat between us. I'm glad it's dark—or, well, almost dark. It somehow makes it easier to interact with him. Especially when he is wearing nothing but a tank top and underwear—yes, he sleeps in boxer briefs, regardless of my presence.

I swallow hard, keeping my eyes on his beautiful profile.

We can be ourselves in the dead of night, can't we? He's vulnerable. Semi-naked. Maybe I can take another layer off. *Metaphorically*, of course.

"Why did you quit working at Scorpio Games?" I try, and then immediately regret starting with *that* question, given how noticeable it's been that he'd rather avoid the subject.

Erik closes his eyes, and for a moment I think he will ignore me and fall asleep right there.

"I wanted to start my own company," he says. "Work on a project I started together with a classmate at university. Make it into a finished product. Sell it. Make a living out of it." His voice sounds mechanical, stripped of emotion, but the fact that his eyes remain closed betrays his need to detach himself from the pain of his failure—because it's clear he didn't succeed.

I want to be positive and supportive, so I say, "That sounds nice. I've always wanted to do the same but never had the idea or the money or the courage." Employment is the safest option, and that's probably what Erik realized. What hurts him. "What happened?" I ask as gently as I can.

"We started, but…"

He stops there. I look at his tightened jaw, his Adam's apple bobbing up and down, and wait, but nothing more comes.

"And now you're looking for jobs?" I keep trying to treat the subject with care and sensibility, even though my curiosity is getting the best of me.

Erik nods, and his silence urges me to start babbling. "I've been there myself not that long ago," I say, trying to meet his gaze, which he keeps anywhere but on me. "It really sucks." I exhale, feeling his pain, and he nods again.

"Yeah."

My mouth doesn't stop, unintimidated by his reserved attitude. "I worked at that Brazilian indie game studio I told you about for five years, but for a large chunk of that period, I wasn't there full-time, or I wasn't being paid and was just helping out to have something on my CV and avoid having to help my mom in her salon." I confess the embarrassing truth about my career before Scorpio Games. "I was looking for jobs all the while, but Brasília doesn't have many good opportunities for designers and close to zero in the game business. So I kept staying at Vortex, even though they didn't have the money to pay me, just hoping for better days, but the projects we worked so hard on were not the success we expected."

"The industry is full of this shit," he mumbles, closing his eyes and pinching the bridge of his nose, weary but likely not tired enough to sleep.

"Yes," I agree with vigor.

"I'm on unemployment benefits, you know." He looks at me at last, and my heart gives a small leap before beating at a significantly faster rate. I keep my gaze steady on his, trying to find the bright blue of his eyes in the shadows covering his face. "It's not exactly lovely."

Erik sighs, leaning back heavily, and I dare to touch his arm. I feel a little tingle, a light jerk when our skin touches, as if we've been coated in static electricity. Erik peers at me, his eyelids, heavy before, now rising fully. We stare at each other.

"Go to the bed now and rest," I say to him, letting my hand stroke his arm once. Maybe the static is still there, because my palm keeps tingling, so I pull my hand away. "I know the thoughts disturb you, but you must give yourself a break."

"I don't want a job." Erik leans his head back on the couch, the corners of his lips stretched up in a nonsmile as he stares at the ceiling. "I want to finish my project."

"Then do it," I say firmly, like a command.

He straightens his posture and looks at me again. The soft glow of the streetlamp outside makes his features discernible—even in the middle of the night. It's as if the dark can reveal what he hides in daylight. I can see what is behind his ocean-blue eyes. There is defeat, hurt confidence, low self-esteem, and a bunch of other harmful feelings.

We stare at each other for long seconds. Nothing shifts in his eyes. His dilated pupils are wells that go deep into a dark, empty space.

"I can't," he answers me at last and then lies down on his pillow, determined to sleep.

That is when I realize he is not a giver because he has nothing to give. Erik Storm can't help others because *he* needs help.

I stand and take his fallen duvet and lay it over his body. Erik doesn't move, but I can see his lips curving in gratitude before I return to his bed.

I make breakfast for both of us. Eggs, toast, and a protein smoothie. When Erik gets up at eight, I'm about to leave for work. I thought he would sleep longer, so I left a sticky note near his portions on the table, saying: *Til dig. Tak for igår.* I translated it on Google. It means, "For you. Thank you for yesterday."

"Thank you, Sol," he says, sitting down to eat. No smile, but last night I learned not to expect one.

"No worries." My gaze lingers on his body—still in tank top and underwear—but only for a second.

I ignore the memory of his remarkable figure by being busy

at work. In the morning, I do my usual tasks, participate in a meeting, and help Chiara and the other QA testers report a bug in a level that was released last week. After lunch, I assist the marketing and customer support teams with player communication after a malfunction in the system. Later, I squeeze in time to help the kitchen assistant clean after we eat cake to celebrate the birthday of the new HR employee. I go as far as carrying some boxes and garbage bags to the dumpsters outside the building.

I can't say no to people. Even when they don't ask directly.

This resulted in a very unproductive day for me in my role, but it made a lot of people happy, so I'm satisfied. Judging by the proud smile Lars flashes at me when he passes by my desk, I can see that my boss is also happy with my proactivity—and I wasn't even trying to impress him.

Near the end of the day, Astrid, the HR lead, a tall woman in her forties with silver-blond hair, gathers everyone for an announcement.

"The Fun Season starts this week! For those of you who don't know what the Fun Season is all about, the slogan summarizes it: 'When the days get colder…'" She prompts her colleagues to continue.

"…our hearts get warmer!" a chorus of about a dozen people utters in unison. The crowd claps and cheers.

Smiling, Astrid goes on. "We have decided to split you into ten groups of eight. We've planned some activities that all groups will do, but separately. All groups will also have a budget for activities they decide for themselves, like eating out and so on."

The room hums with an excited murmur.

"Groups will be formed randomly, but the leads have been picked. Leads, raise your hands!"

Eleven of the most senior employees put their hands in the air. Lars is among them.

"As some of you may already know, it's not a competition…"

"But it is!" someone shouts, and people laugh.

"Well, yes, if you say so." Astrid smirks. "In your groups, you may choose whatever form you wish of giving scores to individual members or sub-teams. The final event of the Fun Season, gathering all employees, is our Christmas party, where we have a talent show and reward the winners of each group."

I look at the enthusiastic faces around me. This Fun Season thing looks like a big deal. Some more veteran employees whisper to each other, anticipating what is to come.

Astrid says we will all receive an email shortly to inform us which group we are in, and then the leader of the group will take over the communication with the members. When I'm packing my things to go home, my email comes.

Lars is my team lead.

My chest flutters, and I smile. This doesn't seem random at all…

Particularly because in my group are also Chiara, Ellen (a very skilled 2D Artist), Simon (the producer for the game I work on), George (the UX/UI Designer everyone loves), Astrid, and…

Martin the Beetle. Of course.

We all work closely together, and we are talented, ambitious people under Lars's leadership. Except for Astrid, the HR Lead, who might help him judge who deserves a promotion…

To be honest, any of us could be a fit for the game director position. Especially Ellen and George. And, well, *Martin*, as I heard from Lars himself.

The threads of excitement in my stomach tie up in a knot.

Five minutes after receiving the first email, I get one from Lars welcoming us into his group and inviting us to our first event—dinner at a Spanish restaurant tomorrow after work.

I take the Metro home, my head brimming with thoughts and concerns. This will be a bigger challenge than I thought—convincing Lars that I deserve the promotion over all these other nice and talented employees who have been in the company, and in Denmark, for much longer than me.

But I can beat the competition. I need to believe in myself. Lars thinks I'm a good candidate. I'll just have to show off in our events. I can do that. *Right?*

I enter my empty room and sigh. Burying myself in bed will have to wait.

Cheer up, Sol! I see all of this as a great sign, Larissa writes to me after I dump my concerns on her. I'm on my yoga mat again, and my back is killing me.

Larissa: You are among this select group, and you'll have lots of great opportunities to shine. Be the sun you are and blind your boss with your awesomeness!

I send her a heart. I love my best friend for always lifting me up when I'm down. After twenty-one years of friendship, living right next to each other, she always knows the right thing to say, even now that we're so far apart.

Larissa: How's Thor?

Me: You mean, Erik? People are actually called Thor here. It's a common name.

Larissa: He's the human incarnation of the god of thunder, Sol. Be careful not to fall under his spell.

If it were up to me, Larissa wouldn't know what Erik looks like. When I showed Erik to the girls at the salon during our video call, my cousin Mariana took a screenshot with my mom's phone and sent it to Larissa because she knew I'd be vague when talking to my friend, and Larissa "deserved the truth."

At least Larissa seems to believe it's safest to not engage in a relationship with him—unlike my cousins, who have been effusively encouraging me to pull Erik by the collar and kiss him with ardent passion whenever I cross with him in the hallway.

The doorbell rings. When I arrive at the front door, Erik is already letting the delivery guys in. I jump in excitement as I watch the parts of my new bed being unloaded in my room.

The guys leave, and Erik stands at the threshold, looking thoughtfully at the boxes as if they are a big puzzle we must solve.

And they are.

"I thought they would help me assemble it," I say, biting my lip.

"Nope. That's the whole concept in Scandinavia. Do it yourself. Or pay a fortune."

I laugh, but there isn't much humor in finding yourself

swimming in huge heavy boxes with pieces you have no clue what to do with.

"We'll do it together, okay?" he reassures me, landing a palm on my shoulder. His warm hand heats the skin under my cotton T-shirt, spreading a boiling wave down the rest of my body. "Teamwork is key."

"Thanks," I say in one breath, my heart thumping with more excitement than should be reserved for a bed.

For one hour, we focus. And we fail.

"Aaargh, this is impossible!" Erik lets out his frustration, dropping a piece of the frame that we simply can't put together. We are both sweaty and exhausted, and only half the frame is completed.

"Break time," I say and go to the kitchen to grab a can of soda for each of us. I bought them. Erik only has healthy stuff in his half of the fridge. When I offer him the Coke though, he takes it.

We drink in silence, sitting on the floor with our backs against the wall, surrounded by tools, screws, and cardboard boxes. Through the window, the setting sun sheds its last rays on the water. It's a beautiful evening. One of those days when, from the heat of your home, you can look out and pretend it's still summer.

"Erik, did you participate in the Fun Season when you worked at Scorpio?"

He lifts his gaze from the instruction manual, brow furrowed. "Yes."

"Was your boss your team lead?"

Erik relaxes his face and throws the manual aside. "Lars Holm was my team lead. He's your boss, right?"

I nod, admiring how the sunbeam through the window crosses his face. The stripe of sunlight illuminates one of his eyes, making it as transparent as the Caribbean Sea and leaving the other in the shadow, dense as a frozen lake on a cloudy evening.

"Yes," I say and lower my gaze to avoid getting too distracted by the pretty view. "Lars is my boss and my Fun Season team lead, and…it might be a stupid thing to think, but…" I debate for a moment whether I should share my concerns with Erik. I then conclude that I need to if I want an honest opinion from someone who knows the other involved party.

I take a deep breath, because even though I do really need that opinion, talking with Erik is nerve-racking. "I'm…" I begin, keeping my eyes lowered. "I suspect that Lars might use the upcoming events to get to know me better and judge if I deserve the game director position or not."

I feel silly saying it out loud, but Erik's expression tells me I'm not saying anything strange. His words confirm it. "It sounds like this is what he's doing, yes."

"You think?" I sit up straighter, my body leaning closer to Erik's. He must be at least three feet away, but I'm so interested in hearing him that I reduce the distance between us. "I mean, Lars said he likes to learn more about his coworkers on a personal level…and I got the impression that if he likes me enough, then…" I trail off, and Erik picks up.

"Yes. That's how Lars is. If he likes people, he rewards them. He cares about job performance, of course, but he's very much about personal relations. He has his favorites, and it's not bad to be on good terms with him."

I drag myself even closer and sit cross-legged in front of Erik. "What can I do to make Lars like me?"

Erik laughs. "Are you asking me how to cheat your way into a promotion?"

I frown. "No. Of course not. I don't want to *cheat* my way in." I drink my soda to its last drops.

Erik keeps smiling. "I'm messing with you, Sol. You want to make a good impression, obviously, and I can tell you how." He lifts a finger as he enumerates. "First, be yourself. Second, be social. Third, be nice."

I wave my hand in the air dismissively. "No pep talk. I want data." He lifts an eyebrow, studying me, and I roll my eyes. "Come on, you know the guy. Tell me what makes him tick."

Erik's gaze travels to the window like he is going to ignore me. "Are you sure that's what you want, Sol?"

"Why are you saying that?" I look at him, suspicious. He said it was his wish to work on his personal project that drove him to quit. But could Lars have been the culprit somehow? Could Erik have been so dissatisfied with the way things worked at the company, he couldn't stand his job anymore?

Like me not that long ago?

"I'm just wondering if you're sure your dream job is at Scorpio." There is bitterness in his voice and resentment in his eyes, and I want to feel empathy for whatever his situation was, but I find myself unable to. He is judging me for wanting to work in the company that no longer suited him. We are so different from each other—we were *born* different, in opposite hemispheres—and he will never know my struggles.

My defensive instincts kick in. "Just because you didn't want to work there, doesn't mean it's not the place for me."

I regret my answer as soon as it's out, and Erik's icy eyes make me feel worse. Maybe he wasn't *judging* me, just trying to warn me, prompting me to think things through. I didn't ask for that kind of advice, but I also didn't have the right to be rude and poke an open wound.

I sigh. "Sorry, I didn't mean to—"

"It's fine."

It isn't. He rises to his feet. Now he will leave me to finish the bed alone.

I stand up too. "Look, I've had my doubts about Scorpio. But game director is my career goal, like I told you. I'll come up with an idea for an original game, and I'll work on it from start to end. No more making similar levels again and again."

He stops at the door and turns around. "It sounds like you hate your job."

Ugh, why does he have to make everything out to be so terrible and hopeless?

"I don't *hate* it. I'm just ready for something more challenging."

He looks at me like he doesn't believe me. But who cares?

"Lars needs to see that I can handle it."

"All Lars will see in the Fun Season is how fun and social you can be."

"But from what you say, that goes a long way."

Erik gazes at me, serious. "Lars favors people who are a lot like him," he says, his eyes narrowed in dislike for the words he's uttering.

The information should surprise me, but it doesn't. "Details, please."

"People who are committed. People in relationships. People who have children. People who live a stable life and have a plan." Erik rolls his eyes as if he thinks this is all ridiculous, but the words keep flowing out of his mouth. "Lars loves Copenhagen and identifies with those who want to stay here for the rest of their lives. He likes competitive people. Extroverts. Winners."

Erik got it all right. That's Lars. It shouldn't be hard to please him when I know all this.

But I don't fit the profile.

You can make it look like you do, can't you? Larissa's voice says in my head, even though I'm not quite sure she would say that to me in real life.

Without another word about Lars or Scorpio Games, we struggle with the bed again and finish it at last. Erik goes to the kitchen to cook his dinner, and I clean my room, put sheets on my brand-new bed, and lie down, exhausted.

I'm determined to make this place home—where I'll acquire my independence, have a prosperous career, and find the version of Sol I could never be in Brasília because there were always too many people and concerns pushing me in other directions.

I already feel like I'm slowly getting there.

Nothing comes without struggle. Nothing comes without proving my value.

My parents taught me that when I was little, and I knew this philosophy would be taken to extremes here in Denmark, where I don't belong.

But belonging is the reward, and there is nothing I want more than to belong here.

Seven

I never had tapas before, and I already love it. I make sure to say that out loud, following my resolve to appear as grateful, extroverted, and pleasant as possible in the first Group Lars event of the season. But as soon as I realize that I'm the odd one out in a group of Europeans who have eaten tapas several times in their lives, I get shy, overly aware of what I do and say.

Lars mentions his latest vacation in Spain, and everyone chats about how nice a country it is, as they have also been there. We are eight at the table, of which five are Danish. Chiara is Italian, but she has lived in Denmark for seven years, and George is English but has been here for three years.

I've never been anywhere on the continent but Denmark. All I know about other European countries comes from movies, books, and news articles, so I just listen when they talk about their favorite Spanish regions, beaches, and dishes.

When the conversation shifts to politics, I have nothing to say. When it's about children and parenthood, I have zero experience to share. When it's about soccer though—European football—I take my chances and participate with my controversial opinions on the latest sold players, especially the Brazilian ones, and why I believe Real Madrid will destroy its opponents in the next Champions League.

I get a few surprised stares. George laughs. "Blimey! You know more about football than me, Sol. Not that I care one bit about it."

"My dad is a big fan of European football," I tell them, trying not to sound too proud or apologetic. "It's a passion we've shared."

Simon, a fervent Real Madrid supporter, gives me a high-five, and Lars lifts his pint for a *"Skål!"*

"We also love *Brazilian* football," I say. "The best of all." I sip my beer. I need to loosen up more. I'm at my best socially when I'm not one hundred percent sober.

"Some of the best players, for sure," Lars agrees. I spend a few minutes discussing soccer with him, and I discover that he knows quite a lot about Palmeiras, the team I've supported since I was a child—again, thanks to my dad.

When we are all full of tapas and more than a bit tipsy, Ellen announces that she got married last week. A round of cheers shakes the table. We toast and congratulate her. George then says he will propose to his boyfriend soon and asks for our advice on how to do it in the most romantic way.

"George, Ellen, you need to introduce your partners to us," Lars says when the brainstorming for George's marriage proposal is getting private-jet extravagant.

Ellen has very fair skin, and her cheeks are red in the heat of the restaurant, matching her fiery curls. "I would love you all to meet Mads," she says.

"And how's your wife, Simon?" Lars asks. "Is she still working at that design bureau?"

"Yes, she's very happy there," Simon answers, a smile buried under his respectable mustache.

"What about you, Chiara?" Lars turns to her. "Any special one?"

"I have a girlfriend. We've been together for eight months."

"Wonderful. We look forward to meeting her!"

Soon it'll be my turn to be under the spotlight. I'm sitting between Lars and Astrid, who is sitting next to Martin. I wipe my sweaty palms on my pants.

"What about you, Martin? Tell us all about the current status of your heart!" George follows the trail led by Lars.

"I'm a happy single!" Martin lifts his glass.

"Cheers!" says Astrid. "Me too!"

This would be my cue to join them. But I'm stuck. I just look at Martin and Astrid's smiling faces as a hole grows in my stomach, sucking in all my air.

Why does being a "happy single" like Martin make me want to poke my eyes out? Why do I feel like I'm joining the loser line by being on equal terms with my rival when everyone else is happily in love? I can't even call myself a *happy* single. That's not a word you can use to describe someone who cries at the end of rom-coms out of pure jealousy.

The more I realize how much behind the others I am in every aspect, the more breathless I feel. The thought that I'm not at all like them makes me dizzy.

I drink a good mouthful of beer until I realize I've emptied my glass. My *second* glass. The dizziness intensifies.

"Sol, darling, I won't believe it if no one has snatched up your heart yet," George says.

I laugh, hoping the conversation will go in another direction before I can answer.

Lars looks at me expectantly. He was radiant to hear about Ellen, George, and Chiara.

I remember what Erik said, about Lars liking people who are in serious relationships. People who want children, who have stable lives and plan to grow old in Copenhagen.

I'm the one who has just arrived. The one with no ties to the country. The one most likely to leave on a whim…

"I have a Danish boyfriend," I hear myself say.

And then it's too late. I can't take it back. Oh gosh.

All the blood in my body rises to my face, burning my cheeks, and I feel like I'll throw up the two pints I've gulped down.

"Ooooh," they say, and I stop listening, panicking as I do whenever I tell a lie.

Odin's beard! Why did I do that?

Oh jeez. *Ugh.*

"Tell us more!"

"How long have you been together?"

"That's wonderful, Sol!"

The last comment is from Lars. I think. My head is spinning as I look from one face to another. I feel as overwhelmed as when the women at my mom's salon all started talking about Erik at the same time.

Oh my goodness—it hits me again. I didn't tell a random

guy in a bar that I have a boyfriend so he can leave me alone. I lied to *my boss*. The person I want to trust me.

What have you done, Sol?

To my relief, the waiter chooses this moment to ask if we need anything else. Some people order more beer and tapas, and I seize the opportunity to breathe and clear my thoughts.

Nothing will come of it. I can sustain the lie for a while. No one will know. And then at some point, we break up. No worries.

"I have an idea!" Lars's booming voice drags all attention his way. "I would love to meet your partners, and I think they deserve to join us in our future events. What if we invite them to take part in our little tournament, and each of the couples can be a team? Astrid and Martin can then join forces."

No, no, NO. My stomach spins, and this time I'm sure all the beer and Spanish food won't stay in my system.

"Brilliant idea, Lars." Astrid approves.

Martin gives her a high-five and says, "We'll team up."

"Alex would LOVE it!" George celebrates. "We'll be Team Georgelex! I'm so in!"

"I'm sure Mads will be up for it. I'll ask him." Ellen smiles.

"I'll ask Anika too," Chiara says, looking excited.

"Lia will join us whenever we can get a babysitter," Simon tells us.

"Lotte will come if there are drinks. Margaritas, especially." Lars laughs.

"Then let's make sure we'll have plenty!" Astrid says.

I hear all this without moving a muscle, completely shocked. I can't believe my ears. I want to vanish from the face of the Earth and never be found.

"Our next event is a trivia contest in my house," Lars announces. He then looks at me and puts a hand on my shoulder. I shrink in my seat, just the ghost of me left on the chair. "I look forward to meeting your boyfriend, Sol!"

I want to scream, slap myself, hide under the table, and never let myself drink a single ounce of alcohol again. Leaving Denmark on the next available flight is also an appealing option. I'm frozen in this restaurant chair, however. Stuck to my lie like chewed gum on the sole of a shoe.

So I do the only thing I can do. I give him a half smile and reply, "Me too."

With the grin of a sober-enough person who won't forget any of this in the morning, Lars turns to talk to the others without realizing the ambiguity in my answer.

I've been checking Cinder every five minutes since I had tapas with my coworkers. In my desperation, I even give likes to guys I would normally not be interested in.

Truth be told, I must have given glass slippers to half the single male population in Copenhagen in the past ten days. I'm like Prince Charming, but my Cinderella seems to be nowhere in this city.

Most of them I discarded in our text conversations. I went out with one last Friday, one on Tuesday, and one yesterday. They were all either weird or impolite, or we had so little in common I would lose that promotion the moment I showed up with them in front of Lars and he noticed we couldn't possibly be a couple.

Today is Saturday, my last chance, because tomorrow is the second event for my group in the Fun Season, and I'm supposed to bring my Danish boyfriend.

I'm sitting at the dining table, desolate, eating a bowl of ice cream while scrolling Cinder, when Erik comes in from the gym. I glance up at him, and he ignores me, as usual.

I watch from the corner of my eye as he enters the bathroom and locks the door. I've been trying to ignore Erik all these days, convinced that I could solve my situation without help. But it's unrealistic now. I mean, it has been from the start—who gets a boyfriend in a few days?

Now I either find someone who will *pretend* to be my boyfriend, or I might as well give up on this promotion. The humiliation of coming up with an excuse for my boyfriend not attending, and all the questions about who he is…

No, I won't do that. At least not without one last attempt.

Erik starts the shower, and the soothing sound of water falling cradles my brain, lulling my thoughts into a decision.

He unlocks the door and heads toward his cave, but my "Hey, Erik" freezes him midway across the dining room, two steps away from my chair.

Wearing only a towel.

I look down, blushing, but my eyes rise back to his chest, pulled by the magnetic view of his well-defined muscles. *Jesus.*

That's a surprisingly accurate description, in fact. With his full beard and long wet hair falling over his shoulders, Erik looks like Jesus. On steroids.

Not that I think he uses steroids. His body looks naturally worked out.

Wonderfully worked out…

"Yes?" He waits for me to say whatever I need.

"Oh." I blink, embarrassed, and fix my posture. "Sorry, I just wanted to…" *God forgive me.*

I lose my thread, my heart hammering against my chest. How does one ask a guy to pretend to be their boyfriend? A guy who is wearing only a towel, with drops of water beading his chest and dripping from his perfect hair—

I clear my throat, feeling my mouth go as dry as the Sahara. It's such a bad idea… But I won't beg for a favor this time. I will *negotiate*.

"I have a work proposition for you."

He squints at me, suspicious. I swallow my nervousness and stand my ground.

"A work proposition?" he repeats slowly, one eyebrow angling.

"Yes. A deal. If you are up for it."

Oh, gods, his smell is fantastic. Fresh citrusy manly cologne spreads through the room, and I take a discreet deep breath to inhale the glorious scent.

"Hmm," he says, and I enjoy the guttural sound a bit too much. "Make some coffee then, and I'll get dressed."

"No," I say, and Erik's eyebrows climb his forehead in disbelief. "No coffee," I continue. "We're getting a beer."

Eight

I get Erik out of the apartment.

He must have realized I'm trying to loosen him up. After all, I'm repeating my strategy from the day we met after matching on Cinder. He knows I'm up to something tricky, but I see it as a good sign that he is going along with it.

Erik is in limbo. He doesn't talk to me, but I know he is frustrated with his fruitless job search and the fact that he doesn't know what to do with his life. Whenever he's not in his room, he drags his feet around the kitchen like a pale ghost sporting jogging pants and tired eyes.

He looks quite decent now, with his long hair down, untangled and still a bit wet, an unwrinkled black T-shirt, and dark blue jeans.

Whenever I'm home, I only see Erik go to the supermarket and the gym. Occasionally, he is at the dining table with his laptop. The few times I glanced at his screen when passing by, I saw him scrolling through job ads, never looking excited or engaged, just bored, frowning, or pressing his temples as if relieving a headache.

He cooks a lot, often elaborate dishes, as if cooking is the moment that gives his day meaning. He never invites me to eat, however. Never chats when we are in the same room. The last time we talked was when he helped me assemble my bed, and I haven't started a conversation since, though I keep my door open and always say hi whenever I cross paths with him in the morning or after work.

I thought he might be annoyed at me for some reason, but he's here with me now.

We walked to a bar near the apartment. It's too cold to sit outside, but we watch the sunset through the windows. It has rained all day, but after five, the sun decided to make a brief appearance before retiring behind the gray clouds, tinting them with artsy orange strokes. It's a Saturday evening, but the crowds haven't swarmed the place yet.

"So, what is your proposition?" Erik looks down at his beer.

"I want to hear about your project," I start, calm and slow to keep my nerves under control. "What it's about, why you abandoned it, and what is stopping you from finishing it."

He looks up as if seeing me for the first time since we left the apartment. It wasn't what he expected to hear. I stay still in my seat, waiting.

Erik drinks his beer. He gulps it down in one go like a true Viking. I laugh.

"Okay, let's do this." I lift my glass and drink up too. It goes to my brain way too fast. I giggle, feeling dizzy. "Are we ready now?" I look at him, grinning.

He nods, surrendering a smile in return. That makes

a surge of heat spread through my chest, comforting and anxiety-inducing at the same time.

"My project was an app. A mix between a game and a..." He stops himself. I lean forward, expectant. Erik clears his throat and says in a low volume, hesitant, "A dating app."

I raise my eyebrows and smile. "So, you're trying to make something better than Cinder, Tinder, and everything similar?"

He nods. "Yeah. I hate those dating apps."

"Then why were you on Cinder?" I give him a teasing smile.

He glares at me as if I don't deserve an answer. "What choice do people have nowadays?" I'm opening my mouth to reply, but he says, "It's what devoted developers do, okay? We look for ways to make something better."

Erik takes a break to drink and realizes that his glass is empty, so he lifts an arm to call the waiter. "Want one more?"

I shake my head. "No, no, I'm good." I can't drink too much tonight. I need to stay in control.

After Erik orders another beer, he resumes. "As I told you, it started as a university project. My classmate and I enjoyed working on it and agreed we would continue with the app after we graduated. I had a couple of temporary part-time jobs that allowed me to keep working on the app for a year or so, then I got employed at Scorpio."

I nod, giving him my full attention. I try to read his eyes as he tries to read mine, and the result is a staring game with no winner.

"Was your working partner in from start to end?" I break the silence after what could be a second or a minute—I couldn't tell, lost as I am in his unintentionally sexy stare.

The waiter puts Erik's beer in front of him, and he starts

drinking it immediately, though a little slower this time. The distraction makes us drop the staring game.

"The idea was *mine*," he says as if there has been no interruption. "My partner joined the project when I had already begun and realized I needed help. I'm mainly a programmer, and I wanted someone with strong design skills."

Erik runs his index finger over the nodes in the wooden table, lost in his past.

"I was at Scorpio for three years, and I tried to keep working on the project in my free time, but it was too hard. I didn't have a life back then. It was all about work." He sighs, smiling a little. "My partner was working at a tech start-up at the time, and then he quit because he wanted to make games again. While he was unemployed, he put a lot of hours into our project. It was coming together nicely, I got excited, and I just… I thought we could do this full-time, you know?"

Erik looks at me in a self-punishing way, like he expects me to say, *Yes, that was a stupid thought.*

But I don't think it was. At all.

"I finally decided to quit my job at Scorpio, and we started the company, Storm Interactive. I mean, *I* did the whole bureaucracy." There is a distaste for his former business partner in Erik's tone, as if the guy didn't just disappoint him but betrayed him.

"I think you were brave," I say, because I suspect he needs to hear it.

Erik lets out a self-deprecating chuckle. "I was an idiot," he corrects me.

We look at each other, my intense gaze piercing through

his. I won't let him hate himself for being a dreamer. I arch an eyebrow. "Because you followed your dream?"

"Life is not a fairy tale, Sol." Bitterness is back in his tone, but I'm used to his defense mechanisms by now. Erik uses scorn and mockery to distance himself from the things that hurt him. Because I now know what is underneath the surface, I can raise a shield and not let any of that bother me.

"He left you, or what?"

Erik blinks as if me following his story with interest surprises him. He nods slowly, disarmed.

"Yes. And I couldn't continue alone."

There is so much more to the story, of course. So many details he is not telling me. But why should I expect him to share that? I didn't even tell him what I want yet.

Erik's left hand closes in a fist on the table, and I watch as his jaw tightens. "Martin left me to go work at fucking Scorpio Games after I quit."

What? My jaw drops. No, this can't—

"Martin? Do you mean Martin Olesen?"

Holy mother of—

"Yes. Martin *fucking* Olesen."

I shriek and cover my mouth. Then I bang a hand on the table. Hard, like Erik did that day at the English pub.

"Oh my gosh, Erik!" I can't believe this. It's so messed up. I stand, disoriented. "Why didn't you tell me before?"

"Why did it matter?" He drinks up, eyes narrowed.

Either he thinks I'm overreacting, or he is not grasping the seriousness of the situation. I rest my hands on the table and lean closer to him.

"Because Martin Olesen is my nemesis." A memory sparks

in my brain. I said this to Erik the day we met at the English pub. He was surprised and, right after, decided to give me the room. Probably because he thought that by helping me, he'd be hindering Martin's success.

Erik's wish to get back at his treacherous former business partner doesn't bother me. In fact, he *should* want that.

"Erik," I say with a grave tone, seeking his eyes with even more intensity. "I'm competing with Martin for that promotion, as you're aware." I take a deep breath before releasing the bomb. "And Martin is going to steal your idea and sell it to Scorpio Games if he becomes the new game director."

Erik stands up too. "What the fuck are you saying?" His brow is furrowed. Very. We stare at each other.

"I had no idea he was your business partner. But this changes everything..."

Or, well, this gives me *more* motive to ask for Erik's help.

We both want the same thing. Martin Olesen to go to h—

"Why are you saying that he'll steal my idea? How can you know that?"

"Here's the thing." I sit down again, and Erik reluctantly settles back on his chair too. "The day Lars told me about the game director position, he said that Martin was talking about a truly innovative idea for an app. 'A dating game of sorts.'"

Erik's face twists into a scowl. "Motherfucker," he mutters, his right hand also clenching into a fist.

"You think he would do that to you?" Maybe I'm jumping to conclusions...

"He would," Erik says without hesitation. "God, how could I've been so stupid?" He hits the table with his fist.

"It's not your—"

"I didn't ask him to sign a contract or a nondisclosure agreement, Sol. I took no legal measures to guarantee the idea would remain secret—and *mine.* I simply…trusted that bastard. *Goddammit.*" He rubs his face. "And he's being considered for the role?"

"Lars hinted at that, yes," I confirm, pained to see his anguish. I would also be crawling out of my skin if I was in his situation. "And Martin is in my Fun Season group."

"Fuck," Erik curses again, brushing his hair back with his fingers in exasperation. "But if he pitched the game to Lars, then it's too late."

"I don't think he gave the whole thing away yet," I say. "Knowing Martin, he's using it as leverage to seem like a more interesting candidate. 'Hey, Lars, I already have an idea I'm ready to pursue if you hire me as game director.'" I imitate Martin's dry, haughty voice.

Erik smiles at my goofy impersonation, which makes my stomach tingle in a funny way. "That sounded accurate," he says.

"I already hated Martin's guts," I grumble. "Now I just…"

Now I want to rip him to absolute pieces. Like he'd done to the last idea I pitched.

Erik looks at me, but I can't tell if he is moved by my concern for his situation or if he is suspicious of why I brought him here to have this conversation.

"Help me understand, Sol. What do you want from me?"

He crosses his arms on the table. His fists are still tightly closed, though his face looks calmer.

"Before I knew…well…all of this…" I make an encompassing hand movement. "I was going to offer help so you could finish your project in exchange for you helping me with something."

I look down, losing courage. He leans forward, pressing me. "And now?"

"Now I want to offer you the same deal. But now I know you have strong reasons to help me."

"And why is that?" He squints.

I keep close eye contact, feeling more breathless by the second. "Because we have a common enemy."

"Hmm," he grunts, and I must stop myself from enjoying the sound for the second time in the day. "So, you want help getting your promotion?"

"That's correct."

We stare at each other, barely blinking.

"And how do you want me to help you?"

I swallow hard. I can never be prepared for this part, so I might as well shoot it out and hope it hits the bull's-eye.

"Tuesday last week was the first event of my group."

He doesn't nod, just waits patiently. Cold, solid, and still—like a marble statue in a museum. There is still anger in his eyes. I remind myself the feeling is not aimed at me.

"We ate tapas…and people started talking about their relationships and…" I babble out, barely breathing between words. "And then people asked about *my* relationship status. I panicked and said I have a Danish boyfriend."

Erik blinks a few times to make sense of my jumble of words. When he speaks, it's in the most boring, disdainful tone one can use. Like his remark when he saw I didn't have a bed. "You lied about having a boyfriend."

I chew on my bottom lip. "Danish. A Danish boyfriend."

Erik rubs his face, looking exhausted. And disappointed in me.

This incites my urge to defend myself, even though I agree I did something extremely stupid. "It's done, and now I can't tell Lars I made it up. I need to impress him, remember?" I wait for sympathy, but none comes. "And, look, the next event is a *trivia night*." I shiver at the thought. "I suck at quiz games, Erik. If I'm bad at trivia questions about Brazilian things, I can't imagine how I'll perform in a game designed for Europeans."

My cheeks heat up. Here I am, admitting more embarrassing things in front of this Norse god look-alike who has the habit of making me feel idiotic. I can't stop my mouth, however, driven by the pipe dream that he'll understand my predicament—and care.

"*If* I say that we broke up or I lied, I'll be put in Martin's 'happy singles' team—ugh—or I'll be alone as a complete loser. That will *not* help me win against the bastard now, will it?" I glare at Erik with the sternness he reserves for me. "Besides, I have to seem like I have roots in Den—"

"Stop." Erik raises a hand. "I don't care about any of that. Sorry, but this is your problem. You lied. Now you fix the situation."

He is getting up. I hold his wrist, and he sits back down, sighing as if to say, *What now?*

"Please, Erik. You're my last hope." He opens his mouth, but I speak first. "I know this sounds very familiar, but listen, it's different this time. You need my help."

"I need your help?" He does the eyebrow thing again.

I nod with vigor. "I'm an expert in dating apps. Besides,

are you forgetting that I'm a designer? I have artistic skills too. I can help you with anything you need. Game design, level design, graphic design, UI design… Name anything design, and I'm there!"

He stares at me, silent, and my chest trembles with the hope that he is considering the proposition.

"I know that Scorpio being your previous workplace makes you hesitant. But you don't have to be. It will be a familiar place, which means *you can be in control*." I lean forward, stressing the words. "You'll show them you're not lying in bed feeling sorry for yourself. You'll show Martin you're *so* much better than him."

A vein trembles in Erik's neck, and I watch him swallow slowly. He's not breaking eye contact. I see that as a reason to continue.

"Also, I'll sign a contract of confidentiality if you need. I'll never steal your idea or talk about it with anyone else. It will still be *your* app. I'll just assist you."

He looks down, blinking rapidly. I sense his stress, but I also sense his hesitation. It's not a quick no. He's thoroughly considering the idea.

I interlace my fingers on the table and lean even closer. "If we work hard enough, we'll have a publishable build by the end of this year, and we can put it in the app store before Lars decides who gets the promotion. That way, even if I fail and Martin ends up becoming the new game director, it won't be *his* idea because it will already be out in the world. You know that's what you need to do, right?" I look at Erik with intent, not giving him time to answer. "When you're done with the code, you copyright it. You trademark the title and logo. Ideas and game mechanics can't be copyrighted, and patents are murky in this industry. People will still copy your idea later, but that's all right if you're the first one to publish it. You'll be known for inventing that app, not Martin. But only if you act now."

I'm starting to believe Erik has indeed frozen into a statue. I touch his arm, triggering an electric tingle that runs from my fingers all the way up to my neck. His fist loosens with a jerk, and he glances at me before staring down at the table again.

"Erik," I say, watching him bite his lower lip in a thinking expression that was *not* meant to make my hormones overload with a warm flush of anticipation. "I know it's a lot to ask. Being my fake boyfriend to impress your former boss and take down your nemesis? Phew." A new wrinkle appears in his forehead, and I instantly regret my arrangement of words. "All I'm saying is, I get that this will be hard for you but—"

"It won't." Erik wakes up from his trance, the corners of his lips quirking up. "It will be a lot of fun."

I lean back, wary. "Are you joking now?"

He shakes his head with the subtlest smirk I've ever seen. My heart thumps in response.

"Same conditions apply," he says, offering me his right hand. "It will all be fake and never, *ever* real. Deal?"

I shake his hand enthusiastically. "Deal."

Nine

The sun is shining on the lakes, and despite the cold breeze, it's a nice morning. When you live in Denmark, you learn to appreciate even the shiest sunrays.

Erik and I had breakfast together while studying trivia cards from the quiz games he owns. I wanted to prepare for tonight, but we realized we could be using our time better—questioning each other about *ourselves*, for instance, since we'll be pretending to be a couple—so we decided to go for a walk.

I stop at the fence separating our building from the bike lane parallel to the sidewalk bordering the lakes. Closing my eyes for a second, I turn my face up to enjoy the modest heat on my skin. Erik touches my shoulder and chuckles, for once not in a scornful way. I turn my head to see his smile.

"You're becoming a Dane already," he says.

"No… I'm just a Brazilian who desperately misses the sun."

He laughs and puts a hand on my back, urging me onward. We wait for bikes to pass before crossing, then we climb down the little steps to the paved way surrounding *Søerne*—three artificial rectangular lakes next to each other housing ducks and swans.

"So, how did we meet?" he asks, and I look at him, puzzled. "In our fake story," he clarifies.

"Oh. Eh... Okay." I straighten up, ready with an answer. "We matched on Cinder. Let's use as much of the truth as possible to keep it simple." I give him an uncertain smile, and as he doesn't say anything, I continue, "But we can say it was two months after I arrived, so we've been dating for four months, which is not a long time but better than only a few weeks."

Erik keeps walking without comment.

"There is, of course, the fact that we live together, and maybe we shouldn't hide that." I scratch my head, thinking. Four months is way too little time to move in with a boyfriend. I probably wouldn't do that even after a year. "Would a long-distance relationship make sense?" I say. "Then we could have met before, when—"

"Met through Cinder four months ago is fine," he cuts me off, practical as usual. "Also fine that you moved in with me when my previous roommate left."

"Who was your previous roommate? Did they leave recently?"

Erik doesn't answer. I'm *so* curious, so I press him. "Come on, I need to know your history."

"My cousin had been living with me for a few months. He moved in with his girlfriend two weeks before you took the room."

His gaze lingers on my face, as if he is overanalyzing my

features under the sunlight. Yes, *overanalyzing*—not *appreciating* them like I am appreciating his. It's Erik, after all.

"And who lived in my room before your cousin?"

"Why does it matter?" He diverts his eyes, getting defensive.

"We need to know about each other's lives. If people ask—"

"We don't need to answer everything people ask, Sol."

His words are not necessarily unkind, but they are clearly dismissive. It's too early to dig into Erik's personal affairs. Especially when I suspect this has something to do with an ex. Perhaps he will never tell me about it, whether we have a fake relationship or not.

"Wait, didn't you get my number from someone who works at Scorpio?" Erik remembers, facing me with a worried look.

"Yes. Mark, a programmer."

"Shit. We need to change our story then."

"Why?" I try to read in his eyes the reason for his concern, and then I realize the problem. "Oh. Mark knows I only just met you because he is the reason why I got your number and heard about the apartment."

"Exactly." He looks at me as if I'm too slow in processing the facts.

"But Mark is not in Group Lars."

"So what? He knows it. People will talk when they hear about us."

I bite my lower lip. I told nearly everyone in the office that I was looking for an apartment.

Erik stops and gazes at me, serious. "Sol. If you want this

to work, you need to think about the holes in your story. Either we fill them properly or we don't go ahead with this."

I take a deep breath. "What about just saying we met when I called you about the apartment? That's what we need to work with, I guess. The truth, or part of it."

Erik doesn't say anything, but his forehead creases. I'm also not a fan of this. Telling the truth—or that part, at least—means I've only known Erik for a few weeks and we are already together. It's a fragile relationship. It doesn't give me the look of roots and stability. It will make me seem impulsive and naive for moving in with someone so quickly.

But better that than no boyfriend.

"We tell them we started texting each other when I got your number," I say. "We met at that pub to talk about the apartment. We had a lot in common. We talked all night and, well..." Shucks, it's embarrassing to make up this story about someone far from fictional who is standing right in front of me. I turn my face to the water, feeling my cheeks heat. "We fell for each other and decided to go ahead with moving in because you needed someone to help you pay the rent and I needed a room, so it was the perfect deal. No one needs to know any details. Just that we are in love and it's all going great."

I glance at him. His forehead is still wrinkled, but he nods.

"Good. That's decided then," I conclude, feeling calmer. We resume walking. "Oh, and I guess we should tell each other some facts about ourselves in case we're asked about each other's favorite food, drink, sport, TV show, game, flower, color, and so on. I'll start," I say, professional and objective. If this is business, let's treat it as such.

"Beans, a Brazilian soda made of guarana, volleyball, *Gilmore Girls*, *The Sims*, violets and cactuses, light blue."

I stop and stare at him, wide-eyed. "What? How do you know all that?"

Erik looks at me with an expression of *This is so obvious I shouldn't even explain.*

"You have so many cans of black beans stocked in the pantry, one might think we're preparing for the apocalypse." I laugh. He goes on. "There's always a can or two of this foreign green soda in the fridge—where do you find that, by the way?"

"They sell it here, can you believe it?" I tell him with excitement. Gee, I was happy to find my good old Guaraná.

"You have a signed volleyball in your room that looks like it's special to you," he continues. "You often watch *Gilmore Girls* or play *The Sims* on your computer while eating at the dining table. You have violets and cactuses at your windowsill and a lot of your clothes and accessories are light blue."

My jaw is on the pavement. He actually pays attention to me. I'm not just some ghost roaming around the place.

"So, I'm not a mind reader," he says with a shrug and a carefree smile. "I simply have eyes."

"It seems like we're more prepared than I thought." I smile back, and we turn a corner when we reach the end of the lake to continue walking by the water.

"Well, not really, when you still don't know about *my* favorite things," he says.

"I know that your favorite food is oatmeal."

He laughs. Erik's breakfast is always a bowl of pure, dry oats that he soaks with milk and gobbles down with pleasure as if it's as tasty as Frosted Flakes. Oatmeal is often his night snack too, and he sometimes eats it as a porridge.

"I eat that a lot, yes, but to say it's my favorite food is a bit of a stretch."

"Then what's your favorite food?"

"Sushi."

"Duly noted." I nod and glance back at him. "You're a tea person. Green tea."

"Yep."

"I don't know what sports and TV shows you like," I say, maintaining eye contact.

"I love playing hockey and watching American football. *God of War* is my favorite game, and I'm a sitcom binge-watcher. Name any sitcom, and I've probably watched it. *Friends* is my all-time favorite, by the way."

"You like laughing?" I tease him. "I thought it was all doom and gloom with you."

Erik laughs louder than I've ever heard. He sounds really… *nice* when he laughs. Now I want to watch sitcoms with him.

"I'm always up for the 'doom and gloom' too," he replies. "The blood, the gore… I love all Tarantino movies."

I shake my head, pretending to shiver. "That doesn't interest me."

"I'll get you to watch them one day," he says with amusement and a confidence that seduces me a bit, but I'm sure that was not his intention.

"You forgot to mention your favorite flowers. And color."

"My favorite flowers are in the lavender fields in Provence," he says with the dreamy tone of someone who remembers a lovely vacation. "And I like them there, where they belong."

I smile. I like that answer.

"Your color is black," I say. There's no way I'm wrong about that.

He grins at me, causing a mild disturbance to my insides.

There are many people out today basking in the sun, going for lazy walks, feeding the ducks, and resting on the benches while eating ice cream. The cafés facing the lakes are full of customers sitting outside, enjoying the view. It's nice walking around here with Erik.

"Hygge," I say out of nowhere, and Erik looks at me, confused, as if I woke him up from a daydream. "I want you to tell me more about hygge. It's what Scandinavians are famous for, right? If it's the base of this culture, I want to learn it. Feel it."

"You *are* experiencing it right now, hopefully." The corners of his mouth tug up. "Or, well, at least a lot of people around us are."

"It means feeling cozy, right?"

He shakes his head in a *sort of* motion.

"Cozy and coziness are translations people attempt, but they don't fully convey the meaning of hygge. It describes a state of being." He keeps his eyes on mine as we walk. "It's a feeling of satisfaction and well-being you experience when you're at peace with yourself and the world at that moment." He smiles at the reflection of the sun on the water. "And it usually happens when you're with people you like or love."

He looks down now, as if embarrassed. What for? Implying that *we* can have hygge together?

"But you can also feel hygge alone," Erik continues. "And you can feel it all over the world. We just invented an expression for this special feeling, and achieving it often is part of our culture. Mostly, we love to tell people that it's nice to be with them by saying, 'This is *hyggeligt*.'"

"So you don't necessarily need candles and hot chocolate?" I ask, smiling.

"No, no… Although certain elements, like coffee, cake, blankets, pleasant smells, laughter…help you be present in a time and place where your usual concerns don't bother you."

I've experienced hygge—or I think I have—a few times since I arrived in Copenhagen. But this moment, right here and now, is the one I'm *sure* is hygge.

We continue our walk for a little longer, until I say, "I want you to help me become more Danish."

"So that you can impress Lars?" There goes his judgmental tone again. It doesn't bother me this time. Nothing does on this beautiful day.

"I'm trying to belong here." I shrug. I want Cristina's life. A life of independence, success, love, safety, and plenty of time for the little pleasures. I want to learn how to properly enjoy the beauty of this country and be part of its culture of trust, respect, and social coziness.

"All right, give me your notepad and a pen."

I look in my purse and pass them to Erik. He sits on the nearest bench and starts scribbling on the first blank page he finds.

I sit by his side. "What are you doing?"

"Making a list for you. You can't consider yourself a true Copenhagener until you've completed these items."

He puts a loose strand of hair behind his ear, taking a break to think about what to write. I look over his shoulder to see what he wrote, the wind carrying his citrusy scent in my direction, confusing my thoughts for a second.

1. Eat pastries from the best bakeries in the city

2. Bike all around, everywhere

3. Visit the parks, castles, and museums

4. Have a picnic on the grass

5. Eat smørrebrød *for lunch (open rye bread sandwiches with a generous layer of traditional toppings)*

6. Shop in the Strøget

7. Go to Tivoli (the second oldest amusement park in the world)

8. Have a beer and fast food at a street food market

9. Discover Freetown Christiania (an independent community in the middle of the city)

"What about the Little Mermaid statue?" I ask him.

"That's a touristy thing. Overrated."

"A lot of the other things are also tourist attractions," I say, although I agree the statue site was a bit less exciting than I imagined. "I might be able to cross some items off the list already."

"What have you completed?"

I try to recall. "Hmm… I saw Amalienborg, the residence of the royal family, of course. I went to the National Museum, Christiansborg Palace… Botanical Garden… Oh, and I've shopped at Strøget many times."

"Good. I would have found it strange if you hadn't. Crossing number six off then." He strikes it through. "I guess you have also done item three to some extent." He draws a line over *Visit parks, castles, and museums.* "Anything else?"

"I've brought chips to eat while tanning on the grass in a

park near my old place during the summer. Does that count as a picnic?"

"I wouldn't say so." Erik clicks the pen, seeming like he isn't done with the list yet. "I missed one thing."

He writes down number ten, and when I see what it is, I laugh in disbelief.

"Winter bathing? Like, getting in the ocean when it's freezing cold?"

"Yes, that's the idea."

I shake my head, laughing. "You people are crazy."

"And yet you want to be like us, so you better join the madness."

I keep laughing and say, "No way."

He throws me the notepad with a mischievous grin. "Too bad. You'll never be a real Copenhagener then."

I shrug. "I'll never be anyway."

"Only if you don't want to."

We keep gazing at each other, and our smiles fade at the same time. A chilly gust of wind shakes our hair, and I press my jacket against my body.

"Trivia night starts at seven," Erik says, checking his watch. "We have a few hours to try some of the things on the list."

I look at him, surprised. Did Erik just say what I thought he said? Is he suggesting we hang out for the rest of the day?

I better not discourage him. I really want the company.

The reason why I explored so little of the city in my six months here was that doing all those things on my own felt strange. Empty. The times I felt hygge alone were at home, wearing my cozy socks, drinking hot chocolate, and watching a romantic movie under my blankets.

Out there, in a beautiful but strange city, I felt like an ant lost from her colony. All I wanted was to be in those wonderful places with someone I liked.

My main motivation to explore was to take pictures or make calls with my family and my best friend and show them what I'd seen and done.

Every time I was out somewhere, observing others, I hoped someone would sit by my side on a bench and start chatting, or that a coworker would cross my path. But it never happened. I made no actual friends.

"Sol?" Erik calls, snatching me out of my thoughts. I look at him, and he smiles. "Let's cross off some items."

Ten

We go back home to prepare for our tour. I put on my pink sneakers and my floral workout leggings. Then I pack a backpack with water, a thermos of coffee, and the cotton *pareo* with a Copacabana sidewalk print that I bought in Rio. It's the perfect blanket for a quick picnic, as it's light and doesn't take up much space in a bag.

I check my phone before leaving and see a message from my dad: Everything good? You've been silent.

I type a quick answer: Sorry, I've been busy with work. Maybe we can have a call tomorrow? But yeah, everything is great.

It's true. Everything *is* great.

Dad types: The big guy next door is not bothering you, is he?

I laugh, imagining Dad in his jealous, protective stance. He doesn't say it, but I'm sure that me living with a man is eating him alive.

Don't worry, Dad, I reply. The last thing on his mind is messing with me.

Sadly.

No. If I love myself and my new life in Denmark, I should never try to turn our fake relationship into a real one. Ruining the mutually beneficial agreements we have would ruin everything.

Dad: You still have the pepper spray I gave you, right?

I giggle at the idea of using that against Erik. I have to go now, Dad. Love you. Then I tuck my phone away and leave the room, smiling.

Erik takes his bike, and I find a rental bike parked close to our apartment and unlock it with an app. Then we set off, me right behind him as he leads the way.

We follow the bike lane. To our left there are buildings like ours connected to one another—old, charming, yellow, white, brick-red, guarded not by high fences but by autumn-colored hedges. To our right, water, benches, and sparse trees, their orange leaves waving with the cool breeze, casting shadows over the people walking their dogs, running, or bringing their babies for a stroll.

We pass by swans with open wings, a little island full of birds, floating restaurants, and couples holding hands. The city vibrates with life and health; bright, fresh, and colorful like an impressionist painting.

At some point, the lane leads us down a tunnel passing under the beautiful Queen Louise's Bridge. When we emerge on the other side, there is no more bike lane—we share a small road with cars, and soon we are taking a turn to enter the biggest park in our neighborhood, Fælledparken.

There is a wide muddy path for bikes and pedestrians to share. It circles around a vast green field where people play soccer, let their dogs run, or sit and enjoy the sun.

I keep following Erik, not talking, not worrying about my concerns, just absorbing the environment and enjoying the exercise and how alive you can feel when outdoors, exploring your city in no hurry and with no predetermined destination.

I pass a couple helping their little daughter steer her tiny bike and pair with Erik to ask, "Where are we going first?"

"I have a good plan," he says, smiling back at me. Birds sing high up in the trees—a calming, jolly melody. "I know a great bakery in the vicinity," Erik tells me. "We can grab a few pastries and come back here to eat."

"Good idea," I say, excited about the prospect of sweets.

He speeds up again, and I do my best to keep pace. I haven't biked in years. I used to go on Sunday rides with my dad as a child. But as a grown-up, if I biked twice a year, it was a lot. At least I'm in good shape, because I've always done some sport as an extracurricular activity, and my passion for volleyball stretched throughout adulthood. Since I came here, I've been doing yoga at home. I used to go running in the summer, but I stopped exercising outdoors when it started to get cold.

I don't know why I haven't bought a bike yet since it is the best means of transportation in this city. I guess I've been scared off by the prices and the traffic. But I realize now that it's easy enough to navigate around, with the bike lanes and dedicated traffic lights, and I'm sure it will be worth the price I pay if I get one. It's not like public transport is cheap here, and now I don't live as close to work. Besides, cycling isn't only good for the body but for the environment too.

I'm so satisfied, so fulfilled, that when we stop to cross a street, Erik notices it just by glancing at me. "You look like you're enjoying the tour."

"It's wonderful! Thank you for bringing me here."

We ride slowly next to each other, passing by a kiosk and entering another part of the park, near a stadium. Then we enter a commercial street, and soon we are stopping in front of the bakery Erik likes.

And he is not the only one. There is a long queue of people outside waiting to enter.

"Is this all to buy bread and cake?" I raise my eyebrows.

"I told you it was a big deal," he says, grinning, and guides me to where we can park our bikes.

We face the line and use the waiting time to draw our plans for the evening. He shows me on his navigation app how to get to Lars's house, where the trivia night will be. Since it would take us about half an hour to walk from our place, compared to ten minutes biking, we agree to ride there at around 6:30 p.m. so we don't risk being late.

"When you have appointments in Denmark, *always* be on time," he tells me.

"Any other tips?" I look at him, avid for more advice.

"Take off your shoes when entering someone's home."

"Oh. It's good you say that. I had no idea."

"When in doubt, just follow my lead, but don't worry too much." He smiles softly. "I think you're doing fine at home."

"I am?" I give him a sideways look, uncertain. "Is Sol Carvalho living up to Erik Storm's standards?"

He gives a short, hoarse laugh. "Well, you clean up after yourself and give me space. I have nothing to complain about."

This lightens my mood. I look in his direction. The sun reflects in his eyes, making them more translucent than ever. He squints and turns his head away to not be blinded, and I catch myself observing his every move, a bit mesmerized. Just a bit.

Who am I kidding? I'm staring. He is gorgeous. Even with all that beard. And I don't see gorgeous people every day.

Well, I do. I see Erik.

"I've been walking around in shoes at home," I comment to get my thoughts away from the danger they are falling into.

"Not when they are muddy, and you vacuum the entrance and the dining room every day," Erik remarks. "So, ten points for you."

"Are we keeping count?" I smile, happy that he didn't forget the game I initiated the day we met.

"According to my calculations, I've got thirty points—ten for knowing about Brasília and twenty for having an orderly bedroom. You are now at twenty."

"You need to be more generous with me," I say jokingly.

"Rest assured that I'll be fair when I recognize a worthy act."

"Now that I think about it, I should remove ten points from you because your mom helped you decorate your room."

"Fair enough. We're even then."

We laugh, and the moment seems surreal. We are actually here, standing in a bakery line on a Sunday afternoon, talking like...friends. Is that what we are becoming? Am I finally making a friend in this city?

We leave the bakery with two pastries each—a *kardemommesnurrer*, a "cardamom roll," and a *spandauer*, the original cake that inspired every pastry named "Danish." The first is a soft, buttery, curly bun with cardamom seeds, and the second is a *wienerbrød* with flaky dough, sugar glaze, and custard crème filling. My mouth is watering just looking at them, but Erik says we should find a nice place to sit. When I tell him I brought coffee and a blanket, he agrees it would be a shame not to cross *picnic* off the list.

We climb on our bikes, and Erik guides us back to the park. We decide to sit under a tree facing the soccer field so we can watch people play. I stretch my *pareo* on the grass for us, take the coffee thermos out of my backpack along with two paper cups, and we enjoy our cakes.

Eating the cardamom roll is like biting into dreams made of cotton candy clouds and unicorn milk. It's wonderfully soft and buttery, and I make loud "mmmm" sounds at every bite. Erik laughs at my enjoyment and joins me in the guttural noises even though he's eaten these pastries several times before. The *spandauer* is also dreamy-licious.

"I can't believe I didn't know how good this could be," I rave over the sound of children yelling on the playground. "I've tried similar pastries since I arrived, but nothing like this!"

"You need to go to the right places. Supermarket cake is nothing compared to these hidden gems."

"Not so hidden, I'd say. Next time I'll join a long line whenever I see one."

He laughs, and we drink our coffee in a peaceful post-cake sugar rush. Brown leaves rustle around us, black-and-white birds springing about, hoping we drop crumbs nearby.

Sorry, little birds. I've eaten every single piece of my lovely snack.

"I think we should get going if you want to visit a few other places." Erik checks his watch. I look at mine too. Half past twelve. "Maybe we can grab some lunch?"

"You're thinking about *more* food?" I use an intonation of incredulity to tease him. Then I say, relaxed, "That's good because I could eat more."

He laughs and stands up. "Let's go then."

We ride across Queen Louise's Bridge, and in a few minutes, we are in front of Torvehallerne, a fresh food marketplace with two covered halls—one with shops selling delicacies, foreign specialties, and other types of fine food, and one hall mostly for fresh fish, cheeses, and meat. In between them, outside, we find rows of stalls with local vegetables, fruits, and flowers, and a couple of food trucks.

We walk around, reveling in the different smells and gladly accepting free samples. I buy a few fruits, biscuits, and juices. It's very crowded inside, and Erik guides me with a hand on my back toward a place selling what is called *smørrebrød*. I take the list he wrote from my bag and confirm that we are about to complete item five: *Open rye bread sandwiches with a generous layer of traditional toppings.*

I squeeze through people to look at the glass displaying the different open sandwiches. They are like art pieces. Erik looks up at the menu with me, and we end up deciding on two each. I get the one with egg and shrimp and the one with chicken salad and bacon. He chooses one with smoked salmon and one with liver pâté.

After facing another long queue, we leave with our recyclable plates and find a table outside. There is so much topping on the bread, and it's all arranged in such an artistic way, it's impossible not to destroy the whole tower of food when eating it—with fork and knife, as Danish people do.

"Do you like it?" Erik asks with a glint in his eyes, hoping for my approval. I nod with a full mouth.

"Very interesting," I say after I swallow. "But it's hard for me to accept not eating hot food for lunch. We get that at work, and I'm happy for it."

"I should prepare you in case you ever need to make your own *smørrebrød*," he says, and I watch as he delicately cuts his food. Eating bread with cutlery is a skill I must learn how to master. "Often, lunch in Denmark is about putting a bunch of possible toppings on the table and giving people a few pieces of *rugbrød*, rye bread," Erik tells me, and I nod, showing that I'm listening. "And we have rules. Things that are good to mix and others you should *never* combine."

I laugh, but he is serious.

"Example?" I say, curious to learn more.

"Well, you saw the flavors on the menu. Those are the iconic combos. Study them and you won't fail. Roast beef always goes well with rémoulade and fried onion, for instance. You can also put rémoulade on a fish fillet, but putting *mayo* on it instead would be frowned upon. Unless you add shrimp. Then it's acceptable because it becomes a *stjerneskud*. A 'shooting star' sandwich, or however you translate that."

"Oh. Okay?" I laugh at the nonsensical rules.

For the rest of our lunch, he tells me all the good combinations and frowns—or pretends to throw up—whenever I mention a blasphemous combo that sounds perfectly tasty to me.

"I'm happy I taught you this lesson so you don't disgust

Lars next time you have lunch together." Erik points his fork at me. I throw a napkin at his face, but he keeps laughing.

When we finish eating, we decide to pass by the King's Garden, as it's basically across the street. It's the park surrounding Rosenborg, a mighty royal castle that is a museum nowadays. The gardens are very Royal-looking, with statues of heroes fighting beasts, and I can easily imagine kings and queens going for lazy walks here in their pompous garments.

Pushing our bikes, as we are not allowed to ride in here, we walk down one of the two straight paths hedged with identical well-trimmed trees tinted with the warm colors of the season. It could have been a romantic walk if we were a couple. My mind drifts to the evening to come, and I start to get nervous.

"What do you think I should wear tonight?" I ask Erik. He looks at me with a slight frown, as if wondering why on Earth I would ask him for fashion advice. "I mean, if I want to blend in," I clarify.

He lets out a snort that sounds a bit like laughter and a bit like disapproval.

"Well, I guess you have noticed by now that dark colors are safe." He glances at me, a bit anxious, and I wonder if he is afraid to offend me in some way.

"You can be honest," I reassure him. "I'm too colorful, I know."

"Your prints are indeed very lively." There's a smile in his voice, but not of mockery, and I laugh, seeing how he's struggling with the words. I look down at the flower pattern of my leggings. "But you're fine, Sol. I like how you have this… *energy* about you."

"I call too much attention." I arch an eyebrow, looking at him, but he doesn't answer, as if he doesn't dare to be honest about this. "It's all right. I guess I already have my answer. Black from head to toe is the way to go."

He laughs, shaking his head. "You don't have to be radical. Danish fashion is about keeping it simple. Muted colors, minimalistic patterns, comfort, and quality. People here tend to avoid being flashy and standing out." His voice lowers, again like he is not comfortable with the subject. "I don't like generalizations," he adds. "People are different. But if you must follow a general cultural trend," he says the words in a dismissive way, "when in doubt, keep it low. Better underdressed than overdressed, and so on."

"Got it," I say, with no hard feelings or anything, just taking mental notes. What he said matches my observations, and I don't think of the differences as a criticism of me. I'm on a mission to blend in with the crowd, and I'm ready to reinvent myself for that. Still, Erik studies me with a hint of concern.

"It all comes from *Janteloven*," he tells me, almost like an apology.

"Jante-what?"

"The Law of Jante. It's a cultural code of sorts. A set of rules Scandinavians follow even if they are unaware."

I look at him, very interested. He notices my eagerness and continues. "It's about thinking you are not better than others. We love being equal in Denmark." I nod, encouraging him to go on. "We don't brag, because we don't want other people to feel bad about not having what we have. And it's not only about that. Thinking about others is not an extraordinary thing—it is a given."

"That's nice," I comment, glad to hear him put into words what I've been observing for a while.

"It's why most of us will clean after ourselves or respect a queue," he says. "We like flat hierarchy. Our minimum salary is quite high compared to other countries, and most academic jobs pay within a similar range."

"This is an aspect where our cultures greatly differ," I tell him. "Don't even get me started on the socioeconomic differences in Brazil."

"Yeah, I know. I've been to your continent. I saw it myself." He looks at me while we walk, the row of trees almost ending. "So, this Law of Jante thing. I would try to impress Lars in a very subtle way if I were you." He gives me a meaningful stare. "Don't do anything that will get you too much attention or put you on uneven ground with others. If someone says you did a good job, you say it was thanks to the team, not only *your* efforts. You get the point."

I nod, thankful for his advice, and we take a branching path toward the exit of the park. I look down at my pink sneakers, trying to picture my wardrobe in my head to see if I have anything discreet for tonight.

On our way to our last destination (item nine of the list), we pass by Nyhavn, Copenhagen's most famous postcard, with the colorful historical buildings in front of the canal filled with boats. It was the first place I visited when I arrived, and it's still one of my favorite spots in the city despite the hordes of tourists crowding the streets.

"What about my hair?" I bring the honey-colored ends to my eyes, wondering if it's time to leave the *ombré* style behind. My roots are very dark, and my hair is quite chemically damaged without monthly maintenance at my mom's salon. Hairdressers are very expensive here, so I've been avoiding them. My mom would make a lot of money in this country. "Should I dye it back to dark brown?"

"You look great as you are, Sol," he says, and then he blushes and becomes a little stiffer. Wait, *what*? He thinks I'm pretty? Is that really what he's saying? My heart races and I try to conceal my smile.

Well, he liked you on Cinder, right? The reminder of how we got acquainted makes my face heat up too. I normally try not to think that he had hoped to date me when we first met.

"But if you *need* an opinion, I think it would be nice if you embrace your natural color, yeah," Erik adds, still careful, but I notice he means it. "And your waves. I know Danish blondes who would love to have dark hair with curls."

"Are you kidding me? They have the silky blond hair women come to my mom's salon begging to get."

Erik shrugs, smiling. "I guess you always want what you can't have."

Eleven

When my boss sees that my boyfriend is Erik Storm, his eyes widen. Then he hugs Erik, claps his back, laughs out loud, and says, "Storm, I can't believe it! How are you? It's so good to see you again!"

They chat excitedly in the foyer. Meanwhile, I stand near the door, clutching my purse in front of my body, smiling like a goth-chic Latina Barbie in a black long-sleeve dress and black tights. An elegant middle-aged woman wearing a beige knitted dress approaches me, and I shake her hand.

"Hi, I'm Lotte, Lars's wife." She smiles kindly, long earrings dangling and shining with a tiny green gem that matches her eyes.

"I'm Sol. Nice to meet you!"

We look at Lars and Erik, both still laughing like two old friends who haven't seen each other in years. Considering Erik's responses whenever I mentioned Lars, I could never have imagined he was so loved by his former boss. I haven't seen Lars have such an effusive reaction to anyone before. And Erik…he's behaving like he loves the man back.

Well, it's good for our act, I guess.

Lars finally turns around and sees me with his wife. While Erik says hi to her, Lars walks over to me.

"Sol, it's great that you came. And holy moly! Erik Storm? Why didn't you tell me?"

I smile weakly, and Erik comes to my side, putting an arm around my shoulders. A shiver runs down my spine the second I feel his warm, massive body touch mine.

"It's all a bit new to us," he answers, which is good, because I've totally lost focus, my mind only understanding one situation: Erik's arm around me. "We wanted the right occasion to tell you guys."

"I can't wait to hear the story." Lars chuckles to himself. "Come in!"

Lars and Lotte enter their vast living room, and Erik and I stay behind to take off our shoes and hang our jackets. It's a relief when he steps away from me, but at the same time, the absence of his warm body next to mine makes me shiver, feeling suddenly cold.

"What was all that about?" I whisper to him as I unzip my boots.

"What do you mean?" he whispers back, looking distracted. A cacophony of voices comes from the living room. We arrived five minutes before seven, but it seems like others were even earlier.

"His euphoria for seeing you," I explain.

Erik smiles shyly. "It's nothing. That's how Lars is."

I'm not convinced, but Erik doesn't wait for me to say more.

He leaves his shoes next to mine and starts walking toward the next room. I catch up with him and hold his hand. We look at each other, and my heart rate increases. His palm is sweaty against mine. Warm. Soft. It's…*weird* to hold hands with him. Good. In a strange, delightful way.

"Ready?" I whisper under my breath.

He nods.

Smiling, we walk to the sofas, where we are met with loud, excited greetings.

"Unbelievable, isn't it?" Lars says, and many people stand up at the same time.

George is the first to embrace us, and we are introduced to his boyfriend, Alex. Then Chiara and her girlfriend, Anika, give us handshakes. Chiara started at Scorpio after Erik left, so she doesn't know him. Astrid gives us each a brief hug, saying that it's good to see Erik again. Simon claps Erik's back with enthusiasm and says he misses him.

We meet Simon's wife, Lia, a petite Portuguese woman who greets me with an *"olá."* As we are still standing in the middle of the room—me asking Lia in Portuguese which city she is from—Ellen arrives with her husband, Mads. She lifts her arms, crying Erik's name wholeheartedly. It takes her a moment to understand that he came as my boyfriend, not a special guest.

"Oh, wow!" she says after we have been introduced to her husband. "This is wild!" She puts one hand on my shoulder and one on Erik's. "How did this happen?"

"I'm also eager to hear!" Lars says.

Thankfully, his wife chooses this moment to call everyone to the table, which is already set with the quiz game, drinks, and snacks. They had warned us to get dinner before, as we would go straight to the game.

When everyone is settled around the table, I start to think Martin won't come. It's ten past seven. He is late. I hold back a smile of triumph.

Then he arrives.

The door is unlocked, so he walks in, announcing himself from the foyer.

It takes Martin a moment to notice Erik's presence. He is heading toward his seat next to Astrid when his eyes land on his former business partner.

"Erik?" Martin opens his mouth in surprise, and Erik stands up. The chatter continues around the table. I'm the only one aware of the tension, it seems. They stare at each other, for an instant completely still. I look from one to the other, waiting for a reaction, so nervous I start biting my nails, something I've never done before.

They hug, at last, a bit awkwardly, and I exhale.

"Long time, no see!" Martin has a strange smile on his face. "What are you doing here?" He takes a seat, and Erik sits next to me. I put a comforting hand on his leg under the table, doing what a girlfriend would do and realize too late that no one can see my gesture. I remove my hand, blushing.

"He is Sol's boyfriend," Lars says as if he still finds it utterly amusing—and wonderful.

"What? Oh! Wow."

People laugh at his reaction, and the murmur around the table grows louder.

"And the two of you know each other too?" Lars talks to

Erik and Martin. According to what Erik told me, Martin got a job at Scorpio after he left.

"Yes, we have worked together," Erik says, and I look at him, concerned. He keeps a smile on his face that might deceive the others, but not me. I'm aware of the turmoil going on inside him.

"Hmm. Small world." Lars smiles, sipping his wine. Martin clearly omitted his experience working with Erik from his résumé and neglected to mention it in his job interview at Scorpio. "And what are you doing at the moment, Erik?" Lars asks him.

I hold Erik's hand on the table to show him my support. I've thrown him in the lion's den, after all.

"I'm working on a personal project." He squeezes my hand, making butterflies dance in my stomach.

This disorients me. I keep my hand where it is, but it takes all my focus to tell my body to stop reacting to Erik's touch. *This is fake, okay? Fake!* I shout at my hormones.

"Oh, is it the same project you left Scorpio to work on?" Lars asks, then quickly adds, "You never told me anything about it. You'll have to fill me in later, Storm." He points at Erik with a piece of dark chocolate. "Now let us understand—" Lars's resonant voice sounds higher than the others "—how did the two of you meet?"

The moment has come. I squeeze Erik's hand harder, relieving my anxiety. Silence has fallen upon the table, all faces directed at us, dying to hear our story.

I'm opening my mouth to start, but Erik gives my hand two quick squeezes before letting go of it and taking the lead. "Okay, okay, here's what happened," he starts, and I lean back in my chair, focusing on my breathing to not freak out. "Sol got my number one day when she was talking to Mark about needing a room—"

"Oh, he told me," Simon interrupts him.

"Did you find a place, Sol?" Chiara asks. We haven't talked about that at work since I got Erik's number. Chiara's eyes then grow wider, and she opens her mouth with understanding. "Or…are the two of you living together now?"

"Yes, we are," I say with a shy smile, and the reactions to this make me want to disappear under the table. Everyone is surprised and thinks it's funny, but Martin's exclamation is what gets me. And Erik. Especially Erik.

"You get a roommate and immediately start dating her, Erik?"

It's supposed to be a fun, teasing comment. But they are not intimate enough for this. It's a provocation, and only I realize it because I know their history, even though I don't know the whole story.

The look on Erik's face after what Martin says makes me think he will throw in the towel and end our charade right here. It angers him. It hurts him. But maybe that's precisely the boost he needs. More fuel for his burning wish to take down his rival.

"Here is where it gets funny," Erik says, concealing his true feelings so well he easily passes as a carefree extrovert sharing an entertaining story. "Sol and I *had* met before."

I try not to frown to avoid giving us away, but I'm wary. Why is he changing the story we rehearsed?

"We actually met through Cinder." He smiles, anticipating the amused reactions. "I didn't have my last name there, and my photo was terrible, so old I was barely recognizable."

"You looked like a bedraggled surfer," I comment to add more credibility, and some people titter.

Simon agrees it's time Erik updates his profile photo, which he uses on all his social media accounts.

"And yet, you gave me a like," Erik remarks, undisturbed.

"I was bored that day," I tease, and the others laugh at our playful exchange.

"Anyway, we started talking, and we kept chatting on the app for a long time without ever going out. For months… since, what? June?"

"June thirteenth," I make up a date. "Thank you for forgetting it."

"I will count our anniversaries from the day you moved in."

"That's inaccurate."

Lars is laughing fondly at us as he drinks his wine, but he interrupts our banter to ask me, "If you had his number, how did you not know it was him renting out the room?"

Erik is the one who answers. "We only talked on Cinder. Sol was Marisol Carvalho in the app. I don't know why, but I didn't connect the names." He taps his forehead with the palm of his hand, reproaching himself. "When she texted me about the apartment, I had no clue it was her, and she had no clue it was me because we hadn't even heard each other's voices before. And, you know, there are a lot of people called Erik in Copenhagen."

I serve wine for both of us, as I see that he needs a dose of alcohol to handle staying in character. After a long sip, Erik continues, "We scheduled a date one day, finally. We had an instant connection…"

Erik drinks up, and I refill his glass. Everyone sees he is preparing to enter an uncomfortably personal part of the story. I hope he stops here. We've said enough.

"She went home with me that night…" He lifts one eyebrow when looking at me, and I hide my face behind my hands. Is he seriously going to tell my coworkers details of a sexy night that never happened? I'm faking embarrassment for the sake of entertainment, but I actually don't want my colleagues picturing me in bed with Erik Storm. I need to make him shut up.

"I think they don't need to hear more, Erik…" I try, but he ignores my appeal.

"Let them hear the finale, honey." He strokes my hand, making me breathless.

Goodness. What is happening? Why is he saying these things and smirking in that tricky way? Why is my body so…*excited* when my mind is on full red alert?

"The day after," he begins, "I was supposed to have a final call with the woman who wanted the room. So, there we are, in my bed at ten in the morning." He gesticulates with his glass, the wine shaking inside. His face is flushed, his eyes energized. It's as if something had possessed him—the spirit of a party animal not afraid to share anything with a group of friends.

I shrink in my seat, my stomach tight with fear and other obscure things.

"Sol goes out of the room to make a call," he continues. "Two seconds later, my phone rings on my night table."

Everyone laughs, some clapping or saying, "Oh my God, what a coincidence!"

Erik nods, enjoying the comments. "Isn't it? Then we laughed about it and concluded that we should go ahead with the rental. It was destiny, after all."

He looks at me with admiration, the sweet scent of grapes and alcohol exhaling from his mouth, which is too close to mine.

And getting closer.

Oh, my God of Thunder.

His lips reach mine.

He kisses me.

It lasts one second.

One second in which I feel a soft pressure on my mouth and forget I'm angry at him for changing our story without telling me.

One second in which my skin tingles and prickles in a thousand different spots.

One second when the butterflies return with full power, lifting my stomach as if I've jumped off a cliff.

I don't have time to react. To grab his neck and hold him there longer. It's a stolen kiss. Fleeting and breathtaking, the aftermath more powerful than the brief instant our lips connected.

Because the *feelings* linger. And they get more overwhelming as I think about what happened.

My heart pounds against my ribs as Erik sits straight in his chair again. I don't hear what is happening around me. The noises at the table are like the humming of static from an old television. Erik is deliberately not looking at me; he's talking to others, drinking, and eating chips.

He can't simply kiss me and ignore me after. He can't make up that stupid story we didn't agree on and talk about us sleeping together with my coworkers without my authorization. Who does he think he is? And I'm sure he didn't just make that up on the go. Who can do that? No…he *rehearsed it* in his head before we came. He hated my version and *betrayed* me instead of telling me what he thought would work better.

And then he kissed me.

I excuse myself to go to the toilet, and Lars tells me I should use the bathroom upstairs because the tap is broken in the one downstairs. I climb to the second floor, glad to be away from the noisy party. It's a big house. I might even be able to make a call and not be heard.

I'm thinking of calling Larissa to seek her advice when I hear footsteps climbing the stairs. I turn around and see Erik on the landing. He gently pushes me inside the bathroom and locks the door.

I turn to face him with my heart in my throat. He is *so* handsome this evening. He has trimmed his beard because I asked him if he could. And *gosh*, he looks hot, wearing a gray button-down shirt I ironed for him, with his hair neatly brushed back and curled in a bun, his jaw even more defined now with only a thin layer of smooth beard covering it. He is no longer a shabby Viking.

He is the sexiest man on Earth.

I swallow hard, cursing my thoughts. He comes closer, the smell of wine reaching me before his face is inches away from mine. I battle the urge to shout at him and the wish to pull him in for a kiss. A proper one.

Everything is exploding inside of me like fireworks, and I try to control myself one breath at a time.

"Sorry about what happened back there," he mutters, his deep voice sounding even more hoarse when he speaks so low. Two of his buttons are open, and I feel like closing them…

Or ripping the rest open.

Jeez. I need to sleep with someone soon. Not Erik. *One little kiss and a few hand touches, and that's how you react, stupid body? Don't you communicate with my brain? With my memories? The ones where Erik says that nothing real will ever happen between us? Did you forget you live with this man, and you will never have peace in your own home if something does happen?*

"Why did you change the story and not tell me?" I try to look harsh. My heart is beating so loud I'm afraid he might hear it.

"I panicked, okay? Sorry." His face looks about as innocent as the devil's would—and God, it's sexy.

I take a deep breath to control my riot of emotions. "You've been rehearsing this new version." I won't let this go. When my annoyance is gone, I don't know what will be left, and I'm afraid to find out.

"What makes you say that?"

"Come on, Erik. We don't trick *each other*," I stress the last two words. Transparency has been our deal from the start.

"Fine, I hated your version. I thought we wouldn't need to use it, that we could just say something vague and lead the conversation elsewhere." He gazes toward the mirror, avoiding me. "I was still working on the story in my head and hating every version I made too. So I had to improvise."

"After Martin was an ass."

Erik chuckles. "Yes." A lopsided grin grows across his face and does strange things to my insides. "This is the closest to an insult I've heard coming out of your mouth. What's up with you and swearing?"

"I don't swear." I shrug, keeping my face serious. He's trying to distract me. Make me forget the kiss.

"Like you don't do drugs." He is looking at me once again, the grin still there, reminding me of things we discussed on our long bike ride.

"Yes. Like I rescue whales, donate blood, and plant trees. I'm a saint."

Erik gives a repressed laugh, his sweet breath tickling my face. He is tilting his head down to stare into my eyes, as he is almost a head taller than me.

"We should get back downstairs," he says.

I won't mention the kiss. It's better this way. It was convincing. He is dedicated to his role. Good. It was very good. For the act.

"Don't let Martin get to you, okay?" Oh no, I'm being sweet now.

Erik blinks at me and I notice a glint of vulnerability in his eyes. It's like he needed to hear my words. I swallow hard, and we stare at each other for an uncomfortable moment.

Until I can't stand it anymore and point a finger at his face to say, "And no more surprises, eh?"

"Yes, ma'am."

He turns around and unlocks the bathroom door.

Twelve

When Erik and I sit back in our spots at the table, Lars and his wife explain the rules of the trivia game, and we are added to the leaderboard Astrid created on her tablet. She asks what we want to be called, and we go for Team Sol & Storm. At the end of the game today, all teams will be scored, and she will update the leaderboard and send it to the group by email. Then we will keep counting points in the next events until a winner is found at the end of the Fun Season.

Erik and I are off to a bad start. We get horrible questions neither of us has a clue about. Lars and Lotte are masters, but I don't mind that they are good. I keep a close eye on my real competitors, especially Martin and Astrid, Team Singles. They are doing better than us, and I squeeze Erik's arm after three wrong answers, telling him we need to get in the game.

Either my pressure works, or the Asgardian gods decide to favor us. Our next four questions are all about Danish things, and Erik nails them. Two are about TV and movies, one about history, and one about the Royal family. I give him a high-five every time he is right. Erik answers the one about history so quickly I even kiss his cheek.

We are suddenly ahead, and Erik is chatting excitedly with the others about topics related to the questions. At some point, the conversation is so heated it even switches to Danish, but George calls their attention with a "Hello, this is an international zone!" and they speak English again.

I'm sipping my third glass of wine, gobbling down candy after candy, when we get a question I can answer. "Who is the only player to have won five UEFA Champions League titles?"

"Cristiano Ronaldo," I answer. It's correct.

Erik hugs me, and I smile. He puts my hair behind my ear, whispering, "We'll win this thing, Sol. Look at Martin's face."

"I can see it."

Martin has been quiet and bitter, bothered by Erik's shiny presence. No clouds are looming over Erik now. Tonight, he's in his element. It's impossible not to want to be like him—or be *with* him.

Our last question is, funnily enough, about Rosenborg.

"We were there earlier today," he says to the others with a smile, taking my hand and locking his fingers between mine. It's such an intimate touch I lose my breath, attacked by the butterflies in my stomach. "It was a wonderful day." I can't tell if he means this for real, but it is true for me.

Erik touches my face with the tips of his fingers, sending shivers down my spine. He brushes my hair away from my face, and I feel an inner mayhem that is amplified by having an audience staring with interest. People I will meet in the office tomorrow who will never see me in the same way again.

I answer the quiz question, still looking at Erik, and Lars drums on the table, announcing that we are the winners. Disappointed groans are heard around the table, Simon moves our pawn to the finish line unnecessarily, and people start talking and standing up.

I see all of this from the corner of my eye because I'm still facing Erik. I hug him to celebrate our victory, happy that he didn't give me another kiss, because I don't know if I would have stopped after one second.

My mind is a mess of thoughts and feelings. On autopilot, I follow Erik's lead and we stand up like the others to stretch our legs and prepare to go home. More chatting takes place in the kitchen and the living room, but I'm no longer interested in joining any conversations. I just want to go home and lie in my bed. It was a long day with many surprises.

Chiara lays a hand on my shoulder when I'm putting on my shoes. "I'm so happy for you, Sol," she says. "The two of you are a beautiful couple."

"Thank you, Chiara," I say wholeheartedly. "You and Anika are also very sweet together," I add, meaning it. "I'm happy to have met her."

"Maybe the four of us could go out sometime." She smiles, and Anika joins her, both ready to get out the door. Anika is as tall as Chiara, her light brown hair so long it can get stuck in her belt. She looks like an elf from *The Lord of the Rings*. I've observed the two of them holding hands, giggling, whispering to each other, and they are indeed a cute pair. I envied them whenever I looked their way during the game. The sincerity of their love...their evident partnership.

Erik and I thank Lars and his wife for the night and say

bye to the rest. We are too drunk to bike, so I abandon the bicycle I rented, and Erik pushes his down the sidewalk. The walk home in the dark is long and silent.

I climb the stairs to the apartment holding the railing, basically dragging myself up. At the last steps, Erik offers me his hand. We trip inside and compete for who gets to the bottle of water in the fridge first, then we elbow each other on our way to the bathroom to be the first to the sink. We end up brushing our teeth together, too tired to care, but I kick him out when I need to pee.

Once I open the bathroom door, I collide with him. Has he been waiting for his turn right outside? I stop with my hands on his chest, and for a moment I think I will be stupid enough to grab his shirt and pull him toward my lips.

The impulse is hard to resist when he is all godlike in front of me, shirt half unbuttoned, hair slipping out of the elastic, golden strands falling in front of glassy blue eyes. But I know that if I surrender to a moment of weakness, I'll be on the street sooner than later. Either because he kicks me out or because I won't be able to stand such a terrifying change in our status as harmonious roommates. That's when I know we should end this charade now.

"Goodnight, Erik." I lower my hands slowly, letting them slide on his Herculean chest for a few more seconds than is appropriate. "Thank you for today," I say in a tired voice, "but I won't be needing your services again."

"My services?" He narrows his eyes, reproachful and amused at the same time.

"Yes." I close one of his buttons, maybe to cover his irresistibly smooth chest, maybe to keep my hands on him a little longer.

"Are you firing me?" His blue eyes pierce through mine, and their intensity makes me hold my breath. I want him to kiss me aggressively—teeth, tongue, and nails—but he just stands there, torturing me with his tantalizing stillness.

"No, I'm releasing you." I gaze at him with as much indifference as I can gather even though I'm ablaze from groin to toes.

"Where did I fail?" His eyes look innocent now, and my wish to cover his mouth with mine increases about two hundred percent. I think of the brief—*too brief*—kiss he gave me out of nowhere earlier tonight. I remember how it made my lips tingle. How it flicked a switch inside me, activating a desire I almost couldn't—*can't*—keep at bay.

"You didn't," I whisper, too shaky, too wobbly on my legs to speak properly. "You were perfect." *And that is the problem.*

I don't know if I can keep pretending without surrendering to my attraction to him. The more *convincing* we are, the more we'll delight Lars, sure, but being around Erik today...

We have to end the situation before it gets out of hand.

I gather what is left of my strength to get back to my room, as far from temptation as possible—which is not far in the confines of our home. I'm almost slipping away when he takes my hand.

"What's up, Sol?"

I turn to face him, my breath stuck somewhere between my lungs and my throat. "We did it," I manage to say. "It's done. They saw you. They love you. I can handle it from now on."

He looks confused. Why is he not more relieved?

"I'm sorry again for changing our story, or if I was too… touchy."

My insides spin. I look into his eyes, trying to read him. There is no sarcasm in his tone this time, only regret.

"I was handling it the best I could," he says.

I tell the butterflies in my stomach to be quiet and find another place to live.

"It's okay, Erik. You were good." *Too good…*

"I still need my payment." He offers me a cunning smile, and I nod when I remember that I must fulfill my promise and help him with his project.

"We'll find some time this week, okay? I need to sleep now. *Godnat.*"

When I'm at my door, he says something in Danish in response to my "good night," which, unfortunately, I don't understand.

"What was that?" I ask, looking over my shoulder as I turn the knob.

But he just smiles and walks to his room without another word.

Thirteen

If I knew I would meet Martin at the coffee machine first thing Monday morning, I would have stayed at my desk and handled my hangover without caffeine.

"Hi, Sol," he says casually, arriving from behind me and placing his cup under the dispensing spout as I move aside to put sugar in my espresso. "Did you and Erik arrive home safely yesterday? You two looked quite drunk."

"We were fine," I say, and Martin sneers like he is above such prosaic things as drinking alcohol, particularly on Sunday evenings.

I know what he's getting at with this. He wants me to talk about Erik and how we are living together—the hottest gossip in the office this morning. I've gotten stares from at least five people who are not in our Fun Season group. Maybe I'm paranoid, but I can usually tell when others talk about me behind my back.

"Are you hungover?" Martin keeps being annoying.

I shake my head, opening another sugar sachet. "Nope. All

good." And I give him a smile that communicates, *Conversation over. On you go.*

His cup gets filled, and he brings it to the counter next to me to add honey. "I'm not sure I believe it," he says when I'm about to go back to my desk.

I look at him. "Believe what?"

"You and Erik. So sudden…"

I stare at him, incredulous. "We *are* together. Why is that hard to believe?"

Keep a calm face, Sol. Don't give yourself away.

Martin's smile is victorious. "You really don't know? Did he not tell you about Lena?"

Lena. Oh my.

"Of course I know about Lena," I say.

I was cleaning my room the other day and found a hairpin deep inside the drawer of the night table the former occupant left there. I already had my suspicions since the day Erik told me he didn't want to live with a woman. I shouldn't judge him when I don't know his history, but my certainty grew after finding the hairpin, and now it has been confirmed.

"I'm glad he's finally moved on," Martin says, stirring his coffee.

I hold my cup tight with both hands to not let them visibly tremble, then I take another sugar sachet just to avoid standing still.

"We used to be good friends, Erik and I, but you must know that already." Martin glances at me. "We haven't talked in a while, but we have a few friends in common, so I hear a little about him occasionally." Martin looks at me again as if expecting me to engage in the conversation. I remain quiet, however, staring at my coffee. "I've heard, for instance, that Erik abandoned his hockey team and hasn't been joining the game jams or any other events of our gaming community."

I wonder what his point is, but I still don't say anything.

"When she left, it was tough on him." Martin looks as emotionless as the beetle I named him after. I register the information. *Lena left Erik. It broke him.* "The last thing I'd expect is that he would commit the same mistake again so soon after."

Anger builds up in my gut, and I must use every ounce of self-control in me to avoid exploding.

Martin is playing a foul game, saying so much crap between the lines of his falsely cordial words that I want to spit in his face.

"*I* am not a mistake," I find myself saying, dry as a fallen autumn leaf.

"It's no surprise you like Erik. Women tend to have a soft spot for him," Martin says with a casual tone loaded with disdain. *Jealousy.* Like he wants that kind of attention. Like he feels invisible when near Erik.

"What people don't usually know," Martin goes on, "is how quickly Erik Storm can discard you—and *disregard you*—when your wants don't align with his."

I swallow hard. *I* have just discarded Erik, breaking our deal at the first sign of trouble.

But Martin is not referring to this kind of backing out. He means *real treachery.* And he's accusing Erik of his own crime.

My face heats up. "*You* left *him*, Martin."

There is so much more I want to say. None of it would be pretty. I must remind myself I don't swear. Or shout at people at work. I'll still need to face him in this office every single day.

"Have you asked him why?" Martin lifts one eyebrow, gazing at me. "But I guess it won't matter. You'll always know *his* version. And what do I care, honestly?"

He turns to walk away, but I can't let him end it here. I hate the guy, but he's giving me a different angle on the facts. Shouldn't I listen to his warnings? "What are you trying to say?" I ask and hate myself a little for taking Martin's bait.

"If you ever think about working with Erik Storm, don't. That's all I can say." Martin chuckles and walks away, enjoying himself for leaving me rooted to the kitchen floor with a cup of overly sweet espresso in my trembling hands.

Just when I find the strength to move, Lars shows up at the sink to get a glass of water.

"Everything okay, Sol?" he asks, not too concerned, as usual.

*No. I've told Erik I don't need him anymore, and Martin is being an even bigger *beep* than I thought he could be.*

I have the impression that it doesn't matter to Lars if I answer or not, but I say, "All good."

"Good. It was nice seeing Storm again. The two of you are…something rare."

I smile wider, laughing and crying a little inside. Is it wrong to want him to be right?

"I must say I'm a big fan of Team Sol & Storm. By the way, the third event is not this Saturday but the next," he says. "A cooking contest. You'll get an email soon."

"Cool. I love food."

Lars laughs. "Perfect. See you and Storm there!"

As soon as he turns around, I exhale heavily. I can't do this without Erik after all. I'll need to get him back onboard. While I'm a great eater, I won't win without a chef.

When I get home, Erik is already cooking his dinner. The smell of fried garlic and mushrooms hits me with full power when I enter the kitchen. My stomach growls, hungry to taste whatever is being made in Erik's expensive frying pan.

Don't get your hopes up, I tell my stomach. *We'll have to settle for a frozen meal as usual.*

"What are you making?" I ask after placing my water glass in the dishwasher. "It smells wonderful."

"Beef stroganoff," he answers, his mood unreadable.

"Mmmm… Stroganoff is my favorite dish," I tell him. "Well, at least the Brazilian version. My mom's, especially." I tiptoe closer and sneak a look over his shoulder, spotting a pot with bubbling water. "Pasta though? We usually eat it with rice."

"Hmm, I never thought of that. I guess you'll have to make me your version one day."

His comment makes my heartbeat rise. Are we at the point where we can eat each other's food? "Does that mean I can try yours?"

He looks at me, and I close the dishwasher, giving him my best hungry-puppy eyes.

"Lucky for you, I'm making enough for two today." He smiles at me, stirring *crème fraîche* into the pan. I smile back, delighted, and stand by his side, watching him work with speed and skill.

"The next event in the Fun Season is a cooking contest,"

I tell him in a casual tone, but my body is tense, full of anticipation. "Not this Saturday, but the next. I hope you can make it."

He looks at me, eyebrows lifted, and my stomach quavers with a mix of hunger and anxiety. "I thought you didn't need my services anymore," his deep, rough voice utters.

A shiver runs through me as I recall our last exchange. How I almost pulled him by the collar for an ardent kiss like my cousins kept suggesting. Me saying he was discharged, and his smirk as he told me something in Danish I didn't understand.

Maybe he hadn't taken me seriously. That smile, the light tone as he said goodnight… The cocky bastard knew I'd come crawling back to him.

Ugh, I can't let him think I need him that much.

"Lars would like you to be there," I say to the counter, as indifferent as I can.

"Lars. Of course."

When I glance in his direction, I see an expression of disappointment. Not like he is disapproving, but like he is…sad?

"Besides, you're a better cook than me," I add. "I'd never win without you."

Erik nods to himself, stirring his dish. It looks done. I wonder if he's overcooking it in his distraction.

"I'll be there, then," his statement is emotionless.

Is he sad because he thought *I* wanted him to go?

But no…of course not. He's just being the usual moody Erik. So I keep speaking. I'm happy he said yes, regardless of his level of excitement.

"Oh, I had the most dreadful conversation with Martin today," I tell him, now with my back to the counter. Erik's alarm rings, and he hurries to drain the pasta before it over-cooks. For a perfectionist like him, one second more ruins an al dente pasta.

"What did he say?" he asks while pouring the pappardelle into the colander.

"He thinks we're lying."

Erik turns his head so abruptly that boiling water splashes outside the colander, and he yells, "Ouch!" I hurry to help him, taking the pasta away and pulling his hands closer to examine them as he keeps complaining. His thumb is a bit red, but it doesn't look like a bad burn.

And then I'm holding his hands in mine.

"Are you okay?"

"It's fine, only stings a little."

I turn the cold tap and put his fingers under the running water. He groans, sounding uncomfortable and relieved at the same time.

"What did Martin say?" Erik insists, turning his eyes to me.

We are too close to each other now, my heart racing from the shock of his cry of pain—and perhaps a little because of my unplanned proximity…

"Martin suspects we might not be together for real because he thinks it's unlikely you'd commit the same mistake again," I say, suddenly very nervous. "You know, so shortly after what happened between you and Lena."

His blue eyes become as wide as saucers, and he turns away, tensing up. A reddish tone spreads across his face, starting with his ears. I retreat a few steps, letting him handle the pasta, which is now the most important task in the world for Erik.

I understand now why Erik had to come up with another

version of the story about how we met. He knew Martin could provoke him about it, and he did. So Erik's improvised version was supposed to free him from the shame of admitting he got involved with a roommate a second time. Like he'd learned nothing. But that version, including Cinder, was still not enough to fully convince Martin.

"He said it was tough when she left you," I continue, but Erik gives me a condemning look.

"I don't want to talk about this."

I face him. "We have to, Erik."

His forehead creases. "So that *Lars* can keep believing your lie?"

"I'm on your side." He serves the food on two plates, ignoring me to avoid a fight, I guess. But I can't let this go. "I can't defend you if I don't know the truth."

He turns his back to the stove, giving me his full attention. At first, his face is tense, angry, but then he sighs and looks down, saying, "Martin loved her."

"What?" My mouth drops open. Holy shiitake mushrooms. "Martin loved Lena?" I'm still processing the information. *Martin's jealous tone earlier makes total sense now...*

Erik nods. "I didn't know." He pulls his hair back, looking unsettled, and ties it in a new quick bun. "She came from Poland to study. Martin had classes with her. He was the one who insisted I give her the room when I was looking for someone to share rent and she needed a place to live." He takes a breath. "I had found this apartment thanks to a friend of my dad's, but I couldn't afford it alone."

I nod to show that I'm listening. I know how big this is for him, and I'm glad he's finally opening up.

Erik looks down with a distant gaze. "I was too stupid to notice, too self-absorbed. Too selfish…"

"*He* is to blame for not telling you how he felt about her." I defend Erik. "Did she like Martin back?"

He shrugs. "They were good friends. The three of us were. Later—too late—I realized Martin wanted her to live here because he would have an excuse to see her often. He was always coming over. We were already working together on the project." Erik turns to grind salt and pepper onto his food. "But Lena never showed signs of liking him more than as a friend. It was *me* she went after."

Erik stops with his palms on the counter, absorbed in his memories.

"I grew fond of her, and we became best friends. Things got…confusing." He seems embarrassed for talking about this with me, but he continues. "She made a move, and I went for it. Headfirst."

I lean my back against the fridge, watching him, bracing myself. This explains it all. His uneasiness when near me. The fear that he'll go through everything all over again.

"She didn't want to tell Martin about us. Whenever he was near, she went away. He noticed something was wrong, and I realized she knew—or suspected—that he had feelings for her."

"Oh my, Erik… I'm so sorry you went through all this," I say, meaning it. I can't blame him for never wanting to go through anything similar again.

There is no third wheel now though. No one else but us.

I frown at myself. Why am I having these thoughts? Would I ever want to be with Erik for real? Physical attraction is one thing—it's another to want to dive into a relationship that would quickly become what he described: confusing.

Besides, he carries too much baggage. I don't want to be Lena 2.0. I don't want him to think of another girl whenever he sees me. A girl he isn't over yet. A girl who lived in my room. Who probably stood here in this kitchen cooking with him.

I hug myself as if a strong wind just blew, freezing me inside.

"This mess," he continues, "it was affecting the three of us. And I did what I usually do—I escaped into my work." He takes two forks and knives from the drawer like he is not even aware of what he's doing. "I worked hard on the project. Alone. All the time. It helped me cope with the things I couldn't cope with. But instead of bringing me relief, it only made things worse, to an unrepairable level, because I…wasn't giving her the attention she deserved."

"Oh, Erik…" I want to come closer and comfort him, but I'm stuck in place, something in my mind telling my body not to move.

"My relationship with Lena deteriorated, and my partnership with Martin ended. We had been working on different things. Apart. Not communicating. Then one day we had a big fight. He showed me the version of the app he had been working on, but his vision wasn't mine, and he said he wanted to leave and asked for permission to keep working on his version alone. I said he couldn't, that it was my company, my idea, but he argued it was just as much his, and, well, it got ugly." Erik laughs darkly. "He brought up Lena. You can imagine how that went."

I nod, my brows knitted. "And then he stopped talking to you and got a job at Scorpio, the company you left?"

"Yes. Three months after our fight."

Ouch. That's heavy.

"And what about Lena?" I ask, almost whispering, afraid my words will open up his wounds.

Erik stares down at the surface of the counter, his back to me.

"She wanted to pursue the academic path. She had finished her master's and was applying for PhD programs all around the country, with no success. This...*chaos* in her personal life was the last straw. The final reason she needed to go back to Poland."

I move one step closer, bringing my hand forward but still lacking the courage to put it on his shoulder.

"I tried to get her to stay, but..."

He turns around, and I'm there, right behind him, breathing unsteadily. I put my arms around his waist, giving him the warm hug I would have liked to receive if it had been me telling this story.

It was one thing knowing he was large and muscular, but *feeling* it flicks the switch again. I'm overly aware of how small I am against his hard chest, and how his warmth spreads through me until my face is flushed and my legs feel unstable.

I slide my hand up and down on his back, caressing it, and he accepts my comforting embrace. It's soothing for me too, as long as I tell myself it's a friendly hug. But once my chaotic blood flow starts concentrating in my intimate parts, I let go.

Safely distanced from him, I stare into his tired eyes, noticing that he is more destroyed inside than I'd realized. He looks numb with pain, exhaustion, and hunger. I give him a quick stroke on the upper arm, breathing to get my pulse back to a resting pace—and failing.

"Let's eat now," I say. "The food is getting cold."

I smile, trying to lighten the mood. I take the plates and carry them to the table, going back for water and napkins. Erik sits on his chair and eats like someone who is not present. After those tough revelations, I let him enjoy some introspection. He's earned it. I'm also so hungry I feel no need to speak until I've devoured my entire portion of stroganoff.

"It was delicious, Erik. Thank you."

"*Tak for mad.* It's how we say, 'Thank you for the food,' in Danish. We always say this to the person who cooked or bought the food."

"*Tak for* the lesson."

He smiles a little, looking slightly better after eating.

"When are we going to work on the project?" I ask him. "I'm available the rest of the evening."

Erik looks at me, surprised and hopeful, as if he expected me to never work with him after all I'd heard today about him and Martin.

"I trust you, Erik Storm," I say, my voice firm and reassuring.

I help people. I don't abandon them when they need me most. And if there is someone who needs me now, it is Erik Storm.

Just as much as I need him.

Fourteen

The autumn weather in Denmark can be truly awful. Especially if biking is your means of transportation.

I love my new light blue bike with a charming basket decorated with fake flowers, but I don't love pedaling her up the bridges when it's raining and so cold and windy my face and fingers freeze to ice. I love my scarlet raincoat, but I don't love dripping half the water pouring from the sky onto the floor whenever I get inside and take it off.

Erik is ready with a cloth for me to clean the floor when I get home soaked on the last Friday of October, the day before the cooking contest. I went to the office earlier than usual so I could be home early to work on Erik's project.

It hasn't been easy to handle both a full-time job and a side project as complex as Erik's app, but I've been managing it. I don't care that I get too tired and there is no time for anything else in my routine. I'm excited about what we've been doing, and I can't wait to shove our wonderful app in Martin's face. Number one most downloaded in app stores. It will happen, I'm sure.

Erik has done a lot already, so I'm jumping in on a half-finished product. He has coded the basic features, and the core structure is there. I should be focusing on UI and UX, on making all the art and animation we'll need. In reality, though, there's so much more he'll need help with. There are advanced features to design, game mechanics to plan and improve, user tests to perform, bugs to find… It will be challenging, but he's well aware of that.

Erik gave me access to the project files, I tested what is playable, then suggested a few things to improve what he's made. He's been listening to me, and when he disagrees, he has strong reasons for it. Most of the time, I end up agreeing with his point of view. I keep in mind all the time that it is *his* project, but he has been so welcoming and open to feedback that it doesn't feel like that.

It feels like something we are building together.

Erik helps me wipe the floor, takes my raincoat to hang in the shower, and hands me a towel so I can dry myself.

"Terrible weather," I complain.

"I'm making tea to warm you up." Erik goes to the kitchen and fetches a teapot and two cups. He puts it all on the table next to our computers, sketches, and notes.

This is what our dining room has looked like for the last two weeks. When we eat, we move things aside to make space for our plates, and often we don't even close the laptops and keep discussing our work between bites.

Erik has also not been cooking to save time. Either he makes a large amount of food when I'm not home to freeze so we can reheat the portions in the microwave another evening, or we make a quick *smørrebrød* with whatever is in the fridge, or we order takeout.

After a quick hot shower, I jump into my cozy pants and favorite home sweater. When I approach Erik from behind to look at the progress he's made when I was away, he says, "You need to change your shampoo."

I smell my hair, frowning. My wavy locks are a little below the shoulders now, a tone of dark brown as close to my original color as possible. When Erik saw me arrive from the hairdresser last week, he gave me a genuine smile and said "perfect" after I asked what he thought.

"What's wrong with my shampoo?" I keep sniffing the ends of my hair, detecting nothing but a lovely fruity and floral scent. The corners of Erik's lips stretch up.

"It distracts me too much."

The butterflies in my stomach awaken, and I smile. He can't see it, his eyes on the computer screen.

Sometimes Erik lets these little comments slip. At first, it seemed he was a bit embarrassed, as if he'd found out too late he'd said the thought out loud. But he doesn't seem to mind anymore.

A lot of bridges have been burned and many boundaries have been crossed since we started working on the project.

In our busy new routine, we don't pay attention to what we wear, which means I often catch him walking around in boxer briefs and a worn T-shirt full of holes, and I might sit at the table for a combo of breakfast and work while wearing pajamas.

We end up in the bathroom together sometimes when I'm late, and he is there with the door open, brushing his teeth or his hair, and I need the sink, the hairdryer, or the mirror. We share the drying rack too, our socks and underwear hanging side by side.

We also started to share expenses. He uses the things I buy just as I use his whenever we okay it for each other—an act that is becoming less regulated the more time passes.

We agreed to clean the apartment together once per week, and on the two Wednesdays we tried it, we listened to music through his powerful speakers, brainstorming for the project while teaming up to dust the shelves and clean the bathroom and the kitchen.

We mock each other's habits now. We say crap and laugh at stupid things when we are both tired and working late at night.

And sometimes he says things that could be flirtatious, but we just laugh at it because our new intimacy allows for it.

It's incredible what ten days of intense work in our living quarters has done for our friendship.

"I need to show you this," Erik says, looking at me. "Took me the whole day."

I take a seat by his side and let him present his work.

We sit shoulder to shoulder many hours per day, but whenever I'm leaning in to look at something on his computer—or he is putting his head next to mine to see what I'm doing—I must force myself to focus. My mind drifts away to dangerous places as my body reacts to his overwhelming presence.

And it's addicting.

I tell myself all the time that it's the project that thrills me. It's the pleasure I feel working on something exciting that makes me impatient to arrive home in the evening.

But it's hard to convince myself of that when *the feels* come.

Sometimes, it takes a while. I can sit at this table for many minutes, or hours, totally immersed in the work before they hit me.

The shivers. The butterflies. The fireworks. The whole darn circus.

It's usually triggered when he leans too close, his breath tickling my skin. When his laugh chimes like Christmas bells next to my ear. When his smile grows until he shows his white teeth, and a little dimple appears on his cheek. When he is freshly showered and his delicious cologne kills a few of my neurons.

Right now, it might have started so quickly because of what he said about my shampoo. *I distract him.* Could it be in the same way that he distracts *me*?

I don't dare let my thoughts go in this direction. Things are going too well. What we have, this new friendship, is uncomplicated. So long as we keep it as is.

He is ridiculously hot, and my body reacts. So what? I can still work with him and silently enjoy the effects. I try not to be greedy. I try never to think that if touching his shoulder with mine feels good, imagine what it would feel like to have his hands on me.

Oh boy. No. Stop.

That's how it goes. Every day. It's tiring, good, scary, and thrilling. I let my heart leap and warm up in his presence. Sometimes I steal a harmless touch with a silly or "accidental" excuse. I allow my eyes to feast on his beauty and my ears to celebrate at the sound of his voice. And it's all good in those hours when I have him all to myself.

"It's great, Erik," I tell him, meaning it.

Unlike how it is at my work, here I'm not afraid to be honest. I don't have a reputation to keep, a status to maintain, or people to please. When something is trash, I tell Erik—in a joking way so it won't hurt, but he doesn't mind. He's learned to expect my truthful statements and even laughs in anticipation, imagining what I will say.

"What's the catch?" He raises an eyebrow, smiling.

"Nothing. I like it. Let's go for it."

He pours tea for us, a smile of satisfaction brightening his face. "We're getting there then."

"We are," I say proudly, and we tea-toast. "It's funny to think that the day I matched with you on Cinder, I thought it'd be cool if there was a dating app in which looks mattered less and it would be more about finding like-minded people."

"That's what Love Birds is about, and now you're helping me fulfill this vision. *Our* vision."

He looks at me with the cup of tea in his hands, steam spiraling in front of him. He is staring, and I stare back, both of us sipping at the same time, spying on each other over the rims of our identical cups. There is almost no distance between our bodies, and something about the way he is looking at me makes my butterflies go wild.

"I think we can make the mini games better though," I say, trying to keep my mind on the project, not on its creator.

"Agreed. Let's try to come up with some new ideas."

Essentially, the app is a game. You are a bird trying to meet another bird, but you don't get other people's profile information right away. You slowly discover who the real person is behind each bird avatar. By interacting with others, you gradually give information about yourself and learn something about the other players. You join matches and tournaments based on your location and interests, so you are more likely to meet a person who will be a good match for you. You then invite another player for private mini games, which might lead to an individual chat room, which might lead to a date.

We still have a lot to figure out, like how to monetize the app. Many of our ideas are good but too ambitious, and we must often take a step back and rethink things we believed were indispensable.

What is essential to us is that people have fun together before talking about themselves. We want gaming pals to fall in love and meet in the real world.

"What really motivated you to create Love Birds, Erik?"

He looks at me, surprised by my question.

"I know you didn't like Cinder and other similar apps," I continue. "But I want to know, why dating apps? Out of all the things you could make."

He rests his chin on his hand, thoughtful. "I don't know, I just..." He pauses, and I wait. "My sister, Frida, was very into those apps some years ago. She was only seventeen back then, and I was twenty-four and living with my parents for a period while I was writing my bachelor's thesis. I ended up, you know, trying to see how the apps worked so I could be a good big brother and protect her."

I mirror his smile.

"Frida told her friends in high school that I'd made a profile on Cinder. She set it up and took my picture, and I let her do it for fun. One day, she made me give glass shoes to a few girls, and later, when I started getting bombarded with matches, I found out that some of the girls knew my sister from school and were lying about their age in the app to get college-age guys interested in them."

He snorts like an old man who lightly reproaches young people.

"After this, a number of Frida's friends I'd never met before started coming to our house all the time. They kept whispering about me, giving me looks..." He shakes his head, uncomfortable. "I hated that kind of popularity. And I hated how my sister's friends were falling in love with me, or being plain obsessed, because I'd made that stupid profile."

"How sad for you, chased by a bunch of girls," I mock, and he makes a dismissive motion with his hand, smiling shyly.

"They were my little sister's friends. Underage teens."

"You can't blame them," I say, shrugging. "You are..." *illegally attractive* "...a well-built guy with a cool degree." I look down, feeling hot in my cheeks.

Erik smirks, shaking his head. "The Erik Storm on Cinder was not *me*," he says. "It was just an enticing bio and a nice picture. Well, at least for them, because I hated it." He laughs, and I follow. "That's when it dawned on me how unlikely you are to meet a partner for life in such a shallow environment, where people are creating fake images of themselves, and we are making decisions on who to meet based on that."

"I once met with a guy who looked like Gaston in his picture, and in reality was more like LeFou. Not that I missed a lot because he *was* a Gaston in the end, personality wise. And that was a no-no for me."

Erik laughs.

"And there was also that time when I matched with a guy who looked like a surfer dude and turned out to be a grumpy Viking."

Erik laughs even more. "Is that me?"

"What do you think?" I support my face in my hand too, each of us facing the other. I blink at him, he blinks at me, and time stands still. "So, you changed your picture into one where people can barely see it's you to check who wouldn't be scared away by an unattractive backpacking surfer?"

"Unattractive?" He narrows his eyes, falsely offended.

I feel myself blushing, but I stand my ground. "Well, there might obviously be people who are into that stuff." I shrug.

"That *stuff*?" He arches one eyebrow now. "You mean backpacking surfer dudes or grumpy Vikings?" There is a glint of amusement in his eyes as he teases me. "You seem to have put a lot of thought into those descriptions."

"And what are you implying with that?" I say, our eyes attracted to each other like magnets. "That I give you too much thought?"

Erik is the one to shrug this time. "That's why I need to make Love Birds. Cinder is all about how you evaluate a picture."

He breaks eye contact at last. I wonder if I escalated our flirting too abruptly and made a pleasant moment turn awkward. *You weren't flirting, Sol*, I tell myself. *And it's more likely that you hurt his feelings than enticed him.*

"I need the birds animated as soon as possible, Sol," Erik says, returning to our work.

I straighten in my chair, taking a deep breath. My mind is

not ready to focus on the project yet. It's still full of Erik—his smell, his voice, his translucent blue eyes, his teasing smile…

I pull my laptop closer and fill my cup with tea. I fight against my inappropriate thoughts.

And eventually, I win.

Fifteen

Erik and I arrive early at the Hut, a fancy restaurant where we are supposed to meet the other teams. The owner is Lars's good friend who's letting us use the place while it's closed to the public before the dinner service. After the cooking contest, we must leave the place clean and ready to receive customers. Everyone is talking about how cool it is that we get to cook in such a fine restaurant, having it all for ourselves.

When all the couples have arrived, Lars explains the rules. "Lotte and I are the hosts, and you guys will be in your teams, each couple responsible for cooking a dish according to our guidelines. I've used a part of our Fun Season budget to buy some ingredients, and they'll be available in the kitchen. Whatever you can find, you can use. What is locked away belongs to the restaurant and shouldn't be touched. Is everything clear so far?"

He looks at the group, and we all confirm by nodding our heads.

"You'll have sixty minutes to prepare your dishes and serve

them on plates for all of us to eat. Lotte and I will be the judges. We'll stay here at our table, and we'll rate your dishes without knowing who made what." He lifts a finger, his voice rising over the excited murmurs. "I have six envelopes with me. Each couple will take one and follow the instructions. They will tell you what kind of dish you must cook." He holds a hand out, offering us six envelopes. I grab one.

"Go, now! You have one hour!" Lars taps his watch.

The couples spread around, putting their heads together to read what is in their envelope. Erik lands a hand on my shoulder, leaning closer to see what we got. My heartbeat instantly rises.

"A hot dish," I read in a whisper, a bit breathless. "You may use the stove, and you can use whatever ingredients and tools you find in the kitchen." I look up at Erik, and he's so close to my face, my stomach flips. "Any ideas?"

"It all depends on what we can find in the fridge," he says with his minty breath. I swallow hard, nodding. "Come on," he calls, adding some distance between our bodies. "Before the others raid it."

He takes my hand, and we hurry to the big industrial kitchen. Chiara and Anika are already choosing pots. Simon and Lia are taking fruits and vegetables from the cold room. George and Alex are organizing their workspace. Ellen and Mads are standing in front of the oven, discussing options, and Martin and Astrid are looking in the small fridge. Erik and I see why: the big walk-in refrigerator is locked.

We come from behind them, trying to peek over their shoulders.

"You guys wait your turn," Martin says, gathering ingredients in his arms.

"What are you making?" Astrid asks us, smiling. "Our dish should be soup."

"Perfect. Then you don't need the beef." Erik sneaks a hand inside the fridge and steals a piece of meat.

"Hey!" Martin protests.

"It's a race, my friend," Erik says and passes an arm around me, guiding me away. We laugh quietly all the way to the stove, and I'm so hyped by his touch, my body trembles and pulsates.

"Nothing like a chance to beat your foe, huh?"

"Martin is not great in the kitchen," Erik tells me with a mischievous grin, his face flushed with the heat indoors and the tension of a tight schedule. There is also a thick layer of excitement around him, and I let myself take it in.

"So, what do we make?" I ask him. "Now we have beef. What about your stroganoff? It's easy enough, right? And delicious."

"Then we make your Brazilian version."

I shake my head. "No, no. I'm not… Yours is better."

"You still haven't made it for me," he argues. "And it will be nice to have an interesting dish the others have never tasted before."

I frown, put off by the idea. "It's not that different from yours, trust me. We should just do what is most likely to please Lars."

Erik turns to the stove, shaking his head, reproachful. "How long will you keep hiding behind me, Sol? When will you show them some of your personality?"

I step closer, frowning. That's one of those things he will

never understand. I don't want to be an exotic bird that people find fascinating. The thing they observe from a distance and say, *Oh, how interesting*, like I'm something that will never belong in their reality.

Is it such a flaw to not want to raise eyebrows and just blend in seamlessly? To not be remembered only for your cultural heritage?

"I'm playing it safe, Erik," I say firmly. "We're making a dish everyone knows. Either you're in or you're out."

Erik is quiet for a second, then he starts looking in the cabinets for a pan. "Go grab some onions, garlic, butter, mushrooms, flour, cream, mustard, beef stock, pasta, and a bit of parsley."

"Ugh, wait," I say, overwhelmed with the long list. "I'll see what I can get."

A few minutes later, I return with all I could find and carry.

"There'll be some replacements. Ketchup instead of mustard. We'll add tomato puree, and no beef stock."

"Great. Then there'll be a Brazilian touch after all." He winks at me, and I surrender a little smile in return.

While Erik cooks the beef and I assist him by cutting the vegetables and measuring the ingredients, the other couples work hard all around us. Astrid and Martin cook their vegetable soup on the second stove, Ellen and Mads make their oven-only dinner, Simon and Lia prepare a salad on the counter behind us, George and Alex make an elaborate sandwich that looks more like art than food, and Chiara and Anika prepare a dessert that fills the kitchen with a delicious chocolate smell.

Although we are all concentrated on our dishes, some of us are curious about what the others are doing and walk around to get glimpses and show support. Drawn by the smell of minty chocolate, I stop behind Chiara and Anika, saying a lengthy "mmmm" that makes them laugh happily.

I'm returning to Erik when Martin approaches to ask if he can use our knife. I'm still a few steps away when he says to Erik in a low voice, "I don't know what you're doing, but it needs to stop."

"Stroganoff." Erik turns to him with an innocent look, stirring his dish. "I can't stop until it's done."

Martin's mood is dark. "If this is because I left you before we—"

"I don't know why you're bringing that up now."

Erik looks very calmly at him, almost like he is bored with the conversation. I stay where I am, pretending to search for spoons to disguise that I'm listening.

"I'm here for Sol. Because I'm her boyfriend."

Martin snorts, showing he doesn't buy our charade. Sensing that Erik needs me by his side, I walk over and drop the stuff I picked up on the counter, smiling as though we are the happiest couple in town.

"Got it all, honey!"

Martin rolls his eyes.

"Anything you need?" I raise an eyebrow at him.

With a last cold glance in my direction, Martin turns on his heel and gets back to his soup. I look at Erik, trying to see his reaction. To my relief, he is smiling.

He interlocks his fingers with mine, brings our united hands to his lips, and kisses the back of my hand. I try to make it look like this is something he does all the time, but my insides are pulsing with the power of ten overworked speakers, a song of temptation and enticement blasting in my brain.

"Would you stir a little while I put the pasta to boil?" he asks, close to my ear, and when I nod, he places me where he was before with a gentle touch on my waist. He lifts my ponytail and gives me a quick kiss on the neck before stepping aside to handle the pasta.

This is so sexy and unexpected that my knees almost give out. Shivers from his kiss on my neck linger, and I feel slightly breathless in the steamy, crowded kitchen.

Oh my. What is he doing? Showing off to Martin? Making *us* believable?

I don't want him to stop.

We touch each other a lot until the end of the one hour—in subtle, excusable ways. But at every brush of hands and deliberate proximity, I fall deeper into the depths of desire.

I'm taking advantage of him, that's undeniable. I'm thoroughly enjoying my fake boyfriend, and from adjusting his shirt to handing him a tool to feeling the electricity of our skin making contact, I don't care if it's all an act.

The *feels* are real.

In the end, Erik is handling the pan from behind me, his mountain of a body heating mine from head to toe. I feel his chest muscles against my back, and it's hard to breathe. Hard. Wait, is he—? I just want to turn around and bring his mouth to mine, and push him down on a bed…

Holy Odin. I'm doomed.

Lars appears at the kitchen door, tapping his watch and distracting me from my uncontrollable emotions. "Time's up, everyone! Now you have five minutes to serve your dishes and bring the plates here for us to enjoy! Remember to bring each other's dishes so as not to let us know who made what!"

At the end of the five minutes, the seven different courses are served on plates for all of us to taste. We all clap, congratulating each other for our good work. We bring it all to the main dining area, serve Lars and Lotte first, and wait for their verdict. They make delighted sounds when tasting the dishes and end up choosing Team Georgelex as the winners, with their Tower of Artsy Wonders Sandwich.

Then it's time for all the chefs to taste the dishes. The tables are placed close to each other so that we are one big group enjoying an early dinner, having a great time.

"Hygge," I say to Erik, who is sitting by my side, both of us feasting on the dessert.

"Yes, it's *hyggeligt.*" He squeezes my hand. I look around to see if Martin is looking, but he is not even in the room, probably in the bathroom.

We help clean. It's a lot of work, given how many utensils twelve people had to use to cook in a hurry. But we work efficiently as a team, and soon the place is shining.

"Good job today, Team Sol & Storm," Lars says to us when it's time to leave. "Interesting stroganoff."

"It had a Brazilian touch," Erik replies, holding my hand and smiling.

"See you guys at the next event? It will probably be in the third or fourth week of November."

"Of course." I give him a bright smile. "Count us in. And *tak for i aften,*" I say the phrase Erik taught me earlier today to thank Lars for the evening.

"Det var dejligt. Tak for mad."

"Velbekomme," Erik replies for both of us.

I understood that Lars thanked us for the food, and then Erik whispers in my ear that Lars first said it was lovely.

We say goodbye to my boss and everyone else and start walking home. Even when the others are long out of sight, Erik keeps holding my hand.

I can barely focus on my steps. My whole being, the entirety of my sensory processing, is concentrated on the hand he is holding. He drops it at some point, and I hide my fingers in the pockets of my coat. We talk joyfully about our cozy afternoon, making comments we've held back in the presence of others, and the closer we get to home, the more nervous I feel.

Something has changed today.

I'm taking off my shoes at the door next to Erik when Larissa calls me on the phone. I ignore it. I want to be in the moment with him, see what will happen... But she calls again and Erik is suddenly engaged on his phone, and I answer the call. I talk with my friend in my room.

And the moment passes.

We are no longer Team Sol & Storm. We are Sol and Erik again, living in their own routines. A room away.

A world away.

Sixteen

"Of course your boss likes you," Larissa says during our video call on Thursday.

I'm eating a Cup of Noodles for dinner, in my bed, supporting my iPad on a pile of pillows in front of me. Erik is at the gym, so I allowed myself a break from the project.

"Why wouldn't he, right?" I try to reason along with her. Lars is always talking about Erik when he talks about me, so I need to hear someone say that my boss cares about me too.

"He's just enthusiastic about the two of you together, and honestly, who can blame him?" Larissa continues, serene and nerdy with her round glasses, fandom tattoos, and the uniform T-shirt of the school where she teaches English as a Second Language. "You're the beautiful and promising new designer, and he's the gorgeous former employee and ambitious entrepreneur everyone loves. The two of you are a power couple. Like Sophie Turner and Nick Jonas."

"Wrong brother. And Sophie and *Joe* are no longer together."

"Really? Oh." She makes an expression of pity. "Then Kim Kardashian and Kanye West," she tries again with reckless certainty.

"Divorced," I say with my mouth half full of noodles. "And he changed his name."

Larissa makes a face, clearly scrambling. "Gisele Bündchen and Tom Brady?"

"Broke up in 2022. You should read more celebrity news."

"And you should read less of it."

"It's just that—" I put the empty noodle cup aside and bring the iPad closer to my face "—Erik takes the spotlight, and I kind of…disappear behind his shiny presence."

How long will you keep hiding behind me, Sol? His words in the restaurant kitchen echo in my head. He's probably right. I've been relying too much on him…

"And you're afraid you won't impress your boss without Erik?"

"Well, yes." I look down, twitching my mouth.

"You just have to show more of yourself, Sol."

Hmm. That again.

"But being me—me without him—means I'm not what Lars prefers."

"Listen, Sol." She brings her face closer to the screen, the tip of her candy pointing at me. "Get your shit together, okay? You're awesome, and yet you keep being insecure. Drop that, girl, please. Like, *immediately*. Or I'll fly there and give you an earful."

"I wouldn't mind you flying here… It sucks to be so far away sometimes."

"I know…" She frowns at her split ends, then picks them apart. A moment of silence follows, until she says, "Now tell me, how is it going with the project? You and Erik?"

I'm not listening, distracted by a notification on my phone. I open the chat named "Fun Season—Group Lars" and see that George has shared a picture with us.

"Sol? Am I talking to a wall?"

"Sorry, I've just received a message in the Fun Season group. Look."

I turn my phone screen toward the iPad, and she squints to make sense of the image.

"Two people at the top of a…"

"An indoor climbing wall. One of the guys from the group with his boyfriend." I turn the phone back to me. "He wrote, 'Wild day! Can any of you be even wilder? I propose a #wildchallenge. The winning team can be chosen at the next event. Are you in? Or are you a bunch of cowards?'"

"Well, I *was* talking to a wall," Larissa remarks.

I laugh, reading the follow-up messages in the group. Everyone is accepting the challenge.

"So, now you and Erik have to do something bolder and take a picture. Hmm. You climbing an *actual* mountain… I look forward to that." Larissa rubs her hands like someone ready for a juicy performance.

"Ha-ha," I fake-laugh. "You know I'm afraid of heights."

The front door opens, and I hear Erik's footsteps at the entrance.

"That's why it'll be fun to witness," Larissa teases me, and I show her my tongue.

"Bye to you. Let me ask Erik if he has any ideas."

"*That* one?" I point at the free-fall tower before me. It's so high I need to tilt my head as far back as it will go to see the top. I have been eyeing the tower's golden teardrop tip since we were outside the amusement park, as it juts toward the sky along with the historical towers in the Copenhagen city center.

"The Golden Tower," Erik says as if announcing a king entering a royal ballroom. "Sixty-three meters high."

"Sixty-three?" I look up, feeling nauseous just watching people ascending slowly and then descending in a high-speed drop. "And you waited to tell me that this is what we're doing until we were right in front of it?"

"Of course, so you wouldn't have a chance to escape."

I narrow my eyes at him, which only makes him smile brighter.

"Well, it was you who wanted to participate in the challenge. And who said that walls were not an option." Erik pulls me sideways for a hug. "You'll be fine, Sol. I can hold your hand."

Caught in his arms, I look up at him. I'm shivering because even though he is heating me from the cold, being embraced by Erik in an amusement park—the second oldest in the world—is romantic. If there was one right thing he could say to convince me, it was that. The idea of holding his hand is so attractive I will even agree to be dropped from a two-hundred-foot height.

"What about the picture? If my phone falls, there'll be nothing left but powder."

Erik laughs. "We can buy the photo they take. Come on, now." Erik pulls me by the hand out of my spot in the middle of a busy Tivoli path on Halloween night.

It's the prettiest amusement park I have ever been to. Everything is so charming—with a thousand lanterns, lush trees, and fairy-tale-like buildings—that not even the creepy Halloween decorations diminish the romantic vibes.

When Erik said we should go to Tivoli for Halloween, to find something wild to do there, I was confused. For some reason, I'd imagined only cute carousels and tiny sailing boats—maybe a fast roller coaster or a haunted house. But then we got in, and my mouth opened in surprise. The Golden Tower is far from being the only wild ride here.

We face the long line, and the closer it gets to our turn, the more I nervously dance to shake off the cold and the fear. Erik laughs at my embarrassing moves.

Finally, we sit on the ride and get locked in place. I test the safety of the seat, fearing I will fly out of it.

"Goodness gracious, what am I doing?" I start to panic, and Erik only laughs more. "You'll pay for this, Erik Storm," I mutter between my teeth.

"Just relax and enjoy the view," he says. "It's wonderful. You'll see the entire city."

I try to do as he says, even though my nerves are killing me. But I only relax for real once he holds my hand. I look at our fingers clicked together like Lego pieces. The shivers are stronger than ever.

When I look at him, he is no longer laughing, just smiling,

serene and encouraging. He squeezes my hand. He can probably hear my frantic breath and feel me shaking.

We ascend, roller-coaster carts becoming moving toys under us. All around me, a beautiful city where old redbrick buildings combine with a lit-up skyline. Cars pass under us like animated miniature models. I tell myself not to look down at my feet hanging in the air.

Erik squeezes my hand. We are reaching the top.

"So far, so good, eh?"

I've trusted Erik. I *do* trust him. I realize I'd go to the end of the world with him.

I nod in response. Because I'm fine. It's all good.

We laugh, hands united, and the moment of suspense comes, when we are left hanging up there for a couple of seconds before the drop. And it's in that couple of seconds, looking at Erik's beautiful profile, long golden hair flying with the cold wind, that I have the realization.

I'm falling in love.

I'm in love with Erik Storm.

I lose my breath. My stomach drops before I do. I'm free-falling, and I scream and scream until my lungs can't take it anymore and my voice won't come out. The city is a blur. It feels as if my soul has left my body and thrown itself back in again.

I'm in love. *Holy ship. Motherfather.*

We keep going up and down. My mind is foggy, my heart hammering in my chest. I look at Erik, pale but joyful, his hair lashing around his face uncontrollably. I feel like screaming more, but I also feel like laughing, a jolt of adrenaline running through my veins.

I did it. I dropped from the tower.

I acknowledged that I'm in love.

Our hands are frozen together. I can't let go. I don't want to let go.

I want him to be my *real* boyfriend.

When the ride is over and we are released from the seat belt, Erik has to help me walk out. My knees are jelly.

He laughs. "It wasn't so bad, was it?"

"It was terrible!"

He laughs even more, holding my hand again even though no one we know is looking. We check our picture. It's horrible, and Erik laughs even more at my expression in the photo—wide-open mouth and tightly closed eyes.

"I can't post this." I cover my face in shame.

"Come on, do you want to win the challenge or not?"

I check the notifications on my phone. There are new messages in the group.

"Oh no, look at this." I show the screen to Erik. Chiara and Anika shared a picture a few minutes ago of the two of them in the tower we've just walked out of.

"Their faces look better than yours," he says, and I push him lightly with my shoulder. "Are they here now?"

I look around as if I'm expecting to see them right behind me. "Weird coincidence," I say, now a bit annoyed that my sacrifice was worthless.

"Not so weird, I'd say. It's Halloween. Everyone is here. And the tower is an obvious choice when you think of 'a wild experience' in this city."

"We need a selfie, at least. Come here." I turn on the front camera and frame Erik and me with the tower in the background. He comes closer, and I take the photo. "Not good enough. More intimate. You're my boyfriend." I must confess, I enjoy saying those words and pretending they mean what they mean.

Erik puts a hand on my shoulder, his fingers tangling in my unruly after-free-fall hair, sending shivers down my spine. Once we have a normal smiling picture, our faces together, we take one where he kisses my cheek. My heartbeat almost goes back to the speed it reached during the free fall.

"Better," I say and discreetly try to catch my breath. Seeing a cute picture of the two of us together doesn't help. "Can I post it on Instagram? I mean, couples post pictures together." That's my rational reason. The irrational one is that I want the whole world to see how great we look together.

"Sure," he says like he doesn't care, and so I post the two selfies, with the caption: Halloween at Tivoli, free-falling from the Golden Tower! #wildchallenge #love #happyhalloween. Then I share the post in the group, saying, @Chiara and @Anika, the two of you beat us, but there will be a round two!😈😉

A few seconds later, Chiara writes back: OMG. Are the two of you still in Tivoli? Let's meet up!

"Are you okay with meeting them?" I ask Erik, a part of me hoping he will say he would prefer to spend the evening alone with me, because that's what I'd like. But I can't refuse to meet Chiara and Anika. They are nice.

"Sure," he says one more time, again like he doesn't really care.

I write them back, and we meet at the bridge. We then

go together to the boats, Chiara and Anika in one, and Erik and me in another.

"Thank you for doing this with me," I say to Erik, now glad that we met with Chiara and Anika since it gave us an excuse to keep holding hands and pretending. I know it's not the same as if it were real, but for a fleeting moment it feels like we're actually dating.

"It's fine, Sol." He smiles more softly and genuinely than I'm used to seeing. I start to wonder if he is enjoying this too.

He looks relaxed, comfortable. He is in the moment, immersed in his role. When Erik is playing my boyfriend, he is confident and cheerful. He is lightning, not thunder. His deception is beautiful.

But it can't be *so* deceptive. He is starting to act like that when we are alone too. When it's just us working on the project, making some quick dinner, or cleaning the apartment to the sound of Scarlet Pleasure. His light shines through the clouds.

And he's being bright and lively today. The way he squeezed my hand at the tower… Could it be…?

No. I can't ask. I can't ruin it all. Better to have fake-boyfriend-roommate-friend Erik than to not have him at all.

After the boats and a quick burger, we follow Chiara and Anika to the light show at the lake and find a spot under a beautiful tree with long ropey branches falling like a cascade over the water. From here, we have a marvelous view of the colorfully lit park, the lights reflecting on the water making me feel like I'm inside Van Gogh's *Starry Night Over the Rhône*.

It's magical, and Erik is holding my hand again. When the space starts to get crowded, Anika moves in front of Chiara, who embraces her by the waist. Erik puts me in front of him too, close to the railing, except that his hands stay on my shoulders. Still, it's good. *Really good.*

When the show starts, with the waters rising, dancing, and changing colors, I feel like I'm in another world. A fantasyland. My Cinderella dream.

And as Cinderella stories go, it ends at midnight.

We won't be apart. We'll go back to the same home, but the magic will stay here.

I try not to focus on that. I stay in the now, letting the soothing, ethereal music touch my soul. I let the lights confuse my senses even more than they already are. I'm dancing inside like those lights. Rising to the sky and falling again, unable to settle.

"Have you guys heard of the tradition?" Anika looks at us. "When the show is about to end and all the lights are dancing at their peak, couples must kiss. It's for luck and prosperity," she finishes, saying this just a few seconds before the music starts escalating to its finale. "It's now. Are you guys ready?"

She holds Chiara's face and kisses her girlfriend. I turn to Erik, nervous. We have an audience. A large crowd packed all around us. On the other hand, it's dark and everyone is looking at the dancing waters… Will he do it?

"For luck and prosperity?" I try.

Erik snorts and smiles shyly. He won't do it. What was I thinking?

I'm spinning on my heels to watch the show again when he takes my arm and turns me toward him. One of his hands digs through my hair, cupping the back of my head, while the other slides along my waist and brings me closer. My palms go to his chest by instinct, and the moment I smell his skin, his candy breath, I know there is no stopping what is coming.

He brings my face toward him, and our lips meet.

At first, a soft little kiss, his wet lips savoring mine. Then a second kiss, longer, stronger, his teeth biting my lower lip with the right amount of pressure. The reactions inside me are so intense, I feel like I'll explode. Butterflies assault my stomach when I press my mouth against his, and his smell—*oh, his smell*—is so delicious that I grip the nape of his neck with uncontrolled power, and he reacts by pushing his tongue into my mouth.

I melt inside. Everything in my body feels like it's on fire. A rainbow of lights passes over my closed eyelids. A celestial song plays in the background, turning more dramatic by the second. As the light show reaches its climax, I suddenly understand why couples must kiss at this point in the show.

Erik kisses me like he means it, the symphony through the hidden speakers orchestrating the rhythm of our lips. Our intimate dance of colorful desire. His fingers trail over the back of my head and my neck, giving me goose bumps. His hand brings me closer, pressing his solid, massive torso against my small frame. I'm touching his chest over layers of winter clothing.

I finish the kiss with a hand on his bearded face, and the texture is wonderful. I want to caress his cheek and scratch his rough chin. I want to go home and kiss him until the sun rises, naked in my bed with him.

The crowd applauds, and I feel like they are clapping for us. Erik opens his eyes too, slowly, and our gazes meet. We are in shock, confused about what happened. Bewildered at how absolutely amazing it felt.

Because he must have felt it all too. I can see it in his eyes. I can feel it in his hand, still on the small of my back. He wants to pull me closer. It was just a teaser for him too.

I'm suddenly eager to go home.

"Wonderful, wasn't it?" Anika asks us with a sly grin.

"There is no kissing tradition," Chiara reprimands her girlfriend, but looks like she found the prank amusing.

"Yeah, I made that up. But look at them." She gestures at us with her head. "They had a wonderful moment."

Indeed, we had.

"We should get going." Chiara checks her watch. "We have to go to work tomorrow."

"Oh, don't remind me," Anika groans. She told us she works as a content creator for a clothing company, and that while she enjoys it, what she truly wants is to be a jewelry designer.

We all walk together to the exit, and I avoid looking at Erik. What happened in the light show affected us both. We don't know how to act now. What we did out there was so convincing that holding hands is not needed at this point.

Chiara and Anika have already left us when we reach our bikes. I'm opening my lock when Erik's phone rings. He looks at it, a line appearing between his brows, as if he's wondering why someone would disturb him at this hour.

"Mor?" He takes the call, his frown deepening.

I watch him as he speaks, increasingly concerned. As the talk is all in Danish, I understand nothing he is saying. When he ends the call, I ask, "What's wrong?"

"My dad fell off a ladder when changing a lamp and is at the hospital now."

I raise my eyebrows, worried. "Is he okay?"

"Just a broken leg, and maybe a rib, they think. But he'll be staying overnight."

"Oh. I'm sorry."

"I'm going there now."

"What, tonight? But don't your parents live, like, three hours away?"

"I'll borrow my cousin's car. My mom shouldn't skip work, ideally, and she'll need help in the next few days. My sister's in Amsterdam, and I don't have a job. So it's not a hassle for me."

I nod, understanding. I'm proud of him. I like that he won't hesitate to help his family. On the other hand, something tells me this is the escape route he wanted to find after what happened between us tonight. It came at the perfect time…

I know I shouldn't think about that when his dad is in the hospital. It's selfish of me. If it were my parents, and I could reach them after driving for three hours, I would have done the same.

"Do you think you'll be safe driving at night? Aren't you tired?"

He shakes his head, and I know what he's thinking. He wouldn't be able to sleep tonight anyway.

I know for a fact that I won't.

Seventeen

I close the calendar app on my computer with a sigh. November 20.

Twenty days without Erik.

When he left to help his parents, I expected to be alone in the apartment for a couple of days. Maybe a week.

Not the eternity it has been.

Every day, I look at the door anxiously. I check my phone every five minutes, but the entire Brazilian population texts me before he sends any news.

At regular intervals, a seed of panic grows in me. The fear that he won't come back. That he will stay where his parents live and find a job there. That I will lose my home—*our* home—because I won't be able to afford it alone.

The fear that I will lose him forever.

Not that he was ever mine. But that's not how it feels in my heart.

Sometimes I feel like texting him and saying how much

I miss him. Most likely, though, this would only make him decide to stay in Jutland for good.

He is running away from me. From *us* and all that we could be.

I do write to him, but we keep it to roommate subjects. And he is incredibly slow at answering. As far as I know, his dad is feeling better, moving around with crutches and some help, and will make a full recovery.

The project is on a halt. Erik brought his laptop with him, but I don't think he's been working. I also can't find inspiration and discipline without him here.

I get home from work exhausted—physically, mentally, and emotionally. All I want in the silence of my too-empty apartment is to lock myself in my room, lie in bed, watch movies, read, or speak with my family and friends on the iPad.

Erik spoiled me. I spent six months getting used to living on my own, but now that I've lived with him, I suddenly find it hard to breathe when I think about being in this city all by myself.

I can't let that defeat me though.

The Escape Room + Pub Night Fun Season event was supposed to happen last week, but it was postponed because Lars got sick. I texted Erik about the new date, and he said he would see if he could make it.

Maybe he won't.

So what if he doesn't, right? That could be my chance to show Lars—and myself—that I'm good enough on my own.

"Are you okay, Sol?" Chiara asks me when she sees me staring at my coffee absentmindedly.

"Yes." I look up quickly and flash a smile in her direction, perhaps with a bit too much effort. "All good."

She might have asked more, but my forced joy dismisses her.

I've opened up to my cousins, my mom, and the women at her salon, at least. I had no choice. That day in Tivoli, when I posted those selfies with Erik, they started bombarding me with messages and comments. I asked Larissa to tell them it was staged, and she answered, "I already did, and they're freaking out anyway."

I had a video call with them the day after to tell the whole story. Edna was almost weeping when I finished. My cousins were shouting that I had to tell him how I felt. Flor was speechless, and my mom put her nose on the screen to tell me up close that one does not simply let a man like that go.

Not that she said it with those words, but her speech became a meme in the private group I have with my cousins. All because I sent them a screenshot of my mom's zoomed-in face and Mariana Photoshopped it on top of a picture of Boromir from *The Lord of the Rings.* When Luana showed her the photomontage, Mom simply shrugged and mumbled something about our hopeless generation who totally misses the point of wise words spoken by elders.

I stare down at my keyboard, wondering what task to tackle next, when my phone vibrates. I retrieve it at the speed of light, even though I know it's probably not Erik.

It's from Cinder.

From Thomas Hansen, a too-good-looking-to-be-real guy I chatted with on Cinder months ago yet haven't seen in person because he never asked me out.

My heart skips a beat. I haven't thought of this dude for a long time. Since Erik came into my life, to be precise.

Thomas: Hey, Sol. How are you doing? Sorry for disappearing. Things have been a little chaotic.

Me: Hey, Thomas! Nice to hear from you again. What have you been up to?

Thomas: I got this new job, and it's been hard to adapt, but I'm enjoying it. I'm also learning to play guitar. What about you?

Me: I'm pretty bored, actually…haha… Work, home. Home, work.

He knows I'm a game designer, but not where I work. I'm careful with people I don't know. I only reveal details of my life once I meet the guy in person and decide I want to keep seeing him. Not that it's particularly hard to find information about people nowadays, but still.

Thomas is a bit of a ghost though. No other social media profiles. Nothing I could stalk. So I won't be showing my cards until he shows his.

What is happening, Sol? Are you actually considering dating this guy? What about Erik? Larissa's voice says in my head. I could text her and get her real thoughts. But I want to keep this one to myself. For now, at least.

It's been twenty days. Maybe it's time I stop dreaming about a future with Erik.

We had a perfect evening. I had the best kiss of my life.

And he *did* feel it too, I know it.

But he chose to be a coward.

I don't need a coward. I need a Prince Charming on a white steed, sword in hand, ready to fight for his love.

We have only been pretending. We are nothing to each other, and as he made clear the day we met, we *never* will be.

It's easier to accept this truth when I have a plan B.

That's why I keep chitchatting with Thomas, and when he asks if I want to go out for a coffee tomorrow after work, I don't hesitate.

I say yes.

He is late.

I write Thomas my third message: Where are you? I can't call him. I don't have his number, just his stupid Cinder chat contact.

When five more minutes pass, I start to feel angry. He might have been run over by a car, or he dropped his phone in the toilet, or he got stuck in traffic. But most likely, what I had suspected from the start is true.

He is a fake.

I get up, my coffee finished, my apple pie eaten. It was a mistake to come here.

And then Thomas Hansen is there, in flesh and bone.

"Undskyld!" he says, which means "sorry" in Danish. He has curly brown hair, blue eyes, and looks like an angel. "I'm so sorry for my lateness, Sol. I got stuck at work, my boss needed something urgent, and my phone died."

"It's okay," I say with a forgiving smile, even though I wanted to punch him just a minute ago.

I sit back down and wait until he orders a coffee—I say "No thanks, I already had one"—and soon he is ready to start the date I had given up on.

It's weird to be here with a guy who is not Erik, but truth be told, he is more my type: slim, elegant, and refined. I like his formal work clothes and silver watch and how his nails are so well kept they look manicured.

Minutes turn into a couple of hours as the conversation shifts from guitar lessons to bands to movies to games to whale-watching and extraterrestrial contact. He's even nicer to talk with in person.

But as we start to talk about ourselves, he says, "I think I should be honest with you."

I look at him, waiting. For almost three hours, I forgot I was lonely. Forgot I was uncomfortable. That being here feels not only weird but…wrong. Suddenly all those feelings are back.

"I've been on and off Cinder because I've had a…well, a complicated relationship."

I nod, showing him that I'm listening.

"We were breaking up and getting back together all the time, and I was unsure about what I wanted."

I keep nodding, appreciating his brutal honesty. His reluctance to accept my date requests makes sense now.

"And now you broke up again?"

"Yes."

"For good?"

He smiles, looking down. "I know this might make you feel insecure, but yes. For good."

He is not convinced. He still loves this girl and is trying to forget her by being with someone else.

I can relate.

I breathe out through my nose, half laughing. "You're tricking yourself, Thomas."

"Excuse me?" He raises his eyebrows.

"You still love her, and you should go get her back."

He snorts and shakes his head in denial. Confused. "Why are you saying this? I thought you—"

"I don't want someone whose heart belongs to another."

"It's not like that." He frowns. "Just because we've struggled to forget someone, it doesn't mean we shouldn't give ourselves a chance to find love again. A better love."

I look down, playing with my bracelet. "I'm here to forget someone too." As soon as the words come out of my mouth, my face burns, but I continue. "He wasn't ready for a commitment, and he backed away."

"Do you still love him?" Thomas asks. I look up to meet his eyes.

"We were never a couple. I'm not sure what we had, but I'm better off forgetting him."

Thomas looks down at his coffee now, awkward silence growing around our table.

"Why did you like me on Cinder, Thomas?"

"I'll be honest with you again." He sighs, avoiding my eyes. "I made a Cinder account a few years ago when I was helping a friend with some research. I went on a few dates, and then my profile was dead while I was in a relationship with my ex-girlfriend. I was on and off the app, like I told you, even when my friend didn't need help anymore. So, in the summer, when I liked your profile and we started chatting, I was at a boring birthday party. My friends started talking about how you can't find a good match online, and I told them I was having a nice conversation with you. They doubted it would result in anything, but I enjoyed talking to you, so I kept in touch."

I'm frozen. Everything has turned to ice inside of me. My heart has stopped beating.

A friend's research. A friend who thought you couldn't find a good match online.

"Thomas, do you know Erik Storm?" My voice comes out shaky.

"Yes, we're acquainted."

OMG.

Is it a problem if Erik finds out about this date from Thomas?

Mental me answers, *Yes! Erik will think I don't like him.*

Mental Larissa: *Why does that matter when he will never know about your feelings anyway?*

"Does he know we've been talking on Cinder?" I ask.

"No, we're not close friends. We just have friends in common."

Don't feel relieved yet.

"Was he the friend you were helping with the Cinder research?" I can't breathe.

"No. That was Martin Olesen."

I suffocate.

Sudden death, it will say in my postmortem.

"Martin Olesen, of course."

For heaven's sake, how could I be so stupid? Why did I not delete this freaking app after I started fake-dating Erik?

I notice Thomas's confused face for the first time since he started breaking me into pieces. "What's happening here, Sol?"

I stand up, moving my chair back noisily. Now all the blood

is back in my veins, pumping with full speed. “Please don’t tell Martin what I told you about Erik.”

If Thomas is Martin’s good friend, Martin will know I was here today. If Thomas also reveals what I told him about never being a couple…

“What did you tell me today about Erik?” His eyes are huge.

I rub my forehead and take a deep breath, struggling for self-control. “Forget about it.”

I’m getting up again, but he holds my arm on the table, stopping me. “No, wait. I understand now. Erik was your boyfriend. No, your *non*-boyfriend,” he corrects himself.

“You can’t tell Martin we had this conversation. You can’t tell him, or Erik, that I was here. *Please.*” I put my hands together to beg.

“I already told Martin I was coming on a date with you today…” Thomas says with a weak voice, looking down.

“You did *what*?” Oh geez. Is Thomas Hansen the one who’s going to ruin my life?

No. That credit is all mine.

“We’re very close, so I mentioned I was finally moving on, you know…after my breakup. Martin was very encouraging, especially after I showed him your profile.”

HOLY CRAAAAB CAKES.

Bastard. Scheming son of a donkey.

I close my eyes tight, tears of anger attempting to leak through my lids.

Then I stop humiliating myself. I rise, take my purse, and storm out of the café.

Eighteen

I wake up to the seductive smell of pancakes.

After a restless night where I skipped dinner and went right to bed, my stomach gives a happy leap when I enter the kitchen and see a shirtless Erik in jogging pants making my favorite breakfast in his expensive frying pan.

"Good morning," I say, sounding sleepy, but my body is fully awake, pumping blood into my veins at a frantic pace.

It's so wonderful to have him back.

And it becomes even better when he turns his head and gives me a big, sincere smile.

"Good morning, Sol." He turns a pancake, and my gut jumps again. *Holy Mjölnir,* his muscles are well defined. He clearly comes from Asgard.

"Did you arrive late yesterday?" I ask.

"Around midnight."

It's early for him to be awake. Usually, he's not up before eight thirty or nine. "Insomnia again?" I lean against the doorframe.

"No, I slept surprisingly well," he says with an upbeat tone, and everything lights up inside me. "It's good to be back."

My heart pounds. Hard. OMG. Did Erik realize this is where he should be? Did he miss me?

"How's your dad?"

"Better. Already back to his workshop, inventing stuff," Erik says fondly, sounding like he's proud of his dad while at the same time thinking he is a hopeless cause.

"Isn't he a physics professor?"

"Yes, but he does handiwork projects in the garage. His profession is a way to earn money, not what he really wants to spend his time doing."

I sense Erik's deep identification with his father—and his fear of ending up like him: doing what he loves only as a hobby, not a career.

He is flipping another pancake, but his hair keeps falling in front of his eyes. "Hey, Sol, could you tie my hair back for me? My hands are dirty."

"Sure."

I move closer. *Thump-thump, thump-thump* goes my heart. How can he be so sexy?

That I thought Thomas could be my plan B now seems laughable.

"Would you kneel a bit, so I can reach your head?" I ask once I'm behind his wall of a body, laughing to disguise how nervous I am.

He kneels on the kitchen floor and leans his head back, blond hair falling over his shoulders like a golden cascade. I ask him where the elastic is, and he points at the counter. I retrieve it, loop it around my wrist, and start gathering his soft hair in my hands. The butterflies in my stomach wake up from their twenty-three-day slumber, and I enjoy this with every cell of my body. I slide my fingers along his scalp, brushing his smooth hair. An almost inaudible groan of pleasure escapes his lips, and he pretends it never happened.

"Ponytail or bun?" I ask, wondering if my voice sounds as choked as my throat is feeling.

"You choose."

I gather the lower half of his hair and "accidentally" caress his neck in the process. He moves as if tickled. I sense the shivers down his spine. I feel them too. The pancakes are slowly burning, but neither of us reacts.

"I think you should change your shampoo," I say. It smells masculine, like a man for whom I would skip work to spend all day in bed.

"Is it distracting?"

"No… It gives you split ends."

He laughs. It's a glorious sound, so contagious it gets me laughing too. I twist his hair up and tie it back. By now, the pancakes are screaming for help. Erik thanks me and hurries back to their rescue.

The pancakes are ready, but I unfortunately don't have time to sit and eat calmly. I gobble two down, thank Erik, and hurry to work.

Chiara isn't well. It's like we switched moods. Or maybe she has been down for a while and I didn't notice, too absorbed in my sadness over Erik's absence.

I didn't want anyone to notice I was having problems in my personal life, but I know *she* noticed. And perhaps those times she asked if I was okay, she expected me to ask her back, but I didn't. I couldn't see her pain. Now it's clear in her red eyes.

"Hey, Chiara. Are you okay?" I ask when we meet in the bathroom, not so much by chance. I went in to wash my hands and reapply lipstick when she left her desk and was gone for almost twenty minutes.

She walks out of a stall and washes her hands next to me. "Anika and I broke up," she tells her reflection.

I turn to look at her, in shock.

"What? No! I mean, oh, I'm so sorry to hear that. You guys were… I mean, I'm sorry." I have no idea what to say. They were so good together, looked so in love. "What happened?"

Chiara sniffs. She's keeping her cool. Pretending her world isn't falling apart. But I know very well what she is going through.

"She got a job in Sweden."

"That's good, right? Sweden is just a bridge away."

Chiara shakes her head.

"That's Malmö. She's moving to Stockholm. Eight hours away by car or bus."

"That must be just an hour away by plane, then?" I need to make her see the light. It can't be that impossible.

"I can't do this, Sol." She looks at me, defeated but with resolve in her eyes. She has obviously thought a lot about her decision.

"Long-distance relationships work for a lot of people," I say.

Chiara snorts. "Not for us."

"What about you moving there? You left Italy to come to Copenhagen. Why not go a bit farther north for her?"

Chiara gives me a humorless smile. "You make it sound so easy… What about my job? All I've built here?"

"She got her dream job?" I ask. "Will she work with jewelry design?" I remember what Anika told us in Tivoli.

Chiara nods. "I don't blame her for going. I know how much she wanted this, and things weren't working out for her here."

"And is *this* your dream job?"

She is silent for a moment. I've cornered her. We are at Scorpio Games, talking about her job not being her ideal.

"I don't want a QA career path," she whispers as if the walls have ears. We both look behind us, and there is no one in the stalls.

A lot of people enter the game industry through quality assurance jobs, but most have other ambitions. I can't judge Chiara, since I'm also aiming for another role. She is probably holding on to the possibilities of the post–Fun Season internal hiring as much as I am.

"Apply for jobs in Stockholm then," I whisper back.

"I'm doing that, but it will probably be too late when I get an offer there…if ever."

I frown. "You think she won't wait for you?"

"We broke up, Sol. It's not fair of me to ask her to halt her life there and wait for something that might never happen."

I hold her by the shoulders. "Chiara. Please think this through. You're unhappy here," I whisper even lower. "If she's the love of your life, take a chance."

Her face looks sculpted in stone. "I'm not unhappy here. I'm safe."

I hug her. I don't want her to be angry at me. All I want

is to help. "Sorry if I'm being harsh," I say over her shoulder. "I understand you so well..."

"Is Erik back? Is that why you look happier today?"

I let go of her, wide-eyed, as if she caught me stealing cookies from the jar on the fridge. She invited us to watch a movie two weeks ago, and I told her we couldn't because Erik was taking care of his dad in Jutland. She and I didn't talk about the subject again, but Chiara is perceptive and understood he's been gone all this time.

"He came back yesterday," I answer hesitantly.

"You should tell the others, Sol."

My heartbeat rises. I know exactly what she's saying, but I pretend I don't. I mean, *how could she know?*

"Tell them what?"

"That you and Erik are not a couple."

I look around, now nearly having a heart attack. "What makes you say that?"

"That day at Tivoli," she begins, dead serious, "it was clear. Anika noticed it too." Her voice breaks when she mentions her ex-girlfriend, but she composes herself quickly.

This is...impossible. I thought we were so convincing!

But, no, of course we weren't.

"That kiss," Chiara continues, her tone more vivid now. "It was, without a shadow of a doubt, a *first* kiss. So full of insecurities and passion..."

Oh dear. Anika was being our cupid with that lie about the kissing tradition. How did I not notice it?

I'm getting so nervous about discussing this in a Scorpio Games bathroom that my compulsive looking around is bordering on paranoia.

"I don't understand why you had to lie about this, Sol, but you must have your reasons." I look down, not wanting to meet her eyes. "Lying is never a good idea though. Especially to your boss."

"Are you going to tell Lars?" I ask, my voice small.

"Of course not. I'm your friend. I'd never do that. I'm just advising you as you advised me about Anika."

I breathe, trying to calm down. "Then let us both think about each other's wise words," I say, and Chiara nods. She puts a hand on my shoulder and gives me a weak smile, ending our exchange in a way that makes it clear we're good.

I'm early for the afternoon design meeting. I take an empty seat next to Lars, a vacuum in my stomach sucking the air out of my lungs as I realize he might know everything because Martin knows everything because Thomas Hansen opened his big mouth.

I keep my gaze on Martin, listening to their premeeting chitchat with a rush of anxiety burning my veins.

Lars then draws my attention when he offers me something from a small package. "Want one? The best licorice in the world."

"What?" I blink a few times, relief washing over me as I stare into his smiling face and realize that Martin hasn't told him anything. Yet.

"Licorice?"

I smile back at him, doing my best not to look disgusted. I hate licorice and can't, for the love of me, understand why Danish people are so fascinated by this horrible salty candy.

But Martin is winning. He's playing all his cards, so I'll

have to play mine too, no matter how much acting I need to do to be loved by Lars.

I take a licorice candy, thanking my boss. He is looking at me with so much expectation it would be an offense not to give the candy another chance. It's almost like a rite of passage. Once you have learned to like licorice, you can be accepted in Denmark as an equal.

"Great, right?"

"Mmmm!" I fake a sound of delight, trying not to gag.

When Lars is chatting with the others again, I discreetly turn around in the swivel chair, spit the candy into my hand and hide it in my pocket inside a crumpled receipt.

"What is your opinion, Sol?" Lars speaks to me, and I turn around, startled. "What is your favorite thing about Denmark?"

Not licorice.

"Oh." I look at them, pretending I'm still chewing the candy. "The design, I guess?" I say the first thing that crosses my mind and has a chance of pleasing Lars. He's design-obsessed.

Although I do appreciate Danish design, that goes below Danish pastries and cakes in my ranking. But Lars is even more of a health maniac than Erik. He allows himself a tiny piece of cake on Fridays, and that's all.

"I couldn't agree more. So many good designers," Lars says, and I smile, satisfied.

"What about the *worst* thing?" Simon asks me.

Licorice.

"The weather." It's not a lie, at least.

They all laugh, agreeing. I mean, who loves Danish weather?

"Favorite *smørrebrød*?" Lars keeps questioning me.

I have the answer ready on my tongue—chicken salad and bacon—but I pretend that all the options are so wonderful that I can't decide. "Hmm… I don't know. They're all great."

"What do you think of *leverpostej*—liver pâté?" he asks me with his eyebrows raised, as if expecting me to be like all foreigners who can't understand Danes' love for liver pâté.

I *am* one of those foreigners, but I won't disappoint him. I can't, not with Martin smiling across the table as if he's already the new game director. I want to show Lars I welcome and appreciate every aspect of his culture—the culture I'm trying to fit into.

"It's great, I love it," I say.

Lars nods, satisfied with my answers. I pray he won't start offering me licorice and liver pâté sandwiches at every opportunity.

"Favorite place in Copenhagen?" Lars continues to interrogate me.

"That's a hard one," I say, this time with honesty. I love the entire city. "Christiansborg Palace." I choose to show I appreciate history and architecture since my real answer—Strøget, the main shopping street—would certainly disappoint someone as cultural and intellectual as Lars.

"Last one now," he says, enjoying the interview and my very suitable replies. "The best restaurant you have dined at with Storm?"

Ai, caramba. We have never been to a restaurant together, but that would be a wrong answer on too many levels…

Fuuuudge. I can't name any fine restaurant. I'm doomed.

Martin is looking at me with a victorious smile on his

beetle face. I wonder why he didn't tell Lars anything. Did Thomas not share with Martin that Erik and I were never a couple? Does Martin just think we broke up? Or is he saving the bomb for later? He looks very pleased with himself right now. He's counting on me giving myself away.

But I won't give him the pleasure of my defeat.

"Noma," I say on impulse. Noma has been nominated as the world's best restaurant many times, which is the only reason I've heard of it.

"Oh, you've eaten there?" Lars sounds surprised—and excited. *Oh no.* "Lotte and I have been trying to get a table there for a long time."

"Yeah, it wasn't easy." I give him the fakest smile humankind has ever witnessed, deeply regretting the snowball of falsehoods I've created.

"Funny, because they have been closed half of the year," Martin says, annoying as always. "I thought you and Erik started dating in October."

All the blood in my body goes up to my face.

I've messed it up. *So bad.*

"I wasn't with Erik. I've been to Denmark before." I try to fix the situation, but it's going from bad to dreadful, and Martin's smile is just growing.

Got you, his eyes say.

Luckily, a mob enters the room at once, and our chatting must end. Lars doesn't seem caught up in my words. I sigh, relieved, even though I know my lie might come back to haunt me.

When the meeting ends two hours later, I'm eager to stretch

my legs, so I grab a coffee just to have a break before returning to my desk.

To my dismay, however, Martin catches up with me.

"Wow," he says in a dry voice, putting a cup next to mine before I start the machine. I move a few steps away and cross my arms over my chest protectively. "What a stack of lies you've accumulated."

"I don't know what you're talking about." *Come on, machine, hurry.* I'm almost ready to abandon my coffee, just to get away from Martin.

But I know he won't leave me alone now.

"You're even dating other guys… I wonder how you're going to keep all those skeletons in your closet."

I swallow painfully. Thomas *did* tell him. *All of it*, for sure.

But I mean, why should he be more loyal to a girl he'd just met than to his good friend?

"I'm not dating anyone but Erik." I keep my composure. He wants to break me down. Get me to confess. I won't give him that. It's his word against mine.

"My sources say Erik has never been your boyfriend."

I'm shaking, my hands closing into fists. I could punch him right now.

Martin takes a step closer, his face uncomfortably close to mine. "Your farce will end, Marisol. You won't get to stay in this company, lying to a dignified man like Lars, winning a position that should be given to me or anyone *honest* who is at Scorpio Games for better reasons than to not be unemployed."

"I deserve to be here," I say, more to myself than to him.

"And that's another lie you tell. But keep that one to yourself."

He turns to take his coffee. I'm stuck in place, breathing hard, my entire body shaking.

"He'll realize at some point," Martin says with eyes on his espresso, the confidence of a winner exhaling through his pores. "Erik, I mean. He'll see he won't achieve his silly revenge and will only get his heart broken if he gives you a chance. Just like it was broken the first time."

The first time... I want to kill Martin. With my bare hands.

"As for Lars," Martin continues, blowing on his coffee and billowing steam that makes his glasses foggy. "I won't leave that to chance. He deserves the truth."

I shake my head, biting my lower lip so hard it almost bleeds. I feel the tears coming, but I can't let him see me cry.

"If you don't tell Lars, I will," he concludes and turns to go back to his desk.

Fuck you, Martin.

I've said it.

But only in my head.

Nineteen

I walk my bike half of the way home because I can't get myself to stop sobbing, and that's probably not considered safe riding.

I look at my surroundings, a Copenhagen blurred by tears, and wonder if this is where the dream ends. My chest is so tight I can barely breathe. I've messed it up, and I don't see a way to fix the situation.

My family is filling my phone with notifications, as always, and I should be feeling in need of support, but I don't want to talk to any of them.

In fact, I feel blessed for not being there, where I can't avoid my mom's scrutiny, my cousins' indiscretion, and my whole family, friends, neighbors, and whoever else the gossip reaches, giving me opinions, judgment, and unwelcome guidance.

I feel oddly separated from everything related to the life I had in Brazil. Denmark *is* becoming my home. I'm more attached to it every day, despite my reservations regarding certain aspects of the culture. None of the people back home know what that's like. None of them have ever been to another country.

They are perfectly fine there and will tell me I'll be fine there and should just go home. None of them truly believed I'd make it here. They're just waiting for me to come back and tell them, *You were right. It wasn't for me.*

That will never happen though. If I do end up having to go back, I won't be *fine*. I would have failed. I would have lost not only the life I have here but the life I *could* have had.

A life that is no longer just a magazine photo collage or a mental picture formed after an enticing conversation—but an image so vivid and full of sounds, tastes, and colors it will follow me for the rest of my days.

When I enter the apartment, I'm still not done crying. My plan is to hide in my room for the rest of the evening with my phone turned off. I come across Erik in the hallway, however. As soon as he asks me, "What's wrong?" I hug him around the waist and bury my head in his chest.

"What's happening, Sol?" He comforts me, pressing me tight and caressing my back as I shed tears.

I say I went out with a guy I met on Cinder when he was away, and that the guy happened to be Thomas Hansen, a friend of Martin's, and now Martin knows we're not together and is threatening to tell Lars if I don't.

I'm not sure Erik can grasp the whole emotional disturbance inside me. While my family doesn't know what it means to live in Denmark, Erik doesn't know what it's like to live in Brazil. I might have told him what I'm afraid to get back to, but he won't feel it in his bones, even if I go into more detail.

Besides, he also doesn't know what I feel for him or how my future at Scorpio means everything regarding *us*.

I want to make sure he doesn't think I'm crying over stupid Thomas Hansen, so I say, "I don't care about the idiot I went out with. But Martin might ruin everything for me at Scorpio now, and he is just so…obnoxious."

I cry a bit more on Erik's chest, shaking with my sobs, and my body can't ignore how close to his heart I am, even when I'm so desolate.

"Yes, he *is* obnoxious," Erik sympathizes, one of his hands running up and down my back, making me less sad but also shakier. "We won't let him get to you, okay? He'll ruin nothing for you."

I snort, drying a tear. Erik's chest is so warm and comforting… I don't want to ever leave this spot.

"Chiara knows too…"

Erik breaks the embrace to look at me, and I dry the rest of my tears with my sleeve. My face must be all red and swollen, and I don't want Erik to see me in this state, but I also can't avoid his eyes.

"We talked in the bathroom today," I tell him before he asks how Chiara found out. "She and Anika noticed we weren't a couple…" I look down, swallowing hard. "And by the way, she and Anika broke up."

"No, really?" He reacts just like I did, disappointed to hear it.

"Anika is moving to Stockholm. She got her dream job there."

"That's nice for her. And they couldn't keep it long distance?"

I shake my head, sniffing. "Chiara thinks I should tell Lars…and now Martin is threatening me. I don't see a way out of this."

Team Sol & Storm will be over—the realization hits me like a punch in the gut. There'll be no more fake dating. No more excuses to spend time with Erik, touching him, kissing him…

I won't get the promotion. My breath gets stuck in my throat, and a new tear rolls slowly down my cheek.

And I'll most likely be fired for dishonesty—the thought slaps me in the face, leaving me red with shame.

I'll be unemployed. Broke. Homeless. Visa-less. And will have no choice but to go back to Brazil.

"Don't panic yet, okay?" Erik sees I'm hyperventilating. "Sol, look at me." He takes my face in his hands and lifts it so I can meet his eyes. They are so blue, so beautiful, so sincere… "Martin is one of those aggressive little dogs that barks loud but never bites."

I laugh at his metaphor. "He looks a little like a Chihuahua."

"Yeah, he does." Erik laughs with me, and for a second, my tears stop falling. "Lars trusts me, and he trusts you too."

"That's precisely why it will be so bad when he finds out…"

"It won't, because he will *not* find out." Erik sounds confident, which calms me. The warmth of his hands on my face also helps. "Martin *could* tell Lars the truth, but then he'd have to hope Lars would believe him. If we continue to be a couple, Lars will believe *us*." Erik looks intensely at me, his hands still framing my face. I hold my breath. "*We* are his favorites, not Martin. If Martin goes down that road and persists, Lars will think he's a desperate man trying all sorts of tricks to beat the competition." He takes his hands off my cheeks, but I still feel the heat of his fingers.

"Martin *would* go down that road though, wouldn't he?" I bite my lip again.

"No, he's bluffing, of course. He's not that stupid. He knows all this, and that's why he hopes he can make you confess."

Erik sees I'm still uncertain and takes one tiny step closer, his body almost meeting mine. I shiver.

"How can you be so sure of that?"

"I know the two men, Sol. And Martin knows me well too. He doesn't expect me to remain by your side to the end. He's scared as hell, feeling threatened by us, and he's making his last desperate move to get you to give up before the finish line. So, this is how we win—we stay the course."

I bite my lip harder. Erik opens my mouth with his thumb to stop me from hurting myself, but the gesture is so sexy I almost pull him toward my lips.

"So, we keep lying?"

"Until the end."

His eyes are serene, assertive. I think of what Chiara said.

"But it's not right…"

"Backing away won't do any good now. You'll just be delivering the victory to Martin. Do you want that to happen?"

I shake my head.

"Let's kick his ass tomorrow. Let's show them who is *not* a couple." He gives me a sly smile, and I almost, *almost* grab his neck and kiss him.

The thought of faking it with him tomorrow is so exciting I decide I can wait. My lust—or at least part of it—will be satisfied in a safe environment.

For once, I have the feeling that he is looking forward to it too.

"How about a movie night? I guess you can't focus on the project today."

Erik mentioning the project gets my heart racing even faster. He *does* want to keep working on the app with me after all. I feel like singing.

"A movie night sounds great," I say.

We make popcorn and sandwiches and sit on his couch. I let him choose the movie, and he picks *Pulp Fiction*. It's his favorite Tarantino movie, the one he says I must watch because of its memorable performances. He puts an arm around me, and I lean on his chest.

It's such a surreal moment. I never imagined we'd reach this level of intimacy. I can hear his heart. My head moves up and down to the rhythm of his steady breathing. His sweatshirt is thick, but I feel his hard muscles under my fingers. His scent is right under my nose, rising directly from his skin. His rough beard is touching the top of my head, scratchy. Irresistible.

It's very hard to stay still, but at the same time, snuggling here is so pleasurable that I close my eyes to enjoy the sensations. I couldn't care less about the movie. It's just an excuse to enjoy *him*. The darkness in the room makes my reaction easier to conceal—my flushed face, my gaze sneaking around his body, discreetly taking in every curve.

I can't hide the irregular pace of my breathing though, and he can't hide his heartbeat. For a lot of the movie, it's accelerated like mine.

I could stay in this cuddling position forever. It's the

warmth and safety I needed after such a tough day. But it's getting hard not to feel lustful.

As the movie nears its end, I move my hands slowly on his chest, with just my fingertips. I wait for a reaction, for him to move my hand away and get up, but he remains still. I watch him and he doesn't take his eyes off the TV, acting as if nothing is happening. His Adam's apple bobs though, and his muscles tense.

This might not be an invitation to continue, but I do. My hand rises, tempting him near the V-neck of his sweatshirt. When my fingertips make contact with his skin, I feel him shudder. He turns to me and we stare at each other in silence for what feels like endless seconds. I don't know if I should go on or not. His serious face could mean he's controlling himself so he doesn't throw me off his couch or so he doesn't pull me toward his lips.

A thousand pictures flash in front of my eyes, all of them involving us naked on this couch. We are both breathing hard, and I notice that's not the only hard thing he is dealing with. I look at the erection in his pants, and my hand begins to slide down into them, but Erik shakes his head in a brief, decisive way.

He swallows visibly and puts his hand over mine, stopping it just above the waistband of his jeans. His eyes are soft and restless—not the eyes of someone telling me no but instead saying, *Not today.* I want him so bad. But I respect his decision. I admire his control, and yet the insecure part of me wonders if I will ever be irresistible to him.

His fingers caress the back of my hand and rise up my arm, teasing me in a way that heats me between my legs, readying me for something that won't happen. His hand comes to rest on my face, and he strokes my cheek briefly before putting my hair behind my ear. I tilt my head back to look into his eyes.

"It was a long day, Sol." His voice sounds so hoarse and unsteady, it gives me chills. "Perhaps we should go to bed."

You in yours, me in mine, is what he's saying.

I nod, trying to put out my fire. I feel embarrassed. Rejected. Inappropriate.

He lifts my face when I look down. "Okay?" The word means a myriad of things in this context.

His eyes glint with repressed lust. He wants to know if I'm fine. He wants me to be all right after the blows I received today, and he doesn't believe us having sex will help. On the contrary.

And he is right.

I nod again, controlling my eyes so they won't start pooling. I love him for stopping me. For not letting his dick make a life-changing decision for both of us.

Because we are still roommates, and I don't want that to change.

He knows very well what happens when we cross that line. And I'm not going to be his second Lena.

I bring my hand to his face and caress him like he did me, then tuck his hair behind his ear.

"*Godnat*, Erik," I say and rise from his couch.

The credits are rolling, and as I turn to walk out of his room, I realize we didn't *technically* cross the line.

But, in fact, we already did.

Twenty

It's a cold and cloudy Saturday morning, and I'm quietly eating toast at the table when Erik sits next to me, full of energy. He crosses his arms over his chest with the smile of a clever programmer who has just had a brilliant idea.

"I know how we can win the wild challenge."

I look at him, taken aback. It's like he is not thinking about last night. We might not have done it, but we did *something*. The intentions, the *attraction*, were clear. Maybe he is willing to discard the whole thing as a moment of vulnerability, like when you are drunk and decorum calls for both parties forgetting what happened.

That takes a weight off my shoulders. If Erik is going to act as if nothing has changed, and we will keep working on the project and acting as a couple in front of Lars, everything can stay as it was. And as much as that means not having Erik entirely, it means having him near me and living here and striving for the life I want.

"How can we win the wild challenge?" I ask him.

"Winter bathing." He raises an eyebrow.

"Ah, no, no, no." I wave my hands in front of me. "We only have until seven in the evening, and look at the weather outside."

"Precisely," he says calmly. "It's called *winter bathing.* And it's not *that* cold now, so we'll be fine."

"Then you want to do what? Go to the beach now and jump in the ocean?"

"Yeah," he says as if I've just asked if he wants eggs for breakfast.

I shake my head, laughing. "You're out of your mind."

"Isn't that the point? A *wild* challenge?"

"I thought winter bathing was common in Denmark. The others must have done it before. It won't be that special."

"Lars hasn't, as far as I know. And he admires people who do it." Erik leans forward, his eyes flickering with the excitement of a mischievous boy ready for action. I keep staring at him, unyielding.

"No, I don't—"

"Come on, Sol. It'll be fun. And you'll get to scratch it off your list."

I must admit it has been bothering me that we didn't complete the ten items he scribbled for me in my notebook.

"All right, let's do it." I throw my arms up, surrendering. I never thought I would say yes to such a thing, but it seems Erik could convince me to go to the end of the world with him. "We need to take an *amazing* picture though. It is a photo contest, after all."

"Deal." Erik jumps to his feet, energy flowing from his

body. He would probably head to the gym now to spend it if we weren't going to swim in freezing waters.

I put on a bikini under my winter clothes—a bizarre combination—then pack my camera and tripod, two towels, a blanket, and a thermos of hot tea.

We bike to the beach, and I make sure to tell Erik how much I regret my decision already. The weather is awful, so windy, and it looks like it's going to rain. The good part is that we're basically the only ones at Amager Strandpark, so I won't have to embarrass myself in front of strangers.

I've been here once during the summer, and it was lovely. A long, winding path shared by cyclists, runners, skaters, and families going for a stroll. A large stripe of sand dotted with people sunbathing. Kite surfers coloring a clear sky, large gatherings of them in the open sea and in the lagoon the bridges cross over, the water brimming with kayakers, swimmers, and rosy toddlers playing with animal floats.

Now it's like braving a postapocalyptic scenario. We are the only survivors.

But I won't remain one after entering these icy waters.

"Usually, people do it there." Erik stops when we have just crossed the main bridge and are about to take the winding path along the shore. He points at a harbor bathhouse with small turquoise structures out on a deck over the water. A Danish flag waves in the wind, and a couple of bathers climb down the wooden steps leading directly into the ocean.

"They have a winter bathing club, and there are saunas, changing rooms… But you need to be a member to use all that, I think."

"So, we're not going there?"

"No. We're on our own."

I swallow hard. "Is it even safe?" I'm more concerned about the temperature than the risk of drowning. The sea here couldn't be calmer.

"Don't worry," Erik replies. "It's healthy. It can boost your immune system, even."

I laugh through my nose. I grew up with my parents telling me I shouldn't eat ice cream when I was sick. Closing every window in the house whenever a gust of cool wind came through. Telling me I'd catch a cold if I jumped in a pool when it was raining.

They would have a heart attack if they saw me do this.

"Tell me it's fine, but don't claim it's healthy," I say as we ride slowly down the cemented path and pass by a couple of runners and skaters.

"But *it is* healthy. At least that's what Scandinavians believe. Why do you think people do it?"

"I don't know. Because they are crazy?"

Erik laughs. "It's supposed to awaken your body in a powerful way and even reduce your stress levels. You should feel great afterward."

"Is that how it feels for you?"

Erik is quiet. I repeat the question in case he didn't hear me, but his lack of response is due to nothing but guilt.

"I've never tried it before."

I press the brake and my bike shrieks. *"What?"*

Erik stops by my side, amused. "I've never done it."

"And you didn't tell me that before?"

"Why does it matter? It'll be the first time for both of us."

My stomach trembles. Hearing "first time" doesn't help with my nerves.

"Where do you want to do it then?" This sounds so wrong…

"Let's go all the way to the last pier. It'll be more private there."

My heart pounds against my ribs, and I climb back onto my bike to follow Erik, who is speeding ahead.

We stop when we reach the end of the large straight path bordering the shore, near post five, where there are toilets and an ice cream kiosk closed for the season.

White wind turbines spin lazily out in the water. The bridge to Sweden is visible at a distance—an impressive piece of engineering with a two-and-a-half-mile underwater tunnel. It's also possible to see a faint Malmö skyline on the horizon. We leave our bikes against the waist-high wall separating the paved path from the sand and walk toward the empty pier.

"If we freeze to death, Erik, I'll kill you," I warn him, and he laughs.

We walk on the wooden planks, farther and farther out. There are a few ladders on the sides at different depths for those who wish to lower themselves into a quick dip.

"Is that how we're doing it?" I point at the nearest ladder.

"It's what people usually do." He shrugs.

I shake my head. "How would that give us a good photo? No, no…we jump."

"What?" Erik laughs. "*That* would be insane. It's too sudden. You could get a cold water shock."

I turn around. "Let's go to the sand, and then we run into the water."

With a husky laugh, Erik follows me. I walk back, then

jump on the sand, heading for a spot where I can get a good shot of us running toward the sea. I take my camera and the tripod out of my bag and start setting up the scene.

I find a great frame with the graphite clouds looking dramatic. When I'm adjusting the shutter speed, Erik stops behind me, his large body towering over my crouched figure.

"Come on, take off your clothes. I'm freezing."

I glance back and then look ahead again, covering my eyes and laughing hysterically. "You're *naked*?" I'm so shocked, my voice sounds shrill. "What are you doing?"

Oh my. I picture the police dropping by and arresting him for indecent exposure.

"We do this naked."

Gosh, he needs to stop talking like that.

"You winter-bathe naked?" I'm scandalized like a conservative eighty-year-old lady.

And I'm feeling tricked. Like, when did I sign up for that?

"It's not a big deal here, okay? People are comfortable in their bodies. Nudity is natural. No one cares."

My eyes are huge, and I'm keeping them on my camera. *Jeez.* That's what I call a culture shock.

"You can do it in clothes or however you want. But if you want to do it like a Viking, then take it all off now before I become an ice statue permanently exhibited on this beach."

I take a deep breath. Okay. I'll do it right. As they say in Brazil: *Quem está na chuva é pra se molhar.* "If you are in the rain, it's to get wet."

I stand up and unzip my coat. "Would you mind turning around, please?"

Erik is dancing in place, trying to handle the cold, and he

does as I say. I quickly take off my boots, my socks, my pants, my sweater, my T-shirt, and lastly, my bikini. The photo needs to reflect my transformation from a prude tropical girl into a brave and confident Viking—with censor bars I'll add later, of course.

I play by the rules. And I go all in.

It's very, very, very, *very* cold, and I'm not even in the water yet.

Erik is already in front of the camera, and I crouch down again to set the timer.

"Ready?" Once I press the shutter button, I'll have ten seconds to join him.

"I'm ready!" He bounces up and down, and I try not to look at his uncensored figure.

I glance over my shoulder. We are still alone and far from any other human. I might have felt a few drops of rain, but it's hard to know now that my entire body has started to freeze.

"Hurry, Sol!" he shouts with a shaky voice.

Adrenaline kicks in. I press the button and run to join Erik. He grabs my hand and looks at me. The red light of the camera blinks.

"Ready? Three, two, one… Go!"

We run, and the camera clicks a couple of shots until our ankles are in and icy water is splashing all around us. I scream, frozen in place, but Erik drags me by the hand, and I have no choice but to enter farther and farther.

"Done," I say, stopping when the water covers my belly, freezing my guts with a punch. "We have the photo, now we just—"

"In with your head, Sol, or it's cheating!" Erik smiles, not letting go of my hand.

"Like we haven't cheated plenty already," I mutter, but he ignores me.

"Together. Three, two, one… Now!"

I do it. I dive in. Once I'm submerged, I feel as though a thousand knives are perforating my body. I lose all air in my lungs for a long, tortured second. *Oh for cod's sake*, it hurts.

Erik pulls me up to the surface with him and signals for us to move toward the pier. Gasping for air, burning with coldness, we reach the nearest ladder, grip its metal bars, and Erik finds his voice again.

"Fuck! This is fucking cold!"

"Oh gosh, I need to get out! Holy cow!"

"Come on, Sol, find the Samuel L. Jackson in you. Release all the shit," he says, his teeth chattering. "I'm not letting you up until you've cursed properly!"

I laugh, a mix of desperation and extreme shivering.

"Shit!" I say and laugh. "Shit, shit, SHIT!"

"Yes! SHIT! Feels good, doesn't it?"

"No!" It's weird to say it. It's wrong.

"Fuck yeah!"

"Fuck no!"

He laughs, enjoying my liberation. He's right. It *is* freeing. I'm dying. But it feels good somehow.

"FUCK MARTIN!" I let it out.

Erik looks proud, and we repeat it in unison.

"Fuck Martin fucking Olesen!" I shout to the gray skies.

Erik quotes Ezekiel 25:17 the way Samuel L. Jackson says it in *Pulp Fiction*, emphasizing the line about great vengeance.

"Fuck Scorpio Games!" I shout next. We're laughing our asses off now.

"Fuck Lars!"

"Fuck working! Let's all do what we love!"

Erik comes closer, his lips purple. I'm afraid there will soon be small ice crystals blocking his nostrils.

"I'm fucking tired of faking," he says, his voice almost not coming out now.

I can't stand it any longer. I can't feel my body. "It's too fucking cold," I say, climbing the ladder. "And you're a bad influence, by the way."

Erik laughs, following me. I try not to think that he's staring at my bare butt, but I feel that he is. I mean, it would be hard *not to* when I'm climbing the ladder right in front of him.

Out of the water, it's even colder. It's so cold, I can't think. We run toward the sand to reach our backpacks and get the towels. I wrap mine around me and throw the other one to Erik. We dry quickly, jumping around, groaning and cursing nonstop.

When I'm dry enough, I get dressed at the speed of light. Still trembling convulsively, I sit on the sand, wrapping the blanket I brought around me and curling into a ball. Erik sits by my side, and I put the blanket around him too. We stay like this, packed together, chattering teeth and shivering next to each other. I remember I have tea in my backpack and reach for it. Erik and I then take turns warming our interiors with the hot drink.

"I'm tired of bullshit too," I say at some point, following up on what he told me in the water—that he was tired of faking.

Erik smiles. "You're tired of me?"

"You're an idiot," I say in a tone that makes it clear I don't mean it. He stares at me with breathtaking intensity, and I add, "But no, I'm not tired of you. I'm just tired of us not being honest with each other."

"That is also what I meant," he says, even more intense, his nose so close to mine, they will touch if I lean just a little more his way. The thought makes my heart leap.

"I don't actually think you're an idiot," I confess, uncontrolled. "You're a sweet person under the tough facade you try so hard to keep up."

I'm trembling so much it's hard to tell if Erik's shivering comes from himself or from sitting shoulder to shoulder with me.

"I don't hate that you live with me," Erik says, and I stare back at him, my pulse quickening. "I love it, actually."

I hold my breath. He keeps staring at me like he...like he...

"You do?"

"I do."

Meu Deus. My insides are vibrating violently. I can't breathe. He leans even closer, and the tip of his nose brushes mine. I adjust the blanket around his neck, my shoulder and arm pressed against his. All the endorphins, oxytocin, dopamine, or whatever hormones awakened in me after winter bathing are working at full speed, making me hyperaware.

"You're not unattractive, even as a backpacking surfer," I correct my statement from the day I trash-talked him out of fear of looking too vulnerable if I said what I really thought.

"And you're the hottest woman in the whole fucking world."

I stop breathing, shivering more than ever. Frozen. In absolute shock. He's looking at me with yearning in those transparent blue eyes, so intense he barely blinks.

Holy shit.

"That is the hottest thing I've ever heard," I say, surfing on our wave of aggressive honesty. "Do you want to kiss me, Erik Storm?"

Holy fucking shit.

"Fuck yeah."

His purple lips press against my frozen ones, and together they warm each other back to life. I hold his neck, bringing him closer, my fingers tangling around his soaked hair. There is no air left inside my lungs, and I can't feel my face, my feet, or the tips of my fingers. I can barely move my joints.

"Let's go home." I interrupt the kiss, speaking with my forehead on his. "I'm too cold."

Right now all the energy in me is being used to stop my body from freezing, and I want to feel this. I need it to be the only thing my mind and my cells can process.

Erik nods in agreement and we run back to our bikes, more eager to arrive at our shared apartment than ever before, and not just because of the cold.

Definitely not just because of the cold.

Twenty-One

We race home, the action slowly heating us. Still, my hair is dripping on my back, and my face is so cold it feels like my brain has been stored in the freezer for a fortnight.

When we open the door to the apartment, Erik and I run for the shower at the same time, both desperate for hot water. I reach the faucet before him and turn it on. Steam spreads, and Erik shuts the door behind him, sealing us both inside.

His eyes lock with mine, and he starts to undress, carelessly dropping first his shirt, then his pants. They pool at his feet as he slowly removes his boxer briefs.

I remain in front of the shower, admiring his naked figure, my chest rising and dropping at the intense pace of my desire. I stare, waiting. Daring him. He stays still like a Greek statue, one of his eyebrows arching as if to say it's my turn. Without a word, I undress before his eyes. Slowly. Shamelessly.

He bites his lower lip and rakes his hungry eyes over my body. My heart thumps harder than ever.

He takes a step closer at last, his sparkly blue eyes burning with lust. His body is glorious, his hairless chest so hard and smooth, it's like he was sculpted in marble. His muscles are defined to perfection. Strong arms that can carry my weight with ease. Ripped abs I want to feel under my fingers. In the foggy, steamy bathroom, he looks like a god emerging from the clouds.

"Together?" I ask, my voice so weak and loaded with passion, it barely comes out. I almost don't dare believe he will surrender. But I can't resist anymore. I'm done pretending I don't want him.

He takes another step forward, painfully slow, provoking me, and his gaze lowers to my breastbone, then to my boobs. He stops a breath away from me, his body almost touching mine. As he moves my hair behind my shoulders for an unobstructed view of my chest, his fingers delicately brush my skin, making me shiver. My nipples harden, ready to be touched. *Hoping* for it. It's the most erotic moment of my life. I'm wet and burning. I'm *aching* for what is to come.

Gentle and careful, as if I'm made of porcelain, he slides his large hand to the nape of my neck and pulls my head back, looking down at me with fire in his eyes.

Our bodies touch, very lightly at first, sparking tingles of pleasure that go all the way down to my toes. When he presses me closer with his other hand around my waist, my blood pumps with savage lust, the powerful flow converging in my center, where it tortures me with a pulsating need that demands to be satiated soon. Really, *really* soon.

His lips brush mine, gentle and soft as a summer breeze—a provocation designed to test my limits, make me react in a fervent haze. But I stay frozen and let him play with my body.

I love the teasing. He opens my mouth with his thumb like he did yesterday, and this time his finger slides over my lower lip as if testing its softness.

He moves the thumb to caress my cheek, then my chin, traveling around my face in full appreciation of my features. *He said I'm the hottest woman in the whole fucking world.* It's hard to breathe. To think. To exist.

Erik puts my hair behind my ear and leans closer to whisper, "Together it is then." His beard is tickly against my skin, and I'm so seduced my legs can barely sustain my body. He wants me. *He fucking wants me.*

I've never desired a man so much in my life, and I've never been so afraid to have him.

I'm afraid of what comes after. I dread what I might become once he claims me and changes me irreparably.

Because there is no way that having Erik Storm won't fuck me up.

Look at what he's already done to me. Imagine when I *literally* open up to him. When he reaches so deep inside, there will be a *before* and an *after* Erik has been in my body.

Because it's too late for my mind.

And for my heart too.

The warmth of his chest pressing against my breasts heats me as no hot water could. I feel his thick erection, and the flames grow, causing my sex to pulse impatiently.

"I want to fuck you, Sol Carvalho," he whispers on my lips. His hand lowers to my ass, and he squeezes it hard. I let out a low, airy moan. "Too aggressive?" He smiles in a seductive way, and it's the last straw. The point of no return. There is no stopping the hurricane about to be released.

"No," I reply through the knot in my throat. "It's fucking hot."

I pull him toward my lips at once, connecting our bodies. Erik groans and lifts my thigh to press it against his pelvis. His palm follows my curves, finding a path between my legs and reaching my center, where his fingers explore my wet folds. I sigh, leaning my head back. The sounds coming out of my mouth get louder once he finds my clit and touches it with perfect, gentle movements. I roll my eyes back in deep pleasure, gripping the nape of his neck with increasing force.

Kissing me passionately, he pushes me into the shower until my back is against the wall. Erik's tongue digs inside my mouth, exploring it with fervor, the taste of salty ocean bringing me back to our moment at the beach. I would jump in those icy waters fifty more times if this would be my reward.

I move my hands all over his body, feeling his muscles as he kisses me with a ferocious need. His lips then move from my mouth to my neck, where he lingers, breathing on my skin, making me purr. He keeps going down, and his lips tempt me most when they reach my nipples, and he licks them with divine circular movements. It's almost too much, but I don't surrender. I don't want to come too fast. I want to get as much time in paradise as I can.

I hold his face—his perfect Viking face—and bring it up to meet mine, eager to feel his rough beard. I'm a big fan of it now. I actually was all along—how could I not love everything about his flawless appearance?—but admitting that to myself would have put me even further down the path of temptation. I love that I can finally touch his beard. I love the feeling of the coarse hairs between my fingers.

Why did I think I wanted a Prince Charming? None would have a chance against Erik Storm. How could I have resisted him for so long? How did I convince myself I could stay away from the sexiest man on Earth when every single part of me was screaming for his touch?

As I caress his face, he runs his hands over my body, his fingers tracing the lines and curves of my breast, slowly moving down over the curve of my waist until he reaches my hips. His hands briefly stroke the plumpness of my butt, then move up my back.

Erik's kisses are powerful, insatiable, and I bite him, thoroughly enjoying the softness of his meaty lips between my teeth. He takes a break to look at me, eyes ablaze, cupping my face with possessive urgency. The hot water slides down his broad shoulders and spreads his hair over his back. It drips from his nose onto mine. It wets his lips and falls into my mouth, and I need—*need*—to feel the entirety of his massive torso.

I push him against the opposite glass wall and kiss every muscle on his smooth, husky chest, down his perfect abs and impressive V line. I close my fingers around his hardness, making him groan with pleasure, and he lifts me in his arms in a sudden, feral move, unable to stand it anymore.

"I need you," his deep, hoarse voice says in my ear, his breath tickling me.

I put my arms around his neck, holding tight, and wrap my legs around his waist, my back against the cold wall once again.

"I want you so bad, Sol..."

I rejoice in his rough voice, his wonderful hands, his Asgardian body.

"Then come in," I say on his lips with urgency, pressing him hard against my body. I'm so ready. I want him so bad too.

"Are you on the pill?" he asks in one breath.

"IUD," I mumble with my forehead on his.

He makes an "mmm" sound that could mean "good" or a million other things, but I interpret it as intense desire that can't wait another second. "I'm tested, okay?" he mutters with his mouth on mine.

I hold his face and kiss him hard. "Me too. Come in now."

He slides in, slowly at first, and I kiss him with passionate fury, closer to combustion with every heartbeat. He's still not close enough. I press my torso against his. *It will never be close enough…*

When I feel Erik filling every inch of me, opening yet more space, it's so overwhelming, so sublime, that I hold my breath and sink my nails into his back. He thrusts into me, and I arch my back, groaning, needing him as I've never needed anyone.

He is strong, keeping me up effortlessly, and I'm so in lust that I hold him even tighter, moving with increasing urgency, the fire consuming me until nothing in the world matters but fucking Erik Storm.

"I can't hold back anymore, Sol…you're too hot." He grabs my hair in a bunch while kissing me. He strokes my clit and kisses my neck, sending shivers down my spine and feeding my flames.

"Oh, Erik," I whisper his name. The heat is stronger than ever. *Oh, it's coming…* I can feel it building up, taking me over. "Together," I say under my breath in the same vulnerable tone I used to utter the word before he kissed me. But it's not a question this time. It's an ardent plea.

We climax at the same time, our cries of delight echoing through the steam. He melts inside of me, throbbing and shuddering. I grip him with all my strength, chin resting on his shoulder. My legs are shaky, my mind foggy with pleasure. Our lips meet in a delicious kiss as he lowers me down to the shower floor. He caresses my face with the tip of his fingers, and we slowly pull apart, breathless, the hot water falling over our heads like a tropical storm.

"That was amazing," I exhale, still feeling as if a thousand fireworks are exploding in my body.

"You can have it again if you want," he whispers suggestively in between kisses. The idea delights me.

"How can I say no to that?" I smile, and he gives me another lengthy kiss.

Erik grabs the bottle of soap, depositing a small amount into the palm of his hand before gently massaging it over my body. My skin is still very sensitive, craving his touch. He turns me around, our slippery bodies meeting. He then lifts my left arm, puts it behind his neck, and soaps me from the tip of my finger, down my arm, stopping on my breasts, where he lingers. It's so good and I'm so aroused, I might be ready again very soon.

We shampoo each other, the tips of his fingers running through my hair in a delicious movement. I sigh, enraptured, then I touch his long, soft hair and massage his scalp. When my fingers tease him behind the ears, he lets out a guttural sound of delight and grows hard again. I want his lips. I'm wild, beastly, so I turn around and claim his mouth once more.

"We should continue this in bed, don't you think?" he

whispers in my ear, cornering me against the steamy glass wall marked with our palms.

"Yes," I say with such certainty, such impatience, he grins, turns off the water, and takes our towels. "Your bed or mine?" I ask, drying as fast as humanly possible.

"Yours. We built it together. Now let's destroy it."

I laugh and drop the towel on the floor, throwing my arms around him again. He lifts me as if we are about to enter our honeymoon suite, our lips locking in a fervid kiss as he carries me to my room.

The blinds are down, blocking any light from spilling in. Erik gently places me in bed and follows me to the mattress, positioning himself between my thighs.

He kisses every inch of my body, moving from my lips down to my neck, my breasts—*oh jeez*—and lowering to my belly, where his beard grazing over the sensitive skin under my navel makes me deliciously ticklish. He skips the middle, then brings the sole of my foot to his chest and caresses my leg with his fingertips before lowering his head to resume kissing me—first ankle, then calf, then thigh…until he is so far up, he is kissing my throbbing center.

No man has ever done this to me, and I almost can't stand how good it feels, not only because he knows what he is doing and his grunts make clear he enjoys it—but mainly because it's Erik. *Erik fucking Storm kissing my pussy.* I never, *ever* thought those words would cross my mind.

His tongue slips through my folds and circles my clit, stimulating me to volcanic heights. I grip the sheets, arching my back with a sigh of pleasure followed by a groan as he continues with his fingers so he can get back to my mouth. I moan and let out a breathy *"Oh, Erik,"* as I press him against my body, aching to feel him inside me.

His sultry kisses snap me into full consciousness, and I realize I want a turn to be in control too.

"I want you on your back," I say with a confidence that doesn't show up often.

Erik looks at me with fire in his eyes, and we roll. Landing on top of him, I shift my hips to position him at my wet entrance, slowly sinking down his hard length until he is seated inside me. I hold my breath all the while, the whole of my body and consciousness halting to concentrate and revel in the wonder, the *deeply* fulfilling sensation, of having Erik fit perfectly inside me. My heart pumps so hard I can almost see the red of the beautiful inferno surrounding me.

"*Shit*, Sol," he groans because it's *so* good for him too, and that turns me on even more.

I move my hips in a slow rhythm first, his hardness sliding in and out. I feel his desire building with mine at each thrust, our breaths growing faster, our hips following the rising beat of our lust. He cups my breasts with his large hands, and the pressure of his fingers on my nipples gives me the last bit of stimulation I need. I ride him even faster, eager for my release. My rapture.

We are synchronized again. We explode together, lips pressed in urgent need, bodies damp, quivering, the scent of soap so mixed with our seduction I will never be able to smell his shampoo without craving him under me. So completely surrendered. So completely mine.

I lie on his chest, our breath recovering, hearts decelerating until reaching a comfortable, steady pace.

"We succeeded," I say at last, and he makes a sound of incomprehension that vibrates in his chest against my ear. "This was the wildest thing we could have done."

He laughs—a full, jolly sound that warms me and tickles me along with the gentle, delicious touch of his hands on my back.

I'm in my bed with Erik Storm.

It's almost like a dream. It can't be happening, can it? He'll realize what he has done and regret it, won't he?

I want to look in his eyes, so I drop from his body and lie on my pillow, facing him. He takes my duvet and covers us both.

What now? I want to ask. But I don't want to ruin it. The moment we talk about it, it will all crumble, I'm sure.

I touch his face, almost as if I want to test if he is real. He puts his hand over mine. Sweet. Loving.

He said he wanted to fuck me, not that he wanted to be in a relationship with me.

Perhaps this is all we'll ever have.

Wouldn't it be enough?

Nothing but *all of him* would be enough.

"You look worried." He half frowns, half smiles, sliding a finger over my nose.

"I'm afraid," I confess.

"Of what?"

"You backing away," I whisper, and my face gets hot. I feel more exposed now than at any other time today.

"There's no going back, Sol." He keeps smiling, and I exhale, calming down. "We've dived in."

I try to smile back, but I can't. He did that with *her*, and he regretted it.

I pass my fingers over his beard. He is so handsome. So… wonderful.

Too good to be real. Too good to be mine.

"Why did you stay with your parents for so long? Why did you barely text me?"

He looks deep into my eyes. "You were right to say I'm an idiot. Or I *was*. I don't want to be an idiot anymore."

I try to smile, but I can't.

"I was scared, Sol, that's the truth." He breathes out and plays with my fingers, his eyes lowered in shame. "That kiss was…*wonderful*," he stresses the word, curving his lips up when he remembers our moment in Tivoli. I can't help but copy his expression. "But I was afraid this wouldn't work… Afraid to get my heart broken…"

"Afraid I would go back to Brazil and never return?"

He smiles, sighing, and answers, "Yes."

Like Lena returned to Poland. I frown when her name crosses my mind. "Do you still think about your ex, Erik?"

He blinks at me, a wrinkle forming on his forehead. "No. Not at all. I've… I've struggled to get over what happened, yes. I struggled to get my life back on track since all that… well, you know the story. But since you moved in, I haven't thought about her once. All I think about is you. All the fucking time."

I smile. Honesty is evident in his silly grin and in the way his eyes shine as he stares fondly at me. His chest rises with energy, his cheeks flushed. My hand is resting on his face. Erik covers it with his own and drives it toward his lips so he can kiss my palm.

"We should give ourselves a chance," he says, and the words

sound like magic to my ears. They sparkle and twinkle. They open my tight chest, making me able to breathe at last. "I can't promise I'll be perfect. But I won't back away."

I kiss him, chasing his salty tongue, biting his honeyed lips.

"There's nothing I want more than to try," I say with my nose touching his, and he smiles—not just with his mouth, but with his eyes too. They are shinier than ever, his pupils enlarged by the passion, the connection that took us both by surprise.

There is so much that can go wrong. There is nothing ideal about us living together. Not to mention that Martin can reveal us at any moment. Lars can fire me. I can lose my visa and return to Brazil like Erik fears.

For a moment, though, I dare hope it will all be just fine.

Twenty-Two

Confined in a mad scientist's lab, solving one puzzle after another before the sixty minutes run out, Erik and I strengthen our cooperation skills together with Lars, Lotte, Chiara, George, and Alex. We make a swift escape while Martin, Astrid, Ellen, Mads, Simon, and Lia remain locked in the other identical room for fifteen more minutes to finally get out when the game master opens the door.

In other words: we beat the hell out of them.

At a table in a nearby pub, drinking beer, we boast about our superiority in the escape room, and Astrid marks victory points for the winning teams on the leaderboard. After today, Erik and I are tied for first place with Team Georgelex.

"Should we vote on the wild challenge pictures now?" Astrid suggests, and everyone agrees.

She has gathered all the pictures on her tablet, including mine and Erik's from our winter bathing experience this morning, which I sent to her privately before we came.

"When did you guys do that?" Chiara asks me, smiling, when it's her turn with the iPad.

"This morning, actually," I say, my cheeks flushing. Erik's face is rosy too.

"Tell us more about it!" Lars smiles. "Are you winter bathers?"

"It was the first time for both of us," Erik answers.

George then jokes, "I hope you guys enjoyed your first time." His words are loaded with insinuation, and we all laugh, me hiding my face in embarrassment. Because this time, it *is* true. I get even shyer when Erik takes my face in his hands and kisses me. Some clap and whoop.

"Aren't they sweet?" Alex lowers his head onto George's shoulder, sighing.

"Let me see the picture," Lars says as he receives the iPad, and I watch his expression. His smile looks approving. "I'd give you guys a high-five if I could." Lars is sitting at the opposite end of the table. "A toast, then!" He lifts his glass.

"To love," Erik says, lifting his beer too, and my heart goes wild in my chest.

Love. *Thump-thump.*

Love? *Thump-thump.*

Ah, if only...

I can't allow myself to be so hopeful.

Everyone toasts to love, and I keep my eyes on Erik's sweet smile. On the soft wavy hair that I helped him brush and tie, only the upper half, in a small elastic. On our fingers interlocked on the table. On the beard that he trimmed again because he knows I like it better like that. On his transparent ocean eyes...

He gives me another quick kiss, then gazes at me, so attractive and suggestive that I get instantly aroused. I'm so in love, so full of lust, I want to snatch him out of his chair, pull him into the bathroom and make out. I can't wait to get home and feel his hands on my naked body—his fingers exploring my breasts, my butt, and then entering me slowly…

My lips stretch into a sly smirk, and he sees where my thoughts are. I can tell his are there too. His fingers trace over my leg under the table, moving under my dress and going farther up. Even though I'm wearing tights, it feels so good I almost let out a moan. It's suddenly so hot in the pub, I have to fan myself with the menu. With my other hand, I seek Erik's fingers under the table and interlace them on mine, stopping him before he makes me jump onto his lap.

I focus on what's going on around me. Although our picture was the coolest—in every sense of the word—Martin wins the voting with his shot midair when bungee-jumping sixty meters down from a crane. I don't mind that Martin gets this one victory. Our winter bathing experience was worthy in every way.

When Erik and I get home, he carries me to his room as soon as I get rid of my shoes and jacket. "You look so fucking sexy in this dress."

He runs his hands over my body, following my silhouette, and I glue my mouth to his with all the passion I had to contain in front of my coworkers.

Now, finally alone at home, there's fire and fireworks. A drumming of heartbeats and grunts of impatient desire. I lift his sweater and T-shirt over his head in a single bundle and throw them across the room. He kisses me, wild, eager. His fingers handle my back zipper blindly. Soon the dress is falling, and I'm stepping on it, hands gripping his strong arms and shoulders until he places me in bed. The flustered butterflies in my stomach join my thudding heart in a riot to lay claim on Erik as quickly as possible, and I obey, bewitched.

He opens his belt, then unzips his pants, and I help him get rid of them. I lower his boxer briefs down his thick, muscular thighs, unveiling his hard cock, and my need to feel it in me makes me ache.

Once he's fully naked, I pull him down with a kiss and roll us around on the bed so I can be on top. I need him under me—under my control. I run my nails over his massive chest and down his ripped abs, biting my lower lip. This *god*, he's all mine. He gives me a sexy smile, amused, aroused, rock-hard against my soft, throbbing folds.

As he teases me at my entrance, his hands go to my breasts. He massages my nipples, stoking the fire in my insides, and I press myself against him, rubbing my clit on his hardness. He keeps touching me, enticing me, and in between moans, I kiss his neck, inhale the citrusy scent of his skin, and run my nose over his rough beard.

"The day you slept in this bed, I couldn't stop thinking about sharing it with you," he whispers in my ear, sending shivers down my spine.

"Is that why you couldn't sleep?" I whisper back as he kisses me on the earlobe. *God, it's amazing…*

"Absolutely." He kisses the skin under my chin. I arch my back, burning, and grip his shoulders with extra strength. I keep rubbing my clit against his cock, and it's getting *so good*, I might come before he's even inside.

"You were a walking temptation, Sol Carvalho." He kisses the skin under my ear and pulls me closer with his hands on my butt as if he's thrusting into me, though he's still outside. I groan, needing more. "I knew I was torturing myself when I agreed to have you here."

And you're torturing me now, making me wait…

I want to hear him though. "So why did you say yes?" My voice comes out between sighs of pleasure.

He holds my face a little above his so he can look into my eyes. "Because I thought I was stronger," he says with a lopsided grin and puts a strand of my hair that had been tickling his face behind my ear. My hair is loosely tied in a ponytail, so as I shake my head and laugh, more rebellious hair slips out of the hair tie and lands on him.

"Being strong is for the weak," I say.

His laugh tickles my ear. Then he uses his powerful arms to roll us around in one swift move so that *he* ends up on top of me. "I guess I knew that all along," he whispers hoarsely, his huge muscular body covering mine, and *God*, it's sexy.

"So, you wanted me all this time?" I say, and it's my turn to take a few loose strands of his hair and tuck them behind his ears. Before Erik, I'd never dated a guy with longer hair than mine, and I thought I would never, ever do that. Why was I so silly?

His big hard cock is right at my opening, pushing through slowly. I'm so wet. So ready.

"Come in already," I say between my teeth, but he ignores the plea to answer my question.

"I wanted you from the day I met you at the English pub," he says on my lips.

A flare of ecstasy pumps my hopeful heart, warming my chest until it matches my burning core.

"When I saw your profile on Cinder—your sweet smile, your dark warm eyes, your beautiful face—I thought I'd doom myself, and I was right."

I smile and grab his cock, aching for him. I'm going to put him in now. He smiles back, and then his fingers enter me, taking my breath away.

"When you told me why you asked me out," he continues as his fingers go deeper, fogging my mind, his hoarse voice even rougher with the vulnerability he usually never expresses. I squeeze his nape, eager for more—of both what he's doing with his fingers and what he's saying. "I was...sad. Disappointed. I wanted it to have been a real date. With the night ending up right where we are now."

His words are as erotic as his movements. My mind is taken over by pleasure, but I manage to say a breathy, "Really?" *Gosh, if I'd known that back then...*

"Oh yeah, *min skat*," he says right as he reaches my G-spot. I shudder and moan loudly, feeling so good I can't be quiet. And Erik calling me his treasure? That's the sexiest thing he could have done.

"I could have said no to you living with me, but part of me knew I had to keep you near," he goes on, not satisfied with my moan. He's aiming for a scream. For a full, long-lasting orgasm. One that will make me wake up all the neighbors.

I'm flaming, throbbing, impatient for the end and, at the same time, dreading the moment it will be over.

He's clouding my thoughts—especially when he lowers his head and starts licking me. I'm shaking uncontrollably, my legs are jelly, but I'm aware of what he's doing. I mean, besides making me burn and yearn for him. He's distracting me. Because he is being more honest than ever, and he doesn't want me to focus on the fact that he is dropping his armor to strip off the layers of truth underneath it.

After all, being metaphorically naked in front of each other is unnerving. More than it is to be literally naked. It's scary because it connects us even more.

He stops licking and kissing my pussy and stares at me for a moment. I lie flat on the mattress, legs spread out, shaking and panting. Hungry for the finale.

"When we met at the pub, I considered moving on with the date and forgetting my stupid idea," I confess.

Erik smiles. "It wasn't so stupid after all."

He kisses me. Hard. Urgent. I slide my fingers up his nape and grip his loose, messy bun, keeping him close. His tongue dances with mine, inebriating me. I can't stand it anymore.

"I need you in me *now*, Erik," I say, urgent, desperate. "Make me come, please."

Finally, *finally*, he penetrates me, deeper and deeper, and our bodies become one. Having his massiveness contained within my tight walls makes me shudder and struggle for air. When he starts thrusting, it's almost unbearable. I'm ablaze, consumed, *so* close…

And as the incoming explosion builds, I conclude that I don't know what makes me most satisfied: Erik filling every inch of space inside me or his admission that he wanted me from the start. His moans and sighs are music to my ears. His skin is my haven. I've never felt so much a part of someone else.

We are one. He completes me.

He's my best friend, my home, my work, my lover. He is part of everything that makes me who I am in Denmark. It's frightening to need someone so much. It's terrifying to know that, without him, nothing makes sense.

Erik starts thrusting harder, deliciously aggressive, and the touch of his hands on my body puts me one hundred percent into the moment. The only thing that matters. Us, here and now, surrendering to our love.

Love. *Love?* Is it love?

I want it to be love.

"Sol," his vulnerable voice whispers, "you're so fucking sexy..." And the burning reaches its peak.

It's *now.*

I scream, reveling in pleasure. My muscles tighten around his cock in luscious spasms and trigger him. My climax lasts slightly longer than his, and I grab onto him with all my power until the world goes back to normal. Or as close to normal as amazing feels.

When he is showering, I sit on the closed toilet seat and look at him through the glass door. He is like a mirage. Like a character from a book come to life.

Erik sees me observing him, smiles, and draws a heart for me with his index finger on the steamy glass. I stand still, heart racing, overthinking. Does he mean he loves me? Is it just a meaningless gesture? Why do I have to worry about this now instead of simply enjoying our delicious affair?

I could use the moment to say I love him. I could peel the last layer protecting me from total exposure.

Because I do.

I love Erik Storm.

Maybe my words would get him to say it back. But what if it's too early for him? He's been giving me more than I expected. He's still afraid he is going down the same destructive path for a second time.

I blow him a kiss instead, and he blows one back. We keep it simple. That's how we'll make it last. We'll pretend we don't see how complicated it is. How tangled together our lives are, and how such commitment at the early stages of a relationship can be too much and break everything.

We must learn how to pull back. How to control our impulses and raise walls here and there. It's a complex mechanic to master, one we might not be ready for. We skipped the first stages. We jumped the learning curve. We dived in.

Now, we are stuck with each other. We gave up our privacy after the first time we had sex. We went from friends to "married" in a day.

What if this doesn't work out? Then I'm homeless. And heartbroken. Then I'm back on the hopeless apartment hunt, which might be even harder this time around. Which might mean my only choice, still, is going back to Brazil. And losing my job. And the promotion. And the entire life I thought I could have here.

Now a life I don't want to have with a nameless Danish Prince Charming. But with Erik Storm.

All the air runs out of my lungs when I hear the disastrous news during my first meeting with the design team on Monday.

The next Scorpio Games project, the one to be directed by the new game director yet to be hired, is Erik's game.

Yes, Love Birds. Except it won't be called that.

And it won't be *Erik*'s game.

It will be a plagiarized version of his idea. Martin's interpretation of it.

"That sounds cool. I love the idea of a mix between a game and a dating app," someone says, and I don't care who it is. My eyes only have one target.

Martin *motherfucking* Olesen. Son of a snake.

Oh, I hate his pretentious smile. He's staring back at me, victorious. He convinced Lars, who was already interested in the idea. I had no clue Lars would choose the game before even choosing the director.

Does that mean Martin won the promotion? Is it over?

I can't let this happen. I can't sit and watch while a traitor sells his partner's idea to the partner's former employer.

Especially when the betrayed person is the man I love.

"You can't do this," I hear myself say. All eyes are on me now. Something inside me is making me speak, and I'm unable to stop it. "This idea is not available. It's Erik's idea!"

The silence is heavy in the room. Lars is looking at me with his forehead wrinkled, and Martin is a stone carved on top of his chair. Did he think I wouldn't have the courage to say it?

"It is actually *my* idea," Martin says calmly and wets his lips as if ready for a juicy meal.

"It's a great idea, so we decided to go for it." Lars interlaces his fingers on the table, blinking in untroubled composure as if they are doing absolutely nothing wrong.

I'm having a hard time hiding the shaking of my hands, both closed in tight fists. I can't believe this is happening. How dare they—how—

Breathe, Sol, breathe...

Anyone who investigates properly will know that Martin was a cofounder of Erik's company and was disgusting enough to abandon him, get a job at Erik's former workplace, and steal his idea... An idea he feels entitled to because he also worked on it. Erik didn't protect himself with an NDA. What Martin is doing is unethical, but not illegal.

Looking at Lars now, serious and tough in his posture, I feel nauseated. I know very well that Scorpio Games is a capitalist powerhouse that takes popular ideas and surfs on their wave of success. But I didn't expect them to be so tricky and disgusting.

Erik's company doesn't have the same money and resources as Scorpio. It's just me and him working for free. No matter how much worse Scorpio's version will be, it will be the one to make thousands, *millions*, and reach the top of the charts...

I'm so furious now I can barely stay in the room, looking at the people acting like it's okay to drive over a tiny car with a tank. How silly was I to think Scorpio wanted to do something original for once!

I take a deep breath. I should keep my cool, at least until the meeting is over. I need time to think things through. If I go mad now, Lars may fire me. Or if he doesn't, I will certainly lose the promotion.

Do I even *want* to work here though? Do I want to direct Erik's game at Scorpio when he's sitting at home, unemployed, working on his own version all by himself for free?

I would be an even bigger traitor than Martin.

Shit. I sigh. The idea of looking Lars in the eye and saying, *I quit*, has never been so appealing, but it's also never been as gut-wrenching.

I'm not the same Sol who sat with Lars in late September with the intention of telling him I had to go back to Brazil because I couldn't find a place to live. Now I not only have an apartment; I have a *home* in Copenhagen, where I'm comfortable and happy.

I have Erik.

Quitting at this point means giving up on him and the life we could build together in this wonderful city. If I don't have this job, the visa, and the money it provides me, I can't stay.

There are no good options. Either I stay at Scorpio and betray Erik, or I give up on my dream and leave him. Neither of the choices give us or our ambitions a fair chance.

So maybe I don't have to choose. Not right now. Not alone.

Controlling my emotions, I stay still and quiet for the rest of the meeting, picturing all the different ways beetle-turned-snake Martin could choke on the venom of his big, poisonous tongue.

Twenty-Three

I forgot my key, and Erik doesn't answer the door. Great.

I text him, and he says he is at the gym, coming home in half an hour, so I decide to walk around the block while I wait.

Instead of taking a stroll by the lake, I walk on the other side of the residential buildings and end up in a public playground. Something makes me open the gate and walk inside. It's getting dark earlier and earlier these days. The sky is already at that mystic cobalt color, going navy within the hour, the streetlamps slowly lighting up.

A handful of kids are swinging, climbing, making sand cakes, and running around loudly. Tired parents call after them, eager to go home and eat dinner. I claim an empty table and watch the activity, knowing that soon I'll be the only one here.

I take my computer out of my backpack and open the latest files in our shared Love Birds folder. I haven't touched them in a while. I'm seeing everything as an external observer—and the idea seems weak and incomplete, like a jumble of pieces that don't connect.

My laptop screen is the lightest thing around when Erik joins me fifteen minutes after texting to ask where I am. When he sits by my side—already showered and equipped for a chilly night—he gives me a kiss and sets a thermos on the table, along with two paper cups.

"I brought coffee."

I force a smile. "You should have brought liquor instead." I rub my face, wondering how to begin. I didn't want to text him about what happened today. This had to be a conversation face-to-face. "We should go inside. It's cold and dark."

"Not that cold—*refreshing.* Not that dark—*inspiring.*" Erik smiles at me. "I thought you were the optimist of the two of us."

"Hard to be optimistic after today," I mumble.

"What happened?" A shadow crosses his face.

I take a deep breath and release the bomb. "They're stealing your idea, that is what's happening. Scorpio's next game is Martin's version of Love Birds."

"What?" Erik stands up. "I thought that…" He loses his train of thought, shocked. I pull him back down, and he sits heavily next to me. His face is pale, his chest rising and falling, panic-stricken.

I've had my visceral reaction. First in the meeting room, then in the bathroom at work, then leaving as early as I could, walking all the way home so I could put on my headphones and cry while blasting aggressive rock. I wasn't in a hurry to arrive and tell Erik the news.

"Erik." I turn his face to me gently with both hands. His eyes are moving around as if he is trying to find a way out.

"Erik, look at me. We won't let them, okay? Martin wasn't chosen as game director yet. It's not over."

The more I think about it, the more it feels like there is no choice I can live with but fighting back.

"It *is* over, Sol." He gazes at me at last, wide-eyed, disturbed. "Lars listened to that asshole. They have the resources *we* don't have. Trying to beat them is stupid. They won't give up."

"Erik, listen." I bring his face closer to mine so he can look into my eyes. I need to be strong to support him, no matter how scared and hurt I am. "We might not stop them from making their version, but we can finish ours and show them how it's done. We'll get it published before them, and *they* will be the clowns."

Erik looks down, sighing. Where is the anger that will fuel him?

"We thought this could happen, didn't we?" I say. "That was the reason we made our deal." I won't abandon him now. "What we feared happened a little before we thought it would. So all we have to do is speed up."

Erik shakes his head and looks down, avoiding my eyes. I let my hands fall, feeling a sudden rush of hopelessness. If he doesn't believe it can be done, doesn't even want to try, how can I?

"You can't help me anymore, Sol." I stare at him, panic rising in my chest. He looks up and meets my gaze. "You can't take up arms on my behalf. You work at Scorpio Games, and I don't want my dream to ruin yours."

I hug him. I press my arms tight around him and bury my face in his shoulder. I need his warmth as much as he needs mine. Nothing we can tell each other now will be easy to say or hear, so we stay silent.

I want to tell him I don't care about my job at Scorpio. But since I don't have any other job opportunities in sight, that would be the same as saying I don't care about *us*.

Erik ends the hug and holds my hands. "Just stay out of it, okay? Focus on your career, on your promotion."

I laugh with disdain. "You mean the promotion that will make me director of *your* game?"

"Love Birds is yours too now," he says, and there is endearment in his eyes. Like he is happy for my involvement in it.

I give him a sad smile. "It's still your app, and I don't want to take ownership of it when Scorpio is in charge, and you're not even there."

"If that's what it takes for you to stay in Denmark, with me, I'll gladly pay the price."

Silence. My eyes fill up with tears. It's sweet, romantic even, that he's willing to sacrifice his dream for mine. For us. But how can I be okay with that?

A gust of wind blows as we look at the empty playground. There is something ghostly about it at this hour. It's gloomy, but also somehow magical, like an abandoned land outside of time.

"What if you talk to Lars?" I say after a while. "You tell him your version of the story and ask him not to go ahead with the project."

"I can't do that."

"Why not?" I raise my head to look at him. There is a single light pole on the perimeter of the playground, casting a weak glow a few feet behind Erik. His eyes are dark in the shadows, their bluish transparency hidden.

"He knows it's my project, and he doesn't care."

I can't argue with that. I heard it from Lars himself.

"I can look for other jobs, you know," I tell him with a weak voice that reflects my discouragement. With so many Europeans in the city, companies are not exactly jumping at the opportunity to hire someone who needs a visa.

Even Erik is still unemployed, and things are different for him. As a Dane in Denmark, he has so many rights that I don't have. An entire support system. A network of people who can help him. A family who will always take him in and even aid him financially.

My parents can't help me when I'm here. They barely make ends meet in Brasília, and I've even loaned them some money when they needed to fix their roof after a storm. I make more money than they do combined. Living costs are different here, much higher, but I'm still way better off than most people I know back home. It's hard to give up on such a thing, even when you hate your job. I know it could be so much worse for me, and then I feel spoiled whenever I find myself loathing Scorpio Games. Even now.

So I understand Erik doesn't want me to give up. He knows he's more privileged than I am. That he could quit his job and live off unemployment benefits.

He knows the country doesn't want me here if I'm a burden. And I know that even if we got married, nothing would change. I'd still need a job, a proven income. You don't get Danish citizenship for marrying a Dane.

"I wish I could hire you in my company," Erik says with

a hint of annoyance, and I get annoyed too, because now the possibility of him making money off his app and kick-starting his business is going down the drain.

No. He doesn't have to give up.

"*You* don't have to stop working on the app, Erik," I say with a hand on his face. "I know how much this project means to you. And you can make it happen. I know you're on a tight schedule, even tighter now. They might start working on it in January. But you're skilled and efficient. You can finish it in a month."

He doesn't reply, biting his lower lip, eyelids lowered. I run a finger over the crease on his forehead, wanting it to disappear. I wish I could make all his concerns vanish. I want to make everything right for him.

And yet, I'm useless. I have to work for the enemy.

But you don't have to be loyal to them, a voice in my head says. Not Larissa's. My own.

My heart is with Erik, and no work contract will change that.

"I'll help you, Erik," I say with sudden determination, "even if that makes me breach the noncompete clause in my contract." I let out a rough laugh. "I mean, I haven't been giving a shit about that anyway all these months."

I'm pretty sure my boss wouldn't be happy to know I've been working on an app that now competes directly with their future product. I haven't been honest, but I don't feel guilty. A war has already begun. And I'll silently fight it at Erik's side.

Erik looks at me with a slightly open mouth, the crease on his forehead deepening. "But Sol—"

"I can't quit Scorpio for now," I interrupt him. "But I won't be loyal to them."

"And what about the game director position?" There is a shine to his eyes as he blinks at me.

"I don't know." I look at my nails, swallowing hard. "Maybe I won't get it."

Erik holds me by the shoulders, making me meet his eyes. There is a new determination in his gaze. An intensity emerging from the shadows. "Sol. You need to get that position."

"But—"

"It was always meant to be yours, and it *will* be." His voice sounds a lot more resonant than it did a minute ago. The familiar Erik Storm fire is awakening in him. And I like that. A lot. The wild, determined Viking is back. "I want you to keep running for the position. You need to beat the shit out of Martin, okay?" I laugh a little and nod, keeping my gaze firmly on his. "If we can't beat them to publication, I want the project in your hands. In *good hands*." He caresses my face, and I cover his hand with mine. "Promise me you won't give up, Sol."

I nod again, hypnotized by his eyes. I can't believe how considerate he is. How strong. How *goddamn* wonderful.

"I won't give up," I say.

"Good." He gives me the tiniest smile, and I wrap my arms around his neck, covering his lips with mine.

His arms close around my waist, and his tongue enters my mouth avidly. His kiss is a consolation amid chaos, warmth in a freezing world, light on a dark road. With some reluctance, I detach my mouth from his after a few seconds, afraid to go too far in a public place, but I smile and pull him by the hand.

"What are we doing?" he asks as I make him follow me.

"We're alone in a nice playground after dark," I say, expecting him to catch up with my excitement. "In fact, the nicest playground I've ever been to. Danish kids must be very happy."

"Happiest country in the world." He shrugs.

"If I showed you the playgrounds I played at when I was a child, you'd cry. Broken swings, rusty slides with missing parts... Whenever I ran to a playground, my mom panicked, and my dad tried to direct me to a field where we could play with a ball instead."

"He would probably like these courts then." Erik points at the lovely basketball court to our left, and the small fenced soccer field with artificial grass and two well-kept goals.

"Yes, he would have loved to come here with me..."

I often have these moments when cultural shock kicks in with full power. I think of all the ways my life would have been different if I had grown up in Denmark. I look at the people here and think, *Damn, they're lucky.*

I sometimes feel like I'm inside a dream, and my past of hardship and deprivation crawls up to the surface, reminding me that life is never this perfect. That this is what you see in movies, not what happens to real people. That all of this—clean streets, beautiful buildings, polite citizens, happy children playing in public wonderlands—must belong in someone's fantasy. *My own fantasy.* I think of all those days in Brazil when I struggled or saw everyone around me struggling and imagined a world like this.

After being in Denmark for so long, I often find myself so caught up in my new life here that I sometimes complain about a minor thing and realize I'm having first-world problems. Then I laugh, and oscillate between feeling happy for myself and bad that my family is not here and will never be, and I'm the only one who will experience this side of reality.

"What are you thinking about? You look so serious suddenly." Erik embraces me from behind, resting his head on my shoulder.

"Just that…when I'm with you, it's like a story someone is telling me."

"Is that good or bad?"

I smile. "I don't know, it's just that… I often look around and have the strange feeling that everything is made of cardboard. That I'm in a movie set. Someone is going to pull me out at some point. I'll hear a 'Cut!' and the lights will dim, and I'll go back to the real world."

Erik turns me to face him, holding my waist. I put my hands on his chest and look up to see his eyes. They are loving.

And there the feeling is. A pressure in my chest, a voice in my head saying everything is fine now, but it won't last. It will fall apart. He won't be by my side forever.

I blink slowly and take a deep breath, fighting against the thoughts. I can't let them ruin this moment.

"I know what you mean," Erik says. "It happens when everything feels too perfect. Then I start to imagine the whole set crumbling until I'm buried under the wreckage."

I lean my forehead against his mouth, and he kisses it.

"But this is real, Erik, isn't it?" I whisper, very low, almost afraid to let the words out, because if said too loud, they might have the power to start the demolition.

"Yes," he whispers back against my head. "It couldn't be more real."

I pull his head down and kiss him with fervor. I need his skin, his essence, his love. I need to feel his soft hair between my fingers, the scent of his masculine shampoo stirring my butterflies. I need to taste his mouth—his soft lips, his coffee-stained tongue chasing and capturing mine. I need to be scratched by his beard, my fingers getting lost in its rough paths.

His hands are on my neck, and I let him bite my lip and turn my head from side to side to enjoy every bit of my face. I stop him before he gets hard in the playground. That must be a sin. I'm already burning, but at least I can hide it easily.

We could run to the apartment, but there will be plenty of time for sex later. I'm not done with my childish dream yet.

"Hey, are those trampolines?" I detangle from Erik, and from the way he adjusts his pants, I realize I pressed the brake right on time. I get closer to the circles I spotted on the ground, confirming my suspicions. "They *are* trampolines! Are you kidding me?" The floor around them is rubbery so kids won't get hurt. "This is so cool!"

I jump onto the nearest one, happy like a little girl. Erik laughs at my contentment and starts jumping on the other circle next to me. I laugh, forgetting everything. For a moment, I'm eight years old again.

"Let's see who jumps higher." I climb on one of the cubes near the trampolines, and Erik does the same. "Ready? Go!"

We jump, and Erik's propulsion is so good he flies up. We trip out of the trampolines, laughing. I hug him by the waist, and he kisses me. We back away together, bodies and mouths connected, until my leg collides with a net swing that looks like a hammock, and I lie down, pulling Erik with me.

We lie side by side, looking up. It's a full moon tonight—a beautiful, sharp silver circle glowing in a clear navy sky. We spend a few minutes admiring the beauty above us, the textures on the lunar surface clearly visible.

"It will all be fine, won't it?" I ask Erik, turning my face to admire his moonlit profile.

"It will," he assures me, trying to convince himself.

I interlock my fingers with his and pray to the skies, *Don't take this away from me. Please, make it last forever.*

The silence is complete and absolute.

Are you hearing me, Odin? Do not take him back, or I'll have to start Ragnarok myself.

"My back hurts." Erik winces. "This is not a comfortable place to lie down for long."

"Then let's find another fun thing to do." I rise to my feet and offer Erik a hand.

We fool around a little. Then I scale the mini climbing wall, making Erik laugh when I say, "Take this, George and Alex!" Then I almost get stuck inside the slide, and Erik pulls me by the leg, which results in me falling on him, both of us rolling ungracefully on the rubbery floor. He chases me, and we play hide and seek. The last time he catches me, he tickles me until I'm crying with laughter. I ask for a break, and we kiss with burning passion in the middle of the dark playground, his hands on my waist, my arms around his neck.

"I miss having this much fun," I say, the butterflies in my stomach as active as the endorphins running through my veins, making me pulsate with life and passion.

"Having fun together is what it's all about, right?" Erik kisses me under the ear, and as I'm feeling goose bumps, his words sink in, triggering an unexpected but welcome chain of thoughts.

"Yes, that's what it's all about!"

"What?" He looks at me, confused.

"Love Birds." I'm grinning, overflowing with excitement. I can't believe I missed that.

"I'm lost. Please explain."

"Erik." I hold his face with both my hands. "You were right when you said it wasn't dark here but *inspiring.* I think I solved our problem with the game."

"Our lack of money, time, and a crew the size of Scorpio Games?"

I smile. "No. The concept itself. 'Having fun together is what it's all about,'" I quote Erik back to him. "We knew this was our point with the app. Getting people to have fun together before going on a date." He nods, showing that he is following. "But what if the playing field, where all the birds are, was a playground?"

He thinks about it for a second, and then our minds connect and become one.

"Yes! That can work. Then the multiplayer matches and private mini games are attractions in the playground."

"Exactly! It's about feeling the way you feel when you are a child. You go to a playground to meet others, play, and make friends. Some might become best friends. Some might even get married later in life."

I sense his excitement. The shadows have left his face. He is fully replenished again, his eyes sparkling.

"All players start as anonymous birds," he says. "And as you win with your team, you learn something new about the other team members."

"Yes," I say enthusiastically. "If we're talking about a playground, the challenges can be inspired by classic children's outdoor games, like marbles, Capture the Flag..."

Erik claps. "Perfect!"

We laugh, now springing, dancing, climbing, and balancing on bars while brainstorming. We talk about the two-player mini games—tic-tac-toe, chess, checkers—and monetization. Everything clicks together like a puzzle we can finally assemble. It's sublime.

"We'll simulate the stages of a real relationship and give people the chance to fall for someone before dating them," I say, walking on a wooden wave and jumping into Erik's arms when I reach the end.

"You're a genius, Sol." He spins me in his arms before putting me down.

"*We* are geniuses together."

Erik kisses me, and I'm so happy, I could fly.

Now we just have to make the dream come true.

Twenty-Four

Eight days until Scorpio Games' Christmas Party. There have been no more Fun Season events since the Escape Room + Pub Night. All that is left is to prepare for the talent show—Group Lars's final challenge.

I thought Erik wouldn't want to show up at Scorpio after everything that's happened, but he said he would attend to support me, and I gladly accepted his offer. For the talent show, he convinced me to choose something to represent my culture. So I suggested a Brazilian partner dance: *forró*.

When a skilled man is directing me, I can dance with grace. My cousins have brought me to *forró* clubs several times, where random guys invited me to dance to the live music. I could usually put on a show when my partner knew what he was doing. So the challenge here was to teach Erik. He watched a few videos, but it was so hard for him that as the days passed, we neglected the training entirely.

Erik's full focus has been on the app. In fact, he is working so hard I basically never see him away from the computer. Despite our close connection not so long ago, our relationship has taken a step back. Perhaps four or five.

We live together. We talk to each other. But there is no time for sex. I sleep in my room, and he sleeps in his. It almost feels like we are no longer a couple.

I hate this new distance. I come home from work, and we work together. Then I go to bed, and he stays awake, working. I wake up and he is on the computer again. I'm not even sure he sleeps. He looks like a zombie. He doesn't cook, doesn't eat, and doesn't go to the gym anymore. All he talks about is code and Love Birds.

He is obsessed.

Is he working so hard because this is how we stay together in the long term? Or is he running away again, as he did after our kiss in Tivoli?

I've been patient, understanding—or trying to. But our conversation at the playground haunts me. It was our last good day. Was it truly *good* though? Or were our kisses, our ideas, like a pretty cover for the wreckage underneath?

Maybe now he's letting go…

Maybe he's doing to me exactly what he did to Lena, neglecting our relationship because he fears it will end the same way, with me going back to my home country.

I'm sitting at the dining table, nibbling on a slice of toast with no appetite, while Erik types frantically on his laptop. It's been days since I stopped working on the project, and he hasn't even noticed.

Suddenly, a wave of anger rises in me, and I'm unable to stay quiet. "I'm tired of this, Erik."

His hands freeze, hovering over his keyboard, and he looks at me. "Tired of what?"

"You ignoring me."

He leans back in his chair with a sigh. He's not surprised. He's been waiting for me to confront him.

"I'm sorry, Sol." His voice sounds tired, like he knew he owed me an apology but simply didn't have time for it.

I keep staring at him, my arms crossed on the table. He rubs his red, watery eyes. He will go down due to the stress. It's what has been keeping me supportive all these days—my concern for him. But by indulging in his harmful agenda, accepting this distance, I'm hurting us both.

"You spend day and night on this project as if I don't exist," I say.

He looks down, silent, and I wait.

"I know I'm not being fair to you," he says.

"So why are you doing that?" I keep my eyes on him, and he still avoids me. He looks embarrassed, but not entirely apologetic.

"You know why."

I take a deep breath, trying to stop the tears from coming out. "Yeah, I know you think I'm going back to Brazil, but I'm trying to figure out if it's because you don't believe I'm getting the promotion or because you don't want me to get it."

Erik reaches for my hand on the table. His gaze meets mine, and he frowns, intense. "I want you to get it, okay? And I believe you can. I've just been thinking...you should do it without me." He swallows hard. "Look at me, Sol. I'm a mess. And it's not because of you."

I shake my head, pursing my lips. "You're obsessed. Even if it's not about us, you can't keep going like this."

He runs a hand over his forehead and his wild, untrimmed beard. "It's my weakness. I'm sorry. I told myself I would finish this project and nothing would stop me, and now I literally *can't* stop before it's over."

I've pushed him. I told him to not surrender, but my wish came true as a botched spell. "Is this how it will be every time you're on a deadline?"

He squeezes my hand. "I'm sorry, Sol. I'm an idiot. I know."

"What should I do about the talent show if you're not going with me?"

I have one week before I'm onstage, and I have absolutely no clue what I can do that will remotely impress Lars.

"You'll figure it out," Erik says. "It's going to be good for you to be there without me for once. You can use the opportunity to show them something about the real you."

I frown. "What is that supposed to mean—'the real me'? Because I lied about us? Because I've been 'hiding behind you' all this time?"

I'm not a sweet person today. Erik may apologize and justify his behavior, but I simply don't have the patience left for his hurtful remarks.

"Well, you did lie, Sol. We both did." His voice is also not exactly sweet. "You've only decided to do that Brazilian dance because I told you it was a good idea. But you keep being embarrassed of your origins, thinking we Danish people can't understand you or welcome you the way you are."

I snort. "Easy for the privileged white man to say."

"This is not about privilege, Sol. It's about you standing up for yourself and who you are." Erik leans forward, his light blue eyes hard like diamonds. "You don't need me. You don't have to be more Danish for Lars to like you. Fuck that. Fuck him. Just show them the fucking amazing person you are, and screw them if they don't like you."

I stare at the crumbs on my plate. He thinks I'm a fucking amazing person. Why does that not seem enough right now, in every way?

"I just can't afford to gamble the way you can," I say.

That's the difference between us. Erik will always be where he belongs no matter what he does or how he plays his "I don't give a shit" attitude. He will always be in his own country while I will be away from mine and at risk of being kicked out of his. I will always have to watch him be at home while I struggle to adapt and belong.

He is right about one thing though. I need to be a separate person from him if I want to succeed in Denmark. I can't let his concerns and dreams get in the way of mine. Especially now that I have seen how he will dive into his ambitions and leave me in second place, regardless of all the sweet things he said that day in the playground.

My phone rings. It's my dad. Glad for the opportunity to leave the table, I lock myself in my bedroom and sit on the bed to answer the video call.

"Hey, Dad," I say, happy that he called. I could use some advice.

Just seeing his face makes my heart warm up—and then become tight and small. As he smiles and says hi, I realize how much I miss him, with his Nike cap and Palmeiras T-shirt, drinking beer on the couch, both of us laughing at the ugly names he keeps finding for the referees when his beloved team is losing. My creativity for finding alternative swear words came from him, as he had to watch his language constantly at my mom's request.

I thought I didn't miss my life in Brazil, but homesickness comes crashing down on me, taking my breath away.

I realize I miss those sunny weekends when we would barbecue in the backyard, gathering the family and the neighbors. I miss the sense of community we always had in our neighborhood. I miss being there with them—watching soccer with my dad, helping Mom in the kitchen, and sitting with Larissa and my cousins in plastic chairs outside to eat beef on a stick and drink Guaraná Antarctica while listening to the corny Brazilian country music my mom enjoys. We'd sing along, loud, until my uncles would come and dance with us. I was the worst *forró* dancer among the girls, but only because they were so good.

"How are you doing, Sol?" Dad's voice comes out of my headphones, loud and clear as if he's sitting next to me. "It's been a while since we talked."

I give him a smile, but what comes out is a sob. I discreetly wipe my eyes on my sleeve, but, of course, he notices it.

"What's wrong, sweetheart?"

His protective-dad tone and the fact that we can't hug only makes me shed more tears. But I keep my composure, barely. "I'm fine, Dad, don't worry."

"Of course you're not fine." His face moves closer to the screen, and the camera makes his nose look disproportionately big. "Tell me what's going on. Are you homesick?"

I nod, sniffing.

"Are you thinking about coming back?"

I can't deny I've considered that option over the past few

weeks. The more distant Erik became, the more I felt the need to be with my family. I realized this would be my life in Denmark. Whenever Erik is not with me, I'll feel lonely and separated from the rest of the world.

"I...can't go back, Dad." I look up to stop the tears that are pooling. "I'm..." But I can't finish my sentence.

"You're in love. I know."

I look at him wide-eyed. He knows I've been dating Erik because the gossip never ends in my family, but we never talked about my feelings. "And you're okay with me dating a Viking who lives on the other half of the world?"

Dad chuckles, and *God*, I've missed the sound of his laughter. I realize I've been avoiding my family to not feel the distance as much. I told myself it was to not have them interfere with my life and my decisions, but I was in fact trying to protect myself on a much deeper level.

This is not so bad though. It's comforting to know that my dad is one call away. Talking like this makes me feel like I'm not alone, no matter how far we are. I get to choose when I want to see my family, and they will be there. *Here.* Right in front of me, in my Danish home.

"We'll support you, sweetie, no matter what you decide," he says, confirming my conclusions. More tears fall, and I smile. It dawns on me that he is never going to judge me—none of them will—or remind me that before I came, he asked if I considered that my Nordic adventure might not work out.

My mom keeps reminding me I can have my old room back because it's the best way she knows to tell me I will always have a place in her house. They want the best for me.

Now I have to figure out what that is.

"We're having problems right now," I tell Dad in a low, shy voice.

"Can you fix them?"

I think for a moment. "I don't know… I mean, we're both focusing on our careers, and we like to say we support each other, but the truth is, chasing those dreams is only making us hurt each other."

Dad scratches his stubble, thinking.

"No couple lives off promises, Sol. The success of a family, even one made of only two people, depends on professional realization. It's like they say, *Amor não enche barriga.*" He quotes a popular Brazilian saying that means: "Love doesn't put food on the table."

I nod, acknowledging that my dad is right. Both Erik and I know this, and that's why we have to put ourselves first.

"So I should focus on my career," I say, more like an affirmation than a question. The air gets thick, almost unbreathable, when I think about leaving Erik. But I can't let him be the reason I breathe.

"You should," Dad agrees, then smiles. "Love is a dance, Sol, and your partner can guide you, but you can't let him carry you all the way. You need to be in control too. And you should know your moves so well you can always dance without him."

His metaphor makes me smile. My dad's wisdom never fails.

I'm going to fight for my career. For the Danish dream I came seeking. I will call Chiara and ask if I can stay at her place until the Christmas party so I can give Erik the space he needs—the break we *both* need.

I will go to the talent show. And I will dance without Erik.

Twenty-Five

Eight days later, we leave our desks at the end of the workday and head downstairs to the Christmas party. I go before Chiara, who is slowly packing her things, and when we meet at the decorated office space reserved for the social event, Chiara grabs my shoulders, flashing a radiant smile.

"I got the Game Designer job in Stockholm!"

We both shriek, and I hug her, saying, "Congratulations!"

We've talked a lot the past few days when I was sleeping at her place. I shared the joys and turbulences of my relationship with Erik, and she told me more about what had been going on between her and Anika. She listened to my advice to not give up on the two of them and kept applying for jobs in Stockholm. I'm so glad she succeeded and that she and Anika will share an apartment there.

On a selfish level, I'm sad to lose the only friend I have in Copenhagen, but the universe would have been unfair if it had denied her and Anika the opportunity to give their love—and their careers—a try.

My smile falters, however. I can't deny I'm jealous. But I try not to blame the universe for being unfair when it came to Erik and me drifting apart. It did its part to make things more complicated for us, but ultimately, it was us who decided we should follow our separate paths.

It wasn't something we agreed upon directly. There was no talk, no official breakup. I just left to stay with Chiara, and he was okay with that. He didn't text me. I didn't call him. We let ourselves focus on our jobs because until we're okay with our own situations, we won't be okay together.

And I'm starting to accept we might never be okay together.

Not that it's an easy thing to accept. It's crushing. My mood swings are a constant reminder of how all of me misses Erik. And how I will be okay without him.

I have to be.

And I'll prove that tonight.

The hall is filled with people sitting on the sofas or on the stairs, serving cups with beer, soda, and mulled wine, and gathering in front of the improvised stage, waiting for their colleagues to embarrass themselves.

The Christmas tree is decorated with beetles from our most famous game and scorpions like the one in the company logo. We all hang out for a while, Christmas songs playing through the speakers, drinks and snacks abounding. Then the talent show begins, and George and Alex are the first couple onstage. They entertain us with a lively performance of "It's Raining Men."

When they are done and people are applauding and whooping, my name is announced. With my heart in my throat, I climb onto the stage and stand behind the curtains. It's the first time I'll do something as attention-getting as dance in front of a crowd. And not just *any* crowd—coworkers who will look at me every single day and remember how I've embarrassed myself onstage.

Oh, Jesus, why am I doing this?

To get promoted, I answer. *To get your dream job.*

To be yourself.

I chuckle inwardly, staring at the silky curtains. I haven't practiced enough; I've switched to samba so I can dance alone. The thing is, when you know how to dance samba, you just do it. You improvise. All I have to do is pretend I'm at a Carnival parade in Brazil.

It's a dance that can be perceived as sexy. You move your hips a lot and your butt shakes as you move your feet to the rhythm of the drums. When you dance samba, it's normal to wear colorful, glittery outfits that cover almost no skin.

I'm wearing my highest high heels and a short green sequined dress. I know I will call attention to myself. But I want to show off dancing like this. It's part of my culture, and I'm proud of it.

When the curtains part, I'm greeted by applause and expectant, drunk faces. I swallow hard, losing courage as I scan the room full of people looking at me. *Please, start the music, or I'll drench my clothes in sweat before I even start moving.*

The drums begin to play, and I press the Start button inside me, forgetting my nervousness and embarking on my samba trip. I try not to look at the crowd, I just dance as if my cousins are behind me, making their own moves, having the time of their lives, and my uncles are in the front row, cheering us on.

Soon I'm letting go, led by the rhythm, enjoying myself. People seem to be enjoying it too. I see a few trying to copy me and dance to the beat, and I smile because their movements are so jerky and awkward. I calm myself with the thought that *I* am not embarrassing myself. I'm just different from them.

And that's good, right?

I'm having fun, and everyone else seems to be having fun too by the end of the song. The final drumming echoes through the walls, and I bow as everyone applauds. *I did it. It was great!*

I'm about to leave the stage when another song starts to play. A tune featuring an accordion and a rhythmic regional beat.

The *forró* song Erik and I had been rehearsing.

I look around, confused. Did I tell them to add this song to the playlist when I thought Erik was going to join me? No… I'm pretty sure I didn't. But then how—

Erik emerges from behind the curtains, and I watch him walk toward me. *What the hell is happening?*

My mouth is hanging open when he positions himself in front of me.

"What are you doing here?" I whisper, wide-eyed.

His reply is a meaningful smirk. One that says, *What do you think I'm doing?*

His left hand holds my right hand, and his right arm goes around my back. He pulls me closer until my chest is pressed against his. I lose my breath. In *forró*, there is no space between bodies.

Feeling the warmth of his muscular torso through the fabric of my dress fills me with desire. My left arm is embracing him at shoulder height, and though our skin is not in contact, this is as close as we can get.

Well, not quite close *enough.* My groin heats up with the way our hips click together. It's scary how fast my body responds to his touch. How quickly it remembers the pleasure and forgets we are not walking in *that* direction.

But we are dancing. Erik starts with the first basic step we learned—one step forward, one step back. We are nailing it like we didn't in our few rehearsals. I'm in awe. *What on Earth is happening?*

Smoothly, he changes to the second basic step—left-left-right-right. He is actually moving his hips. Then he holds both my hands and tries the third basic step, which we didn't practice. It feels easy enough now, both of us opening sideways and stepping back, mirroring each other, until we are back at our starting position.

Suddenly, we are spinning, doing the complicated step he found nice but claimed would be impossible to learn so quickly. I tried to teach him, but he wasn't very patient. Now here he is, dancing with confidence, not afraid to move and be vulnerable. We are caught in a tight embrace, our hips swaying in one flow. It's sexy, fun, and breathlessly intimate.

Dancing here with Erik, who has clearly practiced so much he could be one of the Brazilian men I would find in a club, I feel a heightened sensory experience. I'm touching his solid muscles, observing his mouth, smelling his skin, moving with his guidance. It feels as though all our days apart never existed.

And the time away only increased my longing for him.

I want to touch his face, kiss his neck, and feel his fingers on my naked back. He spins me, and I'm back into his arms. Every boomerang move is a chance to be reunited and feel the butterflies in my stomach assaulting me in a delicious way.

"This is impressive," I whisper to him as we dance. "Who did you practice with?"

"A stiff cousin and a pregnant woman with an eight-month belly. I don't recommend it."

I laugh. I'm so proud of him. And I can't believe he did this for me.

The song ends, and we hear applause roaring. Erik takes my hand, and once we are off the stage, many people acknowledge our good performance. We squeeze through the crowd, trying to find a quiet place where we can talk, but Lars blocks our path and claps right in front of us with a huge smile on his face.

"That was excellent. Very entertaining." He bows his head at me. I thank him with a smile. "Erik, you're a great dancer," Lars says, and Erik laughs dismissively.

"Let's not exaggerate."

"Were both of them Brazilian dances?" Lars asks me, and he looks delighted to have witnessed something so out of what is ordinary for him. Maybe I *was* wrong about him. Maybe I didn't need all the lies.

"Yes," I answer enthusiastically. "The first was samba, and the second is called *forró*."

"Amazing." He puts a hand on Erik's shoulder, still smiling. "Can I have a word with you, Storm?"

Erik looks surprised. He blinks at me, then at Lars.

"Eh…sure."

"Great. Come with me."

And just like that, Lars takes Erik away from me before I get the chance to ask him what this whole dance thing was about. Lars couldn't know we have been living apart, not talking for an entire week, but I can't help but feel frustrated.

Why did he have to talk to Erik in private now? What could he want to say that I couldn't hear?

I hold my breath. *Could this have anything to do with the idea they're stealing from Erik?* Is Lars going to tell him they will not do that after all?

My stomach flips, full of hope. Maybe everything will turn out all right for both of us.

I move through the crowd, trying to spot them, but I don't see them anywhere. Did they go upstairs to a meeting room? I stop myself at the stairs. Erik will tell me what it was about, of course. I just need to wait until he finds me.

I sit down with a cup of mulled wine and wait for what seems like endless minutes. I can't be patient though. My head is spinning. I need to know what is happening.

Today is my last opportunity to convince Lars to choose me for the game director position. We all go on Christmas holiday tomorrow, and then we'll know who he is hiring in early January.

I enter the corridor where the bathrooms are and find Martin leaning on the wall, pressing paper against his nose. He's grimacing. Bleeding.

"What happened to you?" I ask.

"*Erik* happened," Martin says with an angry nasal voice.

An involuntary smile stretches my lips. "Did he punch you?" My expression then changes to concern. "What did you say to him?"

Martin gives me a bloody smile. He's so full of his usual disdain, my insides twist. "You don't know, do you?"

"Know what?" Fear assaults me. I try to keep breathing.

"That you're not getting the game director position."

My body turns to ice, but my heart keeps pulsing, faster and faster.

Shit.

Shit.

FUCK.

"*You* did," I say, because it's the only possible conclusion. That's why Erik punched Martin and left in anger.

But Martin shakes his head, squeezing the bloody piece of toilet paper against his nostrils and smiling wide. "No, Sol, I didn't get it either."

"*What?* Then who did?" My heart hammers like the drums of a samba parade.

Martin snorts with contempt. "Erik got the job."

Twenty-Six

"You're lying," I say to Martin, in denial.

"I'm not," he replies, and his dry tone makes it clear he wished he was.

This can't be happening. Erik wasn't even running for the position. He joined the events as *my boyfriend*, and then suddenly he got the position *I* wanted?

Fuck this. Fuck Lars.

I rub my face, feeling an intense need to scream.

"How long has he known?" I need to know if Erik betrayed me too.

"Lars told him just now," Martin says with his usual expression of disgust. He massages the bridge of his nose and grimaces even more. "Then the fucking bastard broke my nose."

"Why?" I can't understand how Martin was suddenly involved.

"He left the meeting room, came to the bathroom, and I was here. He punched me for 'all the stuff I did,'" Martin says with a scornful smile. "He should have punched Lars though. The decision was his. I didn't even tell him about your lies."

I shake my head. "I don't understand… Where is Erik now?"

"He left."

"Left?" I raise my eyebrows. Did Erik simply go home without talking to me?

"He's pissed." Martin tries to take a deep breath but instantly returns the paper to his nose when he resumes bleeding. He tries to give me a smug look. "I guess you were a real couple after all."

I need a moment to digest everything he's said. Nothing makes sense.

"So, Erik got angry and left? But he was offered a great job…"

"To work on his own project, yes." Martin's voice rises, more nasal and scornful than ever. "And yet, he said no. Because of you."

My eyebrows climb my forehead. "He said no?"

If what Martin is saying is true, Erik just got the opportunity of a lifetime. He can make his app happen. He can direct it at Scorpio Games and turn it into whatever he dreams it could be. He can have the money and resources to do a much better and more successful product than he could ever do on his own.

It's ridiculous to say no.

And yet he said no because of *me*?

I lean against the wall, trembling.

He knew it would destroy me. He knew I would go back to Brazil, because how could I stay here without the job I wanted and knowing *he* got it? Having to work in the same company as him in a role I no longer believe matches my skills?

I laugh like a maniac, and Martin looks at me a bit scared. How dare I think things were going to be fine! It's a ridiculously bad situation. Erik saying no to the job doesn't fix anything.

Maybe him coming to dance with me meant something, but the meaning got lost in the news we just received. The news that changes everything.

I have no wish to work at Scorpio anymore. How can I work for a man who dragged us through the most unorthodox hiring process ever just to end up choosing someone who wasn't even in the picture to begin with?

I simply can't imagine returning to Scorpio Games after the holidays. Especially when Chiara won't be here and Martin will continue to sneer at me every day.

I'm angry. I'm hurt. I'm feeling worthless.

"Erik was an idiot for rejecting the position," Martin says, and I must agree. Erik gave Martin what he wanted because it's obvious that Lars will pick him as his second option. And Martin knows that. It's why he's unbearably smug even with his nose bleeding. "Erik was an idiot for having so much consideration for a liar."

I look up, meeting Martin's gaze. I'm a ticking bomb. He's lucky his nose is already broken, or I might have aimed for his jaw.

"Fuck you, asshole," I pronounce every word clearly. Then I turn around and walk away with feverish determination.

I fear nothing anymore. It's time to tell some truths. I'm going to do what I should have done long ago.

I walk through the party so determined, I don't care who I bump into. Erik is nowhere. He really left.

I can't go home yet though.

I spot Lars and run toward him. I grip his shoulder and turn him around.

"We need to talk."

He sees the fire in my eyes and nods.

We go upstairs, where it's empty and quiet, and sit in a small glass room intended for private meetings. I get straight to the point, and I'm not even feeling nervous. I'm just eager to let it all out.

"I have a couple of things to say. First, I quit."

He raises his eyebrows, though not overly surprised. "Is that because of the talk I just had with Erik?"

I smile with no humor. "Well, you gave him the position you had promised to either me or Martin, even after I did everything right and impressed you. But apparently, you only had eyes for him."

Lars is opening his mouth to reply, but I'm not giving him a chance. I don't want to hear his lousy excuses. *I* am doing the talking today.

"Which leads me to the second thing I want to say." I raise two fingers, gazing intensely at him, as calm and confident as I never have been in front of my boss. "We lied to you. And this is all on me. Erik and I weren't a couple, we just lived together. I brought him to our Fun Season meetings because I felt pressured to have a boyfriend. I felt you would give me more consideration if I had strong ties to Denmark. A reason to stay."

"You didn't have to lie about that, Sol," he says, and it's like he knew the truth already. Martin said he didn't reveal my lies, so maybe Erik did.

"I know that now," I answer.

When I moved to Denmark, I wanted to find myself. I wanted to be my own person, separate from my family and my culture. But that didn't mean I had to become someone I'm not.

"I was too afraid to be myself," I tell Lars. "Too afraid of how I would be perceived by you, with all your standards and preferences. But I shouldn't have bothered. Because in the end, it didn't matter. I still wasn't good enough for you."

"This is not about you, Sol," he says, looking mildly affected. "And I heard you. I thought about what you said at that meeting when you were angry that we were going to work on an idea you claimed belonged to Storm." Lars leans forward, his fingers interlaced on the table. "I realized I made a mistake with Storm. I shouldn't have let him leave Scorpio to work on his project. I should have promoted him and let him make it *here*."

I lean back, studying him. I'm glad he could see his mistake. It's a good reason to have chosen Erik now. Erik deserves the consideration. The recognition.

He should have said yes.

"Yet you didn't consider how I would feel about all this," I say because I can't help it. I'm hurt.

Lars nods, looking down at the table with something that resembles humility. "I know. And I'm sorry."

I nod, accepting his apology in silence. "We were pretending at the start, you know... Erik and me." I look at my own hands, suddenly shy but wanting to let it all out. "And then this whole Fun Season thing brought us together, and what was fake became the truest thing in my life."

Thinking about Erik makes me teary. Because he will be nothing but a memory once I embark on my trip back to Brazil.

But just because I can't be happy here doesn't mean that Erik shouldn't.

"You need to convince him to accept the position, Lars," I say firmly. "It is the right thing. I can't stay here anymore, but that doesn't matter. I wasn't happy at Scorpio, that is the truth." I look down at my green glittery nails. "I hate licorice and liver pâté, by the way. The Strøget is my favorite place in the city. I find black clothes boring, and I love flashy accessories. I suck at quiz games, I only recently started biking, and I'm far from a healthy eater. Ah, and I've never been to Noma. I wouldn't eat ants or live sea creatures even if someone paid me a million bucks."

He laughs, and I let my lips stretch into a smile.

"You're a wonderful person, Sol." Wait, has he learned to pronounce my name correctly? "You are unique and lovely the way you are, and you don't have to change that for me or anyone else. I'm glad Storm found you and you found him. You should be together."

My face goes blank. It's too late now.

"Tell me something, Sol." Lars leans forward again. Yes, he says Sol with the proper accent now! "What is your dream job? Tell me about what you enjoy doing the most."

I think for a moment. If he had asked me this question at our last one-on-one in this room, I would have told him that my dream job was to be a game director at this company.

Why did I want that? Probably because of the salary, the security of a full-time job at a big studio, the creative freedom I would have in the role, and the decision-making power I would be given over a project. But that is not the answer that comes from within. I think about how much I enjoyed working on Love Birds…

"I want to be an indie developer," I tell him. "I want to make my own games and apps with a small passionate team, being free to innovate and have a high level of influence over the whole process."

Lars gives me a large smile. "Now, that is a good answer, Sol. Now I can let you go knowing that I'm doing *you* a favor."

My mouth twitches up, moved by a strange spark of happiness growing in my chest, near my heart. "When can I leave then?"

"You don't have to come back in January if you don't want to."

"There is no notice period?"

He waves his hand dismissively. "Let's not worry about that."

"Thank you, Lars." I'm about to get up, but something keeps me in the chair. "And please, try talking to Erik again, okay?"

We will meet at home at some point. After all, I have to pack my stuff. But I don't want to talk about any of this with Erik. Maybe I can go when he is not there so we can avoid each other entirely. Seeing him now would only make everything harder.

I get up, but Lars is not done. "I want to tell you how our conversation went."

I sit back down, listening eagerly.

"Being a game director at Scorpio Games is also not his dream. That was clear during our chat. And he showed me the app."

"The...app?"

"He finished it."

I stand up. "No way." He could do that in *one week*—while also learning how to dance *forró*?

Wow.

"He did," Lars says, smiling. "And it's fantastic, Sol. The two of you did a wonderful job."

Okay, so Lars knows about my participation, that I'm a traitor.

Who cares? I quit already. And he doesn't seem bothered. In fact, he looks strangely...proud? Amazed?

"We couldn't possibly use the idea in another way. It's *your* idea, and it should remain yours. So, my proposal to him was..." He sits straighter, and my heart is killing me, pumping at the frantic rhythm of my expectation. "I told Storm that Scorpio Games will publish Love Birds if he agrees to a partnership between our companies. Tropical Storm Interactive will remain the creators of the game, while Scorpio will simply invest in it."

My jaw hits the floor. Holy shit.

HOLY. SHIT.

I stand up again. "Are you kidding me?"

"No, I'm not."

And then an important detail gets processed in my brain. "*Tropical* Storm Interactive? Not just Storm Interactive?"

"He changed the name of his company." Lars shrugs.

To include me.

OH. MY. GOD.

Erik loves me.

"I need to go now." I head for the door and glance back

at Lars. I turn the knob and look suspiciously at him again. "You *are* serious, right?"

Lars smiles. "He said yes, Sol." I'm on my way out, but his voice stops me. "Don't forget to take the stuff you have on your desk. And make sure to turn off your computer."

"Sure." I nod hurriedly. "Thanks, Lars. See you."

I don't even wait for his farewell. I rush to my desk to get my stuff as quickly as possible so I can go home to Erik.

I pack my things and sit in front of my work computer to delete any remaining personal files and then turn it off. As my desktop is always clean, I instantly notice the new icon in the middle of the screen.

LOVE BIRDS.

My heart thumps in my ears. Erik shamelessly hacked me. He knows the password I use to unlock all my devices. I giggle into my hands in delighted disbelief.

I click on it and the app opens.

It's the welcome screen we designed. I'm asked to make an account and fill in some personal information. Then I'm on the main screen, my bird avatar walking around in a bird playground surrounded by other identical birds, each one with an anonymous, numbered label.

One of the birds has a name though: ERIK_STORM. We are Acquaintances. A few seconds later, I get a Friend Request from him, which I accept. We are Friends now.

I roam around a little more, wondering what I should do, and a notification pops up in the middle of the screen, reading:

ERIK_STORM has answered your question!
VIEW / IGNORE

I haven't asked him a question. But maybe I did, in the real world? I click on VIEW.

YOU asked ERIK_STORM: Why are you here if you hate dating apps?

ERIK_STORM answered: I don't hate dating apps. It was thanks to Cinder that I found you. And it was right. We are a match.

I smile, my heart pumping so hard, my stomach so full of butterflies, that I can't stay still in the chair.

The app is ready. It's beautiful. It even has music and sound effects. And we can keep working on it. Just us and whoever else we want to bring on the team. We are funded. We are secure.

Another notification pops up.

ERIK_STORM has sent you a Date Request!

"Meet me where we first met."

ACCEPT / IGNORE

Smiling from ear to ear, I click on ACCEPT and get the message: Congratulations! ERIK_STORM is now your Date.

I laugh alone in the dark, sitting at the desk that no longer belongs to me. Tears of happiness stream down my cheeks, and I'm almost getting up to rush to the English pub when my phone vibrates.

It's not him. I have a bunch of unread notifications from my family, as usual.

This time, though, I don't ignore them. I'm in a hurry to meet my date, but I can squeeze in a couple of minutes to answer my messages.

Dad: How did it all go? Did you get the job you wanted?

Sol: No… I got the job I needed. ♥

Mariana: Tell me your HOT boyfriend did something DELICIOUSLY SEXY (and a little romantic) to get you back!

Sol: He became a forró dancer and made a dating app to ask me out. All in one week. Pretty sexy if you ask me!

Mariana: 😮 👄 🌶 🔥

Mariana: If you come back to sleep in this bunk bed with me after this, I'll kick you out of your own room!

Sol: Don't worry. The room is all yours. I intend to stay right here.

Larissa: My family will join yours for Christmas Eve 🎄 and you're FaceTime-invited from 11pm–6am CET for some virtual turkey, dad jokes (involving the pavê dessert of course), corny karaoke, and a Secret Santa with cheap-looking gifts under R$20. RSVP so I can put your name in the Draw Name Generator.

Sol: Count me in! Even if I go to Jutland with Erik, I won't miss that.

Larissa: Are the two of you Thor and Natalie Portman again?

Sol: You could say so.

Larissa: Nice! And cool that you can be at two parties at once and drop out when the jokes become unbearable.

Sol: Not "at once" because you can bet Danish Christmas celebrations don't run that late. They don't eat dinner at midnight like us.

Larissa: Well, I'm jealous anyway. Your Secret Santa gift at our party will not be ugly socks or a crochet magazine. You'll get a GIFT CARD.

Sol: To some restaurant or shop I can't visit.

Larissa: Then you'll give it to me. Hee-hee.

Sol: Or I can make you take pictures of the entire store so I can pick what I want and then make you internationally ship the gift to me for five times the price of the product.

Larissa: You're okay, right?

Sol: With getting a Brazilian gift shipped here? Totally. Include some gummies in the package, please.

Larissa: I meant in general.

Sol: I'm better than ever.

Mom: Should I worry about you, Sol?

Mom: It's fine to come back, you know...

Mom: But it's also fine to stay.

Sol: Thanks, Mom. I'm where I'm supposed to be.

Not quite yet.

I look at the clock. Then I take my things and leave at once.

I find Erik in the English pub standing by the counter. He is as Viking-looking as when I first saw him. But even hotter.

And I have absolutely nothing against Vikings now.

I walk toward him, both of us smiling, and when I reach him, he kisses me passionately, lifting me off the ground. I laugh against his lips, and we kiss more.

"I'm so glad you came," he says. "I'm deeply sorry, Sol, for shutting you out, and for Lars—"

I put a finger over his lips, shutting him up. "I know, Erik. I know it all, and I'm so happy I could dance right here, in front of all these people. With you."

Erik's smile brightens the whole room. He leans closer, a hand cupping my cheek.

"I love you, Sol Carvalho," he whispers in my ear. Hearing his deep voice uttering those words—and saying my name in such a delicious accent—fills me with so many emotions I almost can't breathe. My vision gets foggy, blocked by the tears emerging in my eyes. I grip his nape, pulling him toward me, and he kisses me. Again and again.

"I love you, Erik Storm," I say with every ounce of truth in me. "And I'm going home with you."

With my face between his hands, he gives me another quick, powerful kiss. Then he puts some distance between our bodies.

"Let's travel to Brazil in the summer," he says excitedly, playing with my hair.

I smile. My family will be delighted to hear we're coming. "Only if Rio is in the itinerary," I reply.

"Absolutely. It's about time I do a north to south trip in your country," he says, referencing what we talked about on our first date here.

"And we'll be backpacking surfer dudes. No luxury."

He laughs. "I couldn't agree more." His fingers trace over the edges of my face. "But we won't be the unattractive kind, of course."

"No, of course not. You'll be the hottest Viking dude around even with flower swimming shorts and lobster-red skin."

His hoarse laugh gives me delicious chills. I kiss his sexy lips, but he stops me to speak again.

"Christmas at my parents' place? They can't wait to meet you."

I smile. "Do they know I exist?"

Erik raises an eyebrow in his classic *Are you seriously asking me that?* expression. He then kisses the corner of my lips. "What do you think I talked to them about all those days I spent in Jutland?"

My grin broadens, and he keeps kissing me. I slide my fingers through his hair, enjoying its softness. I imagine Erik opening up with his parents about his feelings for me. It makes me want him even more. I glue his body to mine, not caring that we are in a public place, probably being watched by the people sitting at the bar.

"They will love you," Erik says in my ear, the tip of his nose tickling my skin and giving me goose bumps. "And we'll take care of you. You'll belong here."

I pass my arms around his waist, hugging him tight. "I already do."

He touches his forehead to mine, and we smile at each other, silent for a couple of precious seconds, in which we tell each other everything we want to say without uttering a single word.

Lastly, he stretches out his right hand as if expecting me to give him a handshake. "Partners? For real this time?"

I look at his hand, smiling. "Don't you think mixing love and work is a bit wild?"

He stares seriously at me. "I won't let you down again. Ever. We'll be Team Sol & Storm to the end."

My smile returns, radiating out of my gleeful, sunny soul. "I think we're a great team."

"So…deal?" He moves the hand up a few inches, impatient.

I shake it. "Deal."

★★★★★

Look for Paula Ottoni's next romantic comedy, coming Summer 2025!

Acknowledgments

My writing journey started in Brazil when I was a teenage girl with a big dream. I faced countless obstacles chasing that dream. I couldn't stop writing, so manuscripts kept piling up on my desk next to the homework I never neglected, and I was brave enough to put myself out there despite my insecurities because I knew where I wanted to get.

And—AAHH—I got here now, thanks to so many people! I'd need several pages to list everyone who was part of my decade-long journey, so I'll limit myself to giving a shout out to those who mostly contributed to this moment in my career—my first traditionally published book in English!

I need to start with my husband, Emil. Our love story could be a novel—and it's not this one! But the story of a Brazilian game designer who falls for a (hot, smart, and strong-willed) Dane wouldn't exist if I hadn't found you. I have no words to thank you for your unlimited support of my career. For not only hearing me talk endlessly about my books, but for being hands-on too, reading, critiquing, and revising everything I write because you believe so much in me.

A thank-you the size of Brazil to my brilliant editor, Stacy Boyd, who liked my pitch on DVPit, made me an offer of publication the day I turned thirty (BEST GIFT EVER), and made sure this story reached its best shape. A huge thanks to my amazing agent, Ginger Clark, for believing in my work and always being there with great advice when I need it. My warm, effusive gratitude to everyone at Harlequin and Afterglow Books who worked on this book: Will Tyler, Katherine Rushby, Shana Mongroo, Sara Marinac, and the illustrator Camila Gray and art director Amy Wetton for the cover, which is so beautiful and matches the story so well!

I owe so much to the writing community on Facebook, Twitter, and Instagram. I'm incredibly grateful to all the people I met online who offered valuable feedback on my pages and query. If we've ever talked about writing or critiqued each other's work, feel embraced and know I'm rooting for you—we're all in this together! A special thanks to the writer friends I've made: Heather Ryder, CJ Connolly, Sandra Negrete, and Anna Raven. Your opinions on my early drafts were greatly appreciated, and I hope we can meet in person someday!

I couldn't forget to mention the Brazilian readers and bookish people I've met over the years, in person and online, who read and reviewed my books in Portuguese and keep looking forward to what I'll write next. I hope you liked the piece of Brazil I've sent out into the world. To all those who moved to another country—I hope you've connected with Sol's journey and that you also find belonging if you haven't yet.

I wouldn't have felt so at home in Denmark if it wasn't for

the Danish family I now have. *Tusind tak* to all the Geers, Juels and Rasmussens who took me in as a daughter and sister and make me feel so much hygge. Here, I became a mother, and I'm a happier person because of my wonderful kids. Claire and Noah, this is for you—but please wait until you're way over eighteen to read this book (actually, maybe don't read it, I promise I won't be offended).

I don't know if it's weird to thank a city, but Copenhagen was my muse and is where I found home, so to all the landmarks, businesses, traditions—and yes, the weather even (but NOT licorice)—thanks for inspiring me to write and live the life I've always wanted, full of delicious pastries, bike rides, and cozy cafés where I can be like a writer from the movies.

A summer-hot hug to my "Larissas": Amanda and Laís, the childhood/teenhood friends I can always count on—and text with—regardless of physical distance. You deserve a year-worth of hot chocolate for hearing all my book babbling!

Lastly, to my Brazilian family. You guys followed every step I took toward my dream, and I keep you all close to my heart. *Muito obrigada* to my sister, Natasha. I look forward to the next European country we'll visit and the next "silly game" we'll invent. Dad/Pai, I wish you were here to see what I've accomplished, but I know you know and are very proud.

Mom/Mãe, thank you for dreaming with me—back then, now, and every day to come. I'm crying as I write this because only you know the challenges we've faced to get where we are. You've supported me emotionally and financially when you could and when you couldn't, when we lived together and when we were apart. You've said yes to my every wild idea and traveled with me to book events no matter if we had to sleep in hostels and eat instant noodles for dinner. It's a shame you can't read this novel (yet!) because you don't speak English, but I'll write this in Portuguese for you: *Obrigada por tudo e por sempre acreditar!*

As for you, reader, thank you for giving this book a chance. Please, never stop dreaming and fighting for your happiness. Deal?

Cheers (or maybe I should say, *'Skål!'* *Lifts a mug of hot tea because it's freezing outside*),

Paula

Visit my website: paulaottoni.com
Follow me on Instagram: @apaulaottoni